HUNTING SGT. DUNN

HUNTING SGT. DUNN

A SGT. DUNN NOVEL

RONN MUNSTERMAN

Hunting Sgt. Dunn is a work of fiction. Names, characters, places, and incidents are the product of the author's imagination or are used fictitiously. Any resemblance to actual events, locales, or persons, living or dead is coincidental.

HUNTING SGT. DUNN – A SGT. DUNN NOVEL

Cover Design by

David M. Jones (www.triarete.com)
and
Nathalie Beloeil-Jones (www.nathaliesworkshop.com)

Printed in the United States of America
10 9 8 7 6 5 4 3 2 1

ISBN-13: 978-1-79-755516-4

BISAC: Fiction / War & Military

Acknowledgments

Hello readers! Welcome back.

Both of the main story lines are based on real missions the Germans concocted but never really got the chance to execute. More on them in the Author's Notes. For those of you who love Gertrude, I think you're in for a treat. As we've seen in several books, Nazi Minister of Armaments Albert Speer is sick and tired of Rangers and Commandos interfering with his plans. He decides to do something about it and it's personal.

Thank you to my patient, but ruthless FIRST READERS. They always manage to save me from myself and make excellent suggestions that improve the book. For whatever reason, I had some trouble with technical information this time. Steve Barltrop, Bob Schneider, and Nathan Munsterman pointed out errors in fact, oh my. I talk about this more after you read the book in the Author's Notes . . . please don't skip ahead, the notes always contain spoilers. Here's my hardworking FIRST READER crew: Steven B. Barltrop, Gordon Cotton, Dave Cross, Dave's son and future engineer Jackson Cross, David M. Jones (Jonesy), Zander Jones (Jonesy II), Nathan Munsterman, Robert (Bob) A. Schneider II, John Skelton, Steven D. White, and please welcome one last new FIRST READER: Charlie Shrem, a voracious reader and Sgt. Dunn fan extraordinaire.

Thank you to David M. Jones and his talented wife, Nathalie, for the wonderful cover. This is their fourth one together, and Jonesy's tenth. Their websites are on the copyright page. Check them out.

Thank you to my dear friend Derek Williams for his friendship and support, especially years ago when *Operation Devil's Fire* was the only manuscript written and Dunn's road ahead was a complete blank. Thank you to my wife for her tireless help with the manuscript and with, as usual, help in coming up with a title.

Thank you to the real heroes of WWII, the Greatest Generation. We're losing more and more members of the Greatest Generation as time continues forward. If you know a veteran of

WWII, please say thank you before it's too late. Their courage and willingness to do "what had to be done" will never be forgotten.

Thank you, readers, for your support of the eleven Sgt. Dunn books. I truly appreciate it.

For my wonderful friends Dave and Christine Cross

HUNTING
SGT. DUNN

1

Camp Barton Stacey
60 miles southwest of London
25 November 1944, 1422 Hours

Master Sergeant Tom Dunn raced across the muddy ground, cold rain whipping his face, his prey just a step ahead. He dug deep and with a burst of extra speed caught up, grabbing the man around the waist, tackling him. They fell to the ground and wrestled around until Dunn had his man pinned.

"Got you, Mac!" Dunn chortled as he got to his feet. He was covered in mud from face to boots.

Sergeant Major Malcolm Saunders rolled over onto his back. He stared up at Dunn, a scowl on his face, along with the mud.

"I thought this was flag football, mate!" Saunders got to his knees slowly, and then rose, facing Dunn.

The rest of Dunn's and Saunders' men caught up, gathering around watching their squad leaders face off. You never quite knew what might happen between these two men.

"Well, if you hadn't tied your damn flag to your belt, I wouldn't have had to tackle you!"

Saunders wiped some of the mud off his face with his shirt sleeve. His mustache, which would have normally been red, but was now a dark brown, twitched as he laughed. He held his hands out, one holding the American football, as if to say "what?"

"You mean that's not allowed? You didn't tell us that, Tom."

Dunn's mouth dropped open at Saunders' chutzpah and he shook his head. Instead of pressing the point with a guiltless Saunders, he glanced around for the referee, Sergeant Roy Newman, another Ranger squad leader who Dunn and Saunders had worked with before on missions. He found him just outside the circle of players trying to weave his way to Dunn. He finally broke through.

Newman lifted a silver whistle to his lips, blowing it once. He reached to his belt where he found a yellow strip of cloth. He snatched it and threw it high in the air. It was dead weighted with a stone the size of a large marble. It flew through the air, landing with a squishing sound. He pointed at Saunders and said, "Illegal flag! Ten yard penalty and loss of down."

"What do you mean loss of down?" Saunders shouted, stepping closer.

Newman calmly picked up his flag and held it loosely in his hands.

"You're the worst ref I've ever seen."

"I'm the only football ref you've ever seen."

"Exactly!"

Newman stared at the big Commando. "One more word out of you and you'll get another fifteen yards for unsportsmanlike behavior."

Saunders started to say something, but Steve Barltrop, his second in command, stepped between the two. He grabbed Saunders by the shoulder and turned him away.

"Let's go, Mac."

Saunders looked over his shoulder at Newman, but didn't say anything.

"Back to the line, men," Dunn said, pointing back the way they'd come.

The two teams slogged through the mud back to the line.

Newman paced off the ten yard penalty. He placed the ball on the spot and raised his hand with four fingers extended. "Fourth down and twenty to go."

Under his breath as he passed Newman, Saunders said, "Horrible call."

Newman spun on his heels. "What was that, Sergeant Major?"

"Oh, just saying it was a lovely day in the fall."

"Uh huh. Come here, Sergeant Major."

Saunders groaned, but turned around and walked over to the ref.

"Turn around."

Saunders showed Newman his back.

Newman yanked on the flag. It stayed in place. He bent over and untied it. Walking around in front of Saunders, holding up the red flag—just a strip of cloth—he shook his head. "Forget something?"

Saunders shrugged. "Oops." He tucked one end of the flag between his trousers and his shirt. "Happy now?"

"Incredibly so." Newman laughed as he walked to his position along the line of scrimmage.

Behind him, a large crowd of soldiers from both the U.S. and British armies stood along the sideline to cheer or boo, depending. Dunn's and Saunders' wives, Pamela and Sadie, had chairs to sit on, but they were standing also. Off by themselves were Colonel Mark Kenton, Dunn's commander, and Colonel Rupert Jenkins, Saunders' boss.

The score was Dunn's team twenty-four to Saunders' six with thirty seconds left in the fourth ten-minute quarter. Both teams had tried to run the ball in for two points after their touchdowns, but failed. Without goal posts there could be no kicks after touchdowns, or field goals.

The day had started out cold and wet and had gotten worse throughout with the wind picking up. There was a huge muddy area in the center of the field from one end zone to the other fifty yards away marking where most of the play had been.

Dunn had challenged Saunders and his squad to an American football game about a week ago. Saunders had agreed provided they also played a game of "real" football, known as soccer to the Americans, the next week. Drinks and dinner at the Star & Garter

Hotel's restaurant were on the line for each game. After an hour of going over the rules with the Commando squad and showing the Brits on the field how the game was played, Dunn suggested that Saunders and his men practice a few times before the game. Saunders did that during the week prior.

Saunders and his men formed a circle and huddled up.

Dunn set his men in formation for a punt rush, warning a couple of linebackers to watch for a fake punt. Squad speedsters Al Martelli and Jonesy were back to receive the kick. Dunn played the left defensive end position. Dave Cross, Stan Wickham, and Bob Schneider, the big men in the squad played the defensive line.

Saunders and his men came to the line. Barltrop, who played quarterback, was lined up two steps behind his right guard instead of the center to help block. Saunders was back for the snap and kick.

"Ready, set!" Barltrop shouted. His men took their down positions. "Hut . . . hut hut."

The center, Christopher Dickinson, snapped the ball. It hit the mud about two yards in front of Saunders.

Dunn's team rushed into the line.

Saunders snatched up the ball on a sloppy bounce to his right. It squibbed out of his huge hands and bounded away to his right. He tried to pick it up again on the bounce but instead, booted the ball with his foot. It changed directions toward Dunn's goal line.

"Oh bloody hell!" he shouted.

He heard the splashing sounds of the defense charging him. He dove for the ball and landed on it, tucking it away safely.

Just as he was about to roll over to get up, he felt a hand on his back and Newman blew the whistle ending the play.

Dunn jumped up and waved the muddy red flag triumphantly. "Ha, got you again!"

Saunders got up and snatched the flag away from Dunn, putting it back in place. He smiled.

"You were just lucky. I was about to break free for a touchdown."

"You are so full of it, Mac," Dunn said, laughing.

"Aye."

Dunn patted his friend on the shoulder and the men joined their teams for the turnover on downs.

Dunn huddled his men. With a ten-man squad, they'd had to give up one halfback on offense. Dunn quarterbacked while Wickham, with his football history in Texas, setting all kinds of high school scoring records, played fullback. He was powerful and fast and had scored all four touchdowns. Passing the football had been nearly impossible with the wind and rain. After a bunch of dropped passes, both teams had given up and the game turned into a grind-it-out slog.

Dunn called the play and the men lined up with Dunn taking the spot behind the center, Rob Goerdt.

On the first "hut," Goerdt slapped the ball into Dunn's waiting hands. Dunn pivoted to his right.

And promptly lost his footing. He went down hard. Goerdt, and Cross and Schneider, the two guards, held off the defense as Dunn scrambled to his feet.

Wickham was already in motion for the pitchout play and a few steps farther along than Dunn, who ran toward the right end of the line.

Barltrop, playing left linebacker, saw the play developing and keyed in on Dunn.

Wickham held his hands up.

Barltrop closed the distance and stuck out a hand to grab Dunn's flag on the left hip.

Dunn flipped the ball in a push like a basketball pass.

Wickham caught it in full stride. He tucked it under his right armpit and accelerated.

Barltrop's hand closed on Dunn's flag, but he realized he was too late.

Ira Myers, who was playing cornerback, took a line toward where Wickham would be in a few seconds. He was the only man between the ball carrier and the goal line.

Wickham spotted Myers and, instead of going right to evade the tackler, ran straight at him.

Myers, surprised by Wickham's move, was caught in between. Did he go left and try to grab the flag on Wickham's right hip, or go the other way. He chose to go right and maybe force Wickham out of bounds.

When Wickham was two steps from Myers, he dipped his right shoulder. Myers thought he'd made the right decision and reached for the flag on the left hip.

Wickham planted his right foot, which stuck where he wanted it to stop. He rotated his body counter-clockwise in a nearly complete three-sixty, taking off toward the sideline.

Myers hand closed on nothing but air.

And Wickham was gone.

He covered the distance in incredible time, considering the conditions.

He crossed the goal line and dropped the ball. He stopped and turned around, his hands raised and a gleam in his eyes.

Both teams had tried to follow Wickham, but were yards behind. Everyone finally caught up and Dunn's team hopped up and down around Wickham.

One of Newman's men, enlisted to be timekeeper, raised a 1911 Colt .45 loaded with blanks and fired it into the air, ending the game.

The teams lined up and shook hands. Everyone milled around on the sideline. Dunn sought out Saunders and found him near Sadie and Pamela. He jogged over to join them. A muddy and ornery Saunders was trying to hug Sadie, who took refuge behind Wickham who happened by at the right time.

"I'll kiss you, Mac, but no touching!" She screeched at him from the safety behind a six-foot-three wall.

Saunders pouted, and said, "Okay. I promise." He crossed his fingers behind his back.

Sadie came out from behind Wickham, dashed over to her husband and kissed him a quick one. He made to grab her anyway, but she'd expected it and darted back to safety, laughing at him.

"Nice try," Dunn said.

"You'd think she'd trust me by now."

"I'd say she knows you well enough by now to know better when it comes to something like that."

Saunders snapped his fingers. "Ah, aye, that must be it. So when do you and the lads want to have dinner?"

"The sooner the better. Maybe tomorrow night?"

"Sounds good to me."

Dunn held out his hand. "Good game, Mac."

"You, too, Tom."

Dunn and Pamela walked away from the group holding hands, she keeping a safe distance from his muddy clothes.

"You know, Tom, ordinarily I'd ask you to take me home, but lad, you better wash up before I can even begin to consider it."

He laughed. That was their code word for going home and making love.

"It'll be the fastest bath in history, dear."

"Better be," she replied, and laughed.

2

On High Street
Andover, England
2 miles southwest of Camp Barton Stacey
25 November, 1502 Hours

Evelyn Harris, a voluptuous blond of medium height, stopped in front of the Andover newspaper office. On the main window painted in fine gold lettering under the paper's name were the words: *Published every week since 1802.*

As she opened the door and went in, a little bell tinkled above her.

An older woman seated at a desk behind a counter stood. She smiled at Evelyn.

"May I help you, miss?"

"Yes, please. Evelyn Harris." She held out her hand and the two shook across the counter. "I'm a freelancer out of London. I'm looking for any stories you might have over the past few months about heroic American soldiers. I'm working on a piece that might eventually go to the *New York Times*."

"Oh, my, that would be exciting for you."

"It sure would. Might help get on fulltime somewhere."

The newspaper's office was dark wood with dim lighting. By the window sat a table with one chair. Stacks of the most recent issue were on the counter. Behind the counter, a wall with a single door stood between the front and the heart of the place, the printing presses and the archives.

"So do you have something like that?" Evelyn pressed when the woman didn't answer immediately.

"We surely do. It was very recent. A wonderful story and such a nice couple."

Evelyn raised an eyebrow. A couple?

"Why don't you have a seat at that table and I'll bring you a copy of that newspaper?"

"Thank you."

The woman disappeared through the door to the back and Evelyn sat down. She pulled a notebook and pencil from her purse and laid them on the table.

A few minutes passed and the woman returned with two copies of the same newspaper. She slid them onto the table in front of Evelyn.

"I brought you an extra copy, you know, in case you wanted to buy one for yourself for future reference."

Evelyn looked up at the white-haired lady. "Why thank you, dear, that's so very thoughtful."

"Let me know if you need anything."

"I surely will."

The woman nodded and went back to her desk.

Evelyn pulled the top copy closer. The main story, which was above the fold, showed a picture of a handsome U.S. soldier, a sergeant of some sort, with a gorgeous woman by his side. The headline proclaimed: **Hubby Hero!**

She began reading. When she was done, she looked at the man's face more closely. Could it be him? All she had to go by was that he had dark brown eyes—half the male population thank you very much—was tall, at least six feet-two, and was a U.S. Army Ranger, likely a sergeant because he clearly had been in charge of the mission. Little to go on, but this man might be close enough, because he'd won the Medal of Honor, which was the point of the story. And that he'd married a local gal, Pamela Dunn nee Hardwicke, parents Earl and Florence, who—and isn't this so very helpful?—lived on a farm five miles south of Andover. The article writer stated he couldn't provide any details on the citation for the award, but promised to publish those as soon as possible, given that he was dependent on the Yanks. The Medal of Honor was the equivalent of the Iron Cross. Had to be him.

Rising, she folded the paper under her arm, and put away her notebook and pencil. Last, she put some coins on top of the remaining copy to cover the one she was taking.

"Thank you, ma'am," she called out as she headed for the door.

"My pleasure, miss."

The bell tinkled again.

Five minutes later, Evelyn was at the Star & Garter's check in desk, which was a beautiful, dark walnut. The brown-haired young lady behind the desk smiled a greeting.

"Good afternoon, miss. Welcome to the Star and Garter."

Evelyn removed her coat, draping it over her right arm. She wore a light blue form-fitting suit with a white blouse and black pumps with a bow on the front.

Evelyn smiled in return. Why not? "It's Mrs. Mrs. Evelyn Harris. I believe you have a reservation for my husband and myself. His name is Robert."

"Of course, Mrs. Harris, I saw your reservation earlier. Do you want to sign in, . . . or is your husband coming?" She glanced over Evelyn's shoulder at the front door.

"I will. Robert will be joining me in a day or so. Work, don't you know?"

"Certainly." The clerk spun the sign in ledger around toward Evelyn and handed her a fountain pen.

Evelyn took the pen in her left hand.

The clerk noted the lovely, but simple, gold band on the third finger.

Evelyn signed in, giving a street address in south London. If anyone checked, a Mr. and Mrs. Harris did live there, but were often away in Scotland, as they currently were. They were also thirty years older than Evelyn. She'd driven down from London and parked the car near the hotel's front door.

She laid the pen down. "How much for our entire stay?"

The clerk told her and Evelyn opened her leather purse. She paid, and received a small amount of change in return, which she carefully placed inside a small blue change purse.

The clerk turned around and picked a brass key from the ones available. When she turned back around, Evelyn was looking around the ornate lobby. She faced the clerk. "Lovely lobby. I just love the Greek columns outside."

"Oh, I do, too," gushed the clerk, lying through her teeth.

The owner, who had once visited Greece, upon return, had replaced the posts holding up a small balcony over the doorway with Greek Doric columns. They clashed with the rest of the hotel's white brick and wrought iron décor, but he'd insisted and they stayed. Everyone in Andover hated them, except perhaps the contractor.

The bellhop, an older man of indeterminate age, with white hair and a thick white mustache, stood slightly behind Evelyn, unobtrusively waiting. He wore a black suit, white shirt and black tie. He refused to wear the weird bellhop pillbox hat; he said it made him feel like an organ grinder's monkey. He'd already put Evelyn's luggage, four expensive pieces, on a brass-handled cart when she'd arrived.

"Welcome to the Star and Garter, Mrs. Harris," the clerk said, repeating herself. She handed the key to the bellhop. "Fred will help you to your room."

"Thank you."

Fred took the key and turned the cart toward the lone lift. He pulled the cart toward it, and Evelyn followed.

After Fred placed the largest suitcase on the room's luggage holder, and stacked the others on the floor nearby, Evelyn gave him a decent tip. He thanked her and left, closing the door behind.

Evelyn eyed the room. Comfortable? Yes. Cozy, even. Not as nice as some in Berlin.

She walked briskly over to the door and locked it.

She opened the largest suitcase, leaning the lid against the wall. Turning the brass latches for the leather cover that flipped down over the large bottom section, she lifted it open. She removed a skirt and laid it on the desk. She unwrapped the larger of two oilcloths. A small smile touched her lips.

A German MP40 submachine gun lay on the unfolded oilcloth. The magazines were tucked along the side of the suitcase. Her Luger pistol was in the other oilcloth. A box of 9mm rounds was beneath her lacy underwear, as well as plenty of extra full magazines. Her "husband" would be bringing his own Luger with him, but not the submachine gun, which her group already had in their store of arms.

She rewrapped the MP40, closed the section lid, and closed the suitcase. She picked up the next biggest case and laid it on top, opening it. Inside were more skirts and tops, plus some men's pants and shirts. Her "husband's," of course.

Evelyn Harris, otherwise known as Elsa Hoffman, was a British national by birth, but her parents were German, and had resettled in London after the Great War, where her cobbler father had a good business with a number of shops in the City. She went to public schools, and did well because she was quite smart. When the family took summer trips to Berlin where all their relatives lived, she had fallen in love with Germany, and with Hitler. They'd once even attended a Nuremburg Rally. Evelyn had grown so excited at seeing Hitler in the flesh, she'd nearly fainted.

Having grown up speaking German at home, she spoke it with a Berlin accent, but her English sounded like any other young British woman. A friend of the family in Berlin had talked with her in the garden of her uncle's house for quite some time. By the end of that summer's visit in 1938, she'd been recruited to join the Abwehr at the age of nineteen. She'd been told important work awaited her, but that she'd have to be patient.

Her first assignment had come three years later in late 1941. She was to "befriend" a married man who managed a munitions plant outside London. All she had to do was get his key to the plant's front door for one hour. A simple thing to do, since he always fell asleep after sex. She'd lowered the key from the London hotel's second floor window to a male colleague who made a copy and returned it to her in forty-five minutes. A team of two men later that week used the key to get inside the plant and take pictures of every munitions schematic in the office file cabinets. The man never knew what happened. When she, quite naturally, broke up with him a week later, he was broken hearted. She wasn't.

She was glad she had stopped at the newspaper office first. That prevented her having to change clothes and go to a bar and go through the bothersome chore of seducing some idiot U.S. Army Ranger. Sometimes it truly paid to be smarter than average.

She undressed, washed up, and went to bed. Happily all alone. She was asleep in a minute.

3

Pembroke, Bermuda
25 November, 2344 Hours, Bermuda time, late the same evening

The dark late evening sky was filled with bright and dim flickering lights, and the meandering smoky wondrous line of the Milky Way stretched from the sea to the top of the world. The air was cool and smelled of the salty sea, and was carried on a light breeze from the south. The temperature was still sixty-eight degrees and would remain there until first light.

Nineteen-year-old Gertrude Dunn, an Iowa girl transplanted to Bermuda a few months ago at her government's request, walked the beach with two of her friends. They worked for Bermuda Station as analysts, spending their time reading mail and telegrams going between America and Europe. They were on the look out for anything suspicious; something that might lead authorities to a spy ring working in the States. It had happened.

Their shift typically ended at 11 p.m., but their supervisor had taken mercy on them and let them leave a half hour early, a rarity. The three young women had gone out for a late dinner. Gertrude had filled herself with spicy boiled shrimp, her favorite, something she'd discovered when she'd first arrived on the island. There was live music by a band capable of playing the big band sound quite well. Unfortunately, each of the men there, some from the same place of work as the women, and some expatriates from various friendly countries, was accompanied by a woman. So the three women friends danced with each other, a common sight during wartime.

Gertrude had come to the attention of the Office of Strategic Services when she'd worked at the Rock Island Arsenal near Davenport, Iowa. Two OSS officers had come to the Dunn family home in Cedar Rapids to give Gertrude a written test. She'd scored so high the officers had offered her a job on the spot. And sworn her family and her to secrecy. She'd been sent to St. Louis for training, and while there, caught the eye of someone who suggested she be sent to Bermuda.

The American contingent at Bermuda Station had increased substantially starting in the previous May and vastly outnumbered the British, who'd had about sixty women volunteer to stay on, including the shift supervisors.

A tall woman, Gertrude had a lithe form, a quick wit, and a scathing tongue for stupid or rude people. She had wavy light brown hair that framed her face. At home, the eldest Dunn child, Hazel, lived with their parents while her husband commanded a submarine somewhere in the Pacific. Their brother, who was sandwiched between them in age, Tom, was a U.S. Army Ranger based in England. She'd last seen him when he received the Medal of Honor at the White House the previous month. Prior to that, she had last seen him when he'd returned home on leave following boot camp in the summer of 1942.

Gertrude walked between Frances and Dorothy. All three women carried their shoes, walked barefoot, and carried their small clutch purses in the other hand. Both of her friends were a couple of years older than she, but they'd hit it off soon after Gertrude's arrival to the Atlantic Ocean island. Frances was from the Midwest, too, Kansas City, Missouri, near the famous Plaza and her accent was pretty close to Gertrude's. She was a pretty blue-eyed blond. Dorothy was from Hollywood and planned to try acting after the war. She was nearly as tall as Gertrude's five-eight and she had green eyes that matched the color of the shallow water in the daylight, and long red hair.

Gertrude took a deep breath, savoring the fresh air. "This is wonderful."

Dorothy laughed. "It's so much better than L.A."

"I bet it is," Gertrude replied.

Ahead of them about fifty yards across the sand, a fishing boat was tied to a small dock. The boat appeared to be empty and no one was on the dock.

"Race you guys to the dock. We can dangle our toes in the water."

"You're on, Gerty!" shouted Frances.

"On three," Dorothy said. She counted and when she said three, the women darted forward, sand flying from their heels.

Gertrude took the lead right away, but Frances was only a step behind, while Dorothy was a couple of more steps back.

When they were about ten yards from the finish line, Frances shouted, "I'm catching up, Gerty!"

Gertrude didn't bother looking over her shoulder. She knew that was what Frances wanted because it might cause her to slow down a hair. Instead she strained to increase her speed, pumping her arms in time with her strong legs. She changed directions slightly and flew onto the dock. She raised her hands—still holding her shoes and purse—and did a circular victory dance.

Frances reached the dock two steps later and Dorothy a few more. The women hugged each other as they got their breath back. When they separated, they walked a little farther out on the dock. They eyed the fishing boat. It was definitely empty. The owner would probably arrive around four a.m. to get ready for the day.

The women walked to the end of the dock and sat down side-by-side. The day's second high tide had taken place around eleven p.m., so the water was still close to the level of the dock and their feet were comfortably submerged. They kicked their feet back and forth creating a froth on the water's surface.

Some time went by and they began to feel the fatigue of the day, plus the two alcoholic drinks they'd downed at the club. Someone yawned and that triggered sympathetic yawns amongst the other two. No one wanted to be first to admit it was time to hit the sack. A few more minutes passed and they glanced at each other through sleepy eyes.

It looked like Dorothy was about to give in first.

From behind them came the rhythmic thumping sound of bicycle tires on the wooden dock's planks. They turned to look over their shoulders. A skinny white man maybe in his early twenties rode closer. His white teeth gleamed in the moonlight as he grinned at them. All three assumed he was the boat owner, coming extra early for some reason. The rear brake squeaked and he came to a stop a few feet away. He hopped off the bike athletically and used his bare foot to knock down the kick stand and, oddly, turned the bike around to face the beach.

"Good morning to you, ladies," he said, his tone carrying a friendly British lilt.

"Hello," Gertrude said.

He wore a white short sleeved dress shirt that was tucked into his light-colored shorts. A sheen of sweat glistened on his brow. She thought he might be the son of a British family on the island.

"Lovely night, innit?" he asked, still grinning. He moved a step closer and stopped.

"Is this your boat dock?" Frances asked.

"Ah, no, ma'am. Sure would love to have one as nice, though."

Something in the way he said it triggered an alarm bell in Gertrude's head. She got to her feet carefully, making sure she didn't fall in the water. She stood with one foot slightly ahead of the other.

"Well, girls, looks like we'd better get back home. We have an early morning tomorrow."

Dorothy started to object because they weren't scheduled for a shift until three p.m., but Gertrude's expression stopped her. She was about to ask Gertrude what was wrong, but the man suddenly jumped forward, grabbed Frances, who was closest, by the arm, yanking her to her feet.

In a fluid motion, he drew a knife from behind his back. He stepped backwards dragging Frances with him. He spun her around and caught her neck in the crook of his left arm, while pressing the knife's point against her throat.

Frances squealed in fright.

"Nice and easy, 'girls,' " he said, mimicking Gertrude. "Hand over your fine little purses." He chuckled as if he'd made a wonderful joke.

Gertrude met Frances's eyes, which were wide with fright, looking much like a terrified deer. "Whatever you say, mister. Just don't hurt us," Gertrude said pleadingly. She raised her purse in her right hand and his eyes tracked it.

"Girls, give the man your purses," she commanded.

Dorothy held out hers and the man grabbed it with his left hand. He inadvertently pressed the razor-sharp knife harder against Frances's skin and the blade nicked her. She cried out in pain and fear. The dripping blood looked black in the moonlight.

"Hurry it up!" the man shouted at Gertrude.

RONN MUNSTERMAN

4

Hitler's Office
The Chancellery
Berlin
26 November, 0450 Hours, Berlin time

Ever the night owl, Adolf Hitler conducted his daily—nightly—business at times later than midnight. This meeting with Grand Admiral Karl Dönitz, who was in charge of the Nazi submarine force, and Albert Speer, the Minister of Armaments, would be the last of the night. Hitler would go to bed and sleep undisturbed until noon, when he would arise and have breakfast.

Hitler's office was a monstrosity, as was the entire Reich Chancellery, which had been designed by Albert Speer with the explicit intention of intimidating foreign visitors, although there hadn't been any for quite some time. The office was thirteen meters by thirty and the ceiling was ten meters high. The entrance's double doors were five meters tall. Across from the doors and in front of five floor-to-ceiling windows sat a long gray marble table, one of Hitler's favorite pieces.

Hitler's three-meter-wide desk was on the left end of the office, while on the opposite side visitors could enjoy a sitting area with a massive fireplace. A blue fabric and wood sofa big enough for six people faced the fireplace. An upholstered chair was positioned at each end of the sofa. Between the sofa and the fireplace were four winged chairs. Four floor lamps stood around the sitting space.

Hitler, wearing his dark blue suit, sat behind his desk, which was empty except for a blotter, a black phone, and some engineering drawings.

Speer and Dönitz, whose nickname was *Der Löwe*, the Lion, sat directly across from the *Führer*.

Speer was a handsome man of thirty-nine. He had brown hair and a high forehead. Sharp eyes took in everything at once. He had come to the *Führer's* favor after planning the 1933 Nuremberg Rally. He'd been appointed Minister of Armaments hours after his predecessor, Fritz Todt, had been killed in a 1942 plane crash. Despite telling Hitler he was unqualified for the position, Hitler had said he had faith in him. Speer also wore a suit, but his was brown.

Admiral Dönitz, a slight man of fifty-three with short gray hair always wore his distinguished dress uniform including the Iron Cross, which dangled just below his white shirt's top button. He'd begun his naval service just before the Great War, in 1910. Three years later, he was commissioned as an officer. In 1918, he earned his first *Unterseeboot*, U-boat, command, but it was sunk by the British after it suffered mechanical problems. He was taken prisoner and held first at Malta, then at Sheffield, England until 1920. After the war, his career advanced steadily and in late 1939 he was promoted to *Konteradmiral*, Rear Admiral, and Commander of the Submarines.

Known for inserting himself into the daily operations of submarines, he often radioed them as many as seventy times a day with questions about their locations, fuel, and other day-to-day items. It drove his sub captains crazy and behind the captain's closed doors *Der Löwe* became *Der Maus*, the mouse, for getting into things he shouldn't.

He claimed to have invented the idea of the *rudeltaktik*, pack tactic, otherwise known as the wolfpack, while in the POW camp.

This tactic was specially designed for attacking convoys. The U-boats massed around a convoy, then attacked the escorts, overwhelming them by sheer number and surprise. Once through the protective screen, each U-boat captain could pick his target and use his favored attack tactic. However it came to be, it was a deadly efficient tactic that nearly brought England to her knees. If not for the Americans' interference with their Liberty ship convoys, England would have been forced to surrender. Nearly two years ago, he'd been promoted by Hitler to Grand Admiral and he replaced Erich Raeder as Commander in Chief of the Navy.

Having already dispensed with the "*Heil* Hitler" greetings and a little small talk, Dönitz got right to it.

"*Mein Führer*," he began, "I'm pleased to report we will be ready for sea testing of the platforms by the first of December."

Hitler gave a rare smile and leaned forward unabashedly showing his excitement. These days any good news was welcome. "All is well with the towing apparatus?"

"Yes, it is. The platforms are robust and strong and have held up to underwater tests with no leakage."

"How is U-2508 performing?"

"Excellently. As you know, she's a Type Twenty-One class *U-boot*. She was launched on the thirteenth, just twelve days ago. I expect to commission her in two days."

Hitler beamed.

"I estimate the trip across the Atlantic to a point five hundred kilometers from New York City will consume eight days." Dönitz looked at Speer. "Can you confirm that the three V2 rockets will be ready and delivered to us within a few days?"

Speer nodded. "They are being prepared for shipment as we speak. The train should leave at sundown tonight arriving at Blohm and Voss's shipyard four hours later."

"Thank you," Dönitz said.

"Of course."

"Explain the launch process for me," Hitler said.

Dönitz was thoroughly prepared for Hitler's request because the *Führer* was a naturally inquisitive man, which unfortunately, led to his sticking his fingers into operational details. This was a constant source of consternation among the military leaders of the Third Reich. It was long believed that Hitler's interference cost the

Germans hundreds of thousands of soldiers especially at Stalingrad the year previous. However, no one dared explain this to him. How could you when it could mean your life? That he himself was guilty of the same thing by contacting his sub captains daily seemed lost on the admiral.

"Certainly, *Mein Führer*. The submarine will tow three of the submersible launch platforms at one time. The platforms are designed to float horizontally with the V2 rocket aboard. The platforms will automatically submerge about twenty minutes after the submarine begins a forward motion.

"One of the platforms will also carry extra fuel for the submarine. When the *U-boot* reaches the launch point and stops, she will surface as will the platforms. The rocket launch crew will board each platform, fill the ballast tanks so the platforms rotate to make the rockets vertical and stable. They'll set the launch parameters, distance and direction, and the timer.

"They'll return to the submarine, which will submerge and move to a safe distance from the rockets. From there they will monitor the launches. We have people near New York City who will report on the effectiveness of the rockets when they explode in Manhattan. That is still the primary target, is it not?"

"Absolutely, yes, Manhattan's Wall Street, is the target. It is the heart of American money. Destroy that and their economy will come to a crashing halt. I envy our agents who will be able to witness this. It's as perfect an example of *schadenfreude* as I can think of."

Dönitz and Speer smiled at the *Führer's* use of the German-specific word for relishing someone else's troubles.

"After launch, the submarine will head home to Hamburg. In the meantime, Blohm and Voss will continue building new platforms, since they are for one-time use only."

Hitler nodded his understanding and sat back in his chair. He steepled his fingers together and dipped his chin to touch the fingertips as he thought.

Speer glanced at Dönitz, but neither man said anything.

"How long to build a set of three?"

"Now that they've perfected the manufacturing process, about five days for each one, so just over a fortnight," Speer said.

"Plus the eight days to get to the launch point."

"Yes, sir. A total of twenty-three days."

"I want it done in three weeks."

Speer cleared his throat. "I believe the fifteen days manufacturing time is the lowest they can go."

"Tell them their *Führer* personally demands an improvement to thirteen days. Surely they can do that." Hitler clapped his hands together as if that settled it.

"Ja, Mein Führer." Speer exchanged another look with Dönitz, this time one of helplessness.

"I'm looking forward to this, gentlemen." Hitler stood and offered his hand to each man across the desk. When they finished shaking his hand, they stepped back and gave the Nazi salute saying, *"Heil* Hitler!"

Hitler, so excited by the prospect of bombing the United States, snapped off a rare perfect Nazi salute instead of his usual, lazy hand flip. He beamed at his underlings as they turned and walked toward the doors.

After they closed the doors behind them, he marched over to the marble table in front of the dark windows. A large map of the world was laid out on it. He leaned over, placing his left hand on the cool, smooth surface of the table for support. He held a fountain pen in his right hand. He found New York City, Manhattan in particular, and drew three X's on the island.

"This is for you, Roosevelt," he said happily.

RONN MUNSTERMAN

5

Gertrude's face was a mask of fear. "I'm hurrying, I'm hurrying." She took a couple of steps closer and held out the clutch purse so it was a few inches out of his grasp. She bent her knees slightly.

As she'd expected, the robber moved his left hand closer to grab the prize.

In a flash of motion, Gertrude dropped the purse, stepped forward and snagged his wrist with both hands.

She rotated to her right with incredible speed and power.

The man, completely caught off guard, also rotated clockwise. As his right shoulder spun on his body's axis, it pulled the knife blade away from Frances's neck. Taking advantage of the freedom, she scrabbled sideways away from the attacker.

Meanwhile, Gertrude had the man's left arm under her armpit. She clenched it in place by snugging her bicep against it. Still rotating, she placed her right hand just in front of her left shoulder.

He struggled against this unexpected power and tried to slice at Gertrude with the knife, but he was still rotating and being pulled in the wrong direction. His head was tilted forward toward Gertrude's right side.

She snapped her right elbow back and a sickening crunch came with a smashed nose.

The robber's head flew backwards. The knife clattered to the dock.

"Grab the knife!" Gertrude shouted.

Dorothy kicked it into the water.

He grabbed his face with his right hand. Gertrude still had his left arm trapped under hers.

Gertrude's muscle memory was still firing. She spun the opposite way, to her left. This caused the robber to flail forward behind her. He took two quick steps to keep from falling to the dock.

Just as she'd expected, the backs of his legs were exposed to her as she looked over her left shoulder. She shifted her weight to her right foot, raised her left knee to the waist and stomped backwards. Her foot smashed into the robber's left knee. It hinged as it was designed and he collapsed to the dock, moaning in pain.

Gertrude kept rotating and stopped when she was directly above the prostrate man, his left arm still trapped. She dropped onto his back with a crash, folding his left arm behind his back. She grabbed the wrist with her left hand and leaned forward to trap it.

"Dorothy, sit on his legs!"

Her friend jumped onto his flailing legs, pinning them against the dock.

"Frances, take off your belt and tie it around his left wrist."

Frances hesitated, then untied her belt. She knelt to Gertrude's left and tied one end around the wrist.

Gertrude leaned forward and grasped his right wrist and yanked it behind his back. Frances tied his wrists together, tying several knots in the cloth belt.

"Go find a phone and call the station's security office. Run, Frances!"

Her friend jumped to her feet and dashed away toward the beach, and the road beyond.

The robber, realizing there were only two women left, started to struggle.

"Stop that," Gertrude said, kneeing his back as a reminder of who was on top.

"Make me, you little bitch," he snarled.

Gertrude sighed.

Dorothy leaned forward and said, "He didn't really just call you a 'little bitch,' did he?"

"Yep." Gertrude grabbed an ear in each hand like they were handles on a pot. "Okay, buster, time for a lesson in courtesy, American style."

She pulled back on his ears and his head followed, as did a scream. She slammed his forehead down into the hard wood. The loud crack made her wonder whether it was his head or the wood that broke. Hopefully the wood.

"I give up," he said, his voice muffled.

"What's that? A little louder."

"I give up!"

She patted him on the shoulder. "There's a good boy."

"So what do we do now?" Dorothy asked.

"We enjoy the view while we wait for security."

The robber lay perfectly still, and Gertrude wondered if he'd simply fallen asleep.

Frances returned and smiled at the sight.

"Frances, I have a handkerchief in my purse. Better put it on your cut to stop the bleeding."

Frances picked up Gertrude's purse. She held the cloth against her throat. "Thanks."

"Sure."

About ten minutes later, just when Gertrude was trying to figure out how much longer she could stay in her position, a car stopped on the road. A spotlight came on, swinging about until it settled on two women, who were sitting on top of a man.

The three Bermuda Station security officers were armed with Webley .38s, nightsticks, and carried handcuffs. They ran across the beach and the dock. The leader, a short man in his thirties, walked around so he could see Gertrude's face. He looked down at the robber who managed to turn his head to look up.

"Help me, please."

The officer laughed. "Hello, Rodney. Causing trouble again?"

"Just minding my own business. They attacked me."

"Wait, you know him?" Gertrude asked.

"Yeah. We get local crime information from the police, so we know what's going on. He's been arrested several times for robbery, particularly female tourists. He's the kind of guy it's always good to get off the street."

He knelt and slapped a pair of cuffs on the man's wrists, leaving the makeshift binding of the belt in place for the fun of it. His partners joined him, one on either side of the robber.

"Okay, ladies, you can get off him," the leader said, mirth in his voice.

After the two young women got to their feet and stepped away, he said, "Okay, boys, get him up and by the car." He noticed the bike. He turned to Gertrude, eyeing her carefully. Wow, he thought, what a beauty. And tall. She was his height. "Is that bike his?"

"Yes, sir."

"Boys, I'll bring the bike. It's probably stolen anyway."

The two officers manhandled the robber, who appeared to be grateful to escape the crazy women, toward the car.

"I'd appreciate it if you'd tell me what happened here. Later in the day, after you can get some rest, I'll need a full statement for the Pembroke Police."

Dorothy spoke up. "I'll fill you in." While she did that, the officer listened quietly. Until she got to the part where Gertrude physically attacked a man who had a knife to her friend's throat.

His mouth dropped open. "You're kidding me," he said to Gertrude.

She shrugged. "No. That's how it happened."

He seemed to suddenly notice their accents. "You're American."

She nodded. "Yes, sir. All three of us."

"Hm." His eyes narrowed as he peered at her. "Where did you learn to fight like that?"

"My brother taught me when he came back from boot camp a few years ago."

"I see. Where is he now?"

"Based in England. He's a Ranger."

The man's eyebrows arched at this. "A Ranger? You mean like a Commando?"

Gertrude huffed a bit. "No," she said, drawing out the vowel. "I mean like a U.S. Army Ranger."

"I stand corrected. And you remembered this lesson from a few years ago?"

"Well, of course. I remember everything. And it wasn't just one lesson. It was a week-long training session. He wanted me to be able to protect myself." She waved a hand at her two friends, who were beaming in pride. "And my friends."

He smiled for the first time. "Well, I'd say you did that all right." He pointed at Frances and said, "We'll take your friend who was injured to the infirmary for treatment and perhaps a tetanus shot."

He checked his watch. "What time does your next shift start?"

"Second shift; three p.m."

"I'd like you all to come to the security office at one to give your formal statements. Also, just so you know, you'll be called to give testimony in court when his case goes to trial. Do you have any problems with that?"

"None at all."

"A copy of my report will go to your supervisor."

"Oh, okay."

"I better drive you all back to your quarters. Don't worry, I'll have the attacker stay behind with the other two officers so you don't have to share the car with him."

"Thank you, sir. That's quite thoughtful."

He nodded and walked away. He kicked up the bike's kickstand and rolled it along with him.

Gertrude's friends each gave her a hug and thanked her profusely.

The three women grasped hands and walked toward the car.

"Your brother taught you how to do that? Really?" Frances asked.

"Yep, he really did."

"Wow. Well, I'm certainly grateful."

"Me, too," chimed in Dorothy.

Gertrude took it all in stride. Her brother had been an unforgiving taskmaster when he'd been teaching her. She'd gotten angry at him so many times she'd lost count, but now was extremely thankful for his tenacity. She'd have to write him about this and hoped it would make him proud.

She missed him deeply and had been thrilled to be invited to the White House for the Medal of Honor ceremony. That was certainly a once in a lifetime event. He'd been so nice to her when she and her new boyfriend, Alan Finch, broke the news they were seriously dating. Dunn had met Finch through his work as a Ranger when Finch first started working for the British Prime Minister, Winston Churchill. She grinned to herself recalling Tom's reaction to finding out someone he knew was dating his little sister. Priceless.

Finch had arrived at Bermuda Station and had given a talk to all the new analysts. They'd literally met by accident when he'd nearly knocked her down running to a meeting. A dinner led to a mutual attraction. Although he'd panicked and tried to quit things when he learned she was Dunn's baby sister. She had set him straight and it had been smooth sailing. Except that she was in Bermuda and he was in Canada on special assignment somewhere; he couldn't tell her where. She missed him sorely, too.

6

Colonel Rupert Jenkins' office
Camp Barton Stacey
26 November, 1255 Hours, London time, the next
afternoon

Sunday in England brought cold air and yet more rain. The sky was gray, the clouds low. In spite of the day, a normally taciturn man with a mane of white hair had a smile on his face. He'd made a decision earlier in the morning, while shaving, and was about to do something he hadn't done since he was a cadet at Sandhurst, England's Royal Military College. Even though he was nervous about it, he marveled at how steady his hand was as he reached for the black telephone on his desk. He dialed zero, told the operator he wanted another operator in London, and asked
the second one for a phone number. He wrote down the number and asked for a long distance operator. Eventually, the line began ringing. Someone picked it up on the third ring.

"Clayton residence."

Jenkins pictured a man who would be in his late sixties now: black suit, white shirt, and black tie.

"Alice Clayton, please. Colonel Rupert Jenkins calling."

"Ah yes, Colonel Jenkins," the man replied as if Jenkins was a regular caller. "I'll see if Lady Alice is in." The phone clunked down on a table. Footsteps echoed growing fainter.

Jenkins smiled. It used to be "miss" twenty odd years ago.

Lighter sounds of footsteps came closer after a few minutes.

"Colonel Rupert Jenkins, you say?" said a woman.

Jenkins' heart seemed to seize up at the sound of Alice's soft voice. He found his own voice and replied, "Yes, Alice, it's me, Rupert."

"A colonel?"

"Yes."

"Hm." A clicking sound came across the wire. He recognized it as her tapping her front teeth with her long fingernails as she thought. An old habit.

"I'm quite sure I don't know a Rupert Jenkins, colonel or otherwise."

Jenkins swallowed. What had he been thinking?

"Please, Alice."

She went on as if he hadn't said anything. "Of course, I *did* know a Rupie Jenkins, but my goodness that was, oh dear, how long ago was that? Hm?"

Jenkins cringed at her nickname for him.

"Oh, yes, that was twenty years ago, uh, last May, I believe. When Rupie told me he had chosen the army life over me. I never understood, don't you know?"

Jenkins took a deep breath. A few beads of sweat formed on his forehead.

"Alice, please let me explain."

"Explain? You want to explain away a girl's broken heart? Is that what you're saying, Rupie?"

"No, that's . . . no, I want to see you. To talk to you face to face."

"You want to talk to me. Now? Today? Is today convenient for you?"

"I was thinking tonight. Perhaps after dinner."

"Should I invite my husband along?"

Jenkins frowned. Husband?

"You're not married, Alice."

"How do you know that? Have you been checking up on me?" Her voice grew shrill.

"No, not really . . . yes. I read the marriages column every day."

"So you *have* been checking up on me. Do you know why I don't have a husband?"

"Alice, please."

"Because, my dear Rupie, you broke my heart permanently."

"I want to fix it, Alice."

She gave a dry laugh at that.

"I'm not some car you can tune up with a wrench, you know." Jenkins closed his eyes. "Yes, I know. May I come see you?"

"Give me your phone number."

He rattled off his number.

"I'll think about it. I may ring you. I don't know when. Or if. Do you understand?"

"Yes, Alice."

The phone clicked dead. He held the handset out and stared at it. Hanging up slowly, he wiped his sweaty brow with his hand. He held up the same hand as earlier. It was trembling. He laid it on the desk and sighed.

Colonel Rupert Jenkins commanded a company of British Commandos. He'd been the commandant of the Commando School at Achnacarry House for some time prior to this assignment. And a phone call to a former fiancé had reduced him to a quivering lump of flesh.

He checked his watch. He had a few minutes before his meeting with one of his squad leaders. He jumped to his feet and left the office, glad he'd had sense enough to close the door before the phone call. After a quick face washing in the bathroom, he was back at his desk, the door open.

Feeling somewhat better, he unlocked and pulled open his lowest desk drawer. From it he lifted a folder, which he laid on the desk and flipped open. Across the top of the first page was a red stamp: Top Secret.

A knock at the door came from a six-foot redhead who filled the door. The red hair caused Jenkins to think of Alice again. He pushed the thought aside and said in his usual gruff voice, "Come."

Sergeant Major Malcolm Saunders glided into the office. On his heels came a smaller man, Sergeant Steve Barltrop, his second in command. The two Commandos saluted, and when the colonel returned it, sat down in front of his desk.

Saunders looked around the office, surprise on his face. "No Lieutenant Mallory, sir?"

Mallory was Jenkins' aide.

"Day off."

Saunders lifted an eyebrow. "You gave Lieutenant Mallory the day off?"

Jenkins gave Saunders a pinched look, but shrugged. "Deserved one."

"Yes, sir," was all Saunders could think of to say.

"I have a very unusual mission for you." Jenkins fiddled with the papers in the folder.

Saunders and Barltrop exchanged a look. Jenkins seemed . . . out of sorts. "All right, sir."

"The Germans have been forging British currency, especially in five, ten, and twenty pound notes. They plan to flood the country with millions of pounds of worthless money, hoping to wreck the economy."

"You've got to be bloody kidding, sir," Saunders replied.

"Wish I was."

"Where are they making the money?"

"A concentration camp in eastern Germany. According to Bletchley Park and their Enigma codebreakers, the money is about to be shipped to Bremerhaven by truck, and stored in a warehouse. When a submarine and infiltration team are available, they'll send it here. The Chancellor of the Exchequer, Sir John Anderson, says it would indeed wreak havoc on the economy. So it must be stopped. Find the warehouse—Bletchley Park has identified three possibilities—and blow it all up. Burn it all. It cannot get on that sub. Sir John wants you to get a few of each denomination and bring it home for evaluation."

"I'm trying to picture how big a pile of money it's going to be."

Jenkins grinned. "I know the answer to that. I asked Sir John. Based on the Ultra intelligence, they've forged close to a hundred and twenty-five million pounds, most of which is in fivers. Anyway, his staff estimates the notes will fill twenty-two pallets that measure four feet by five feet, four feet in height. Several truck loads for certain."

"Twenty-two?" Barltrop asked. "That's unimaginable."

"Aye, it is," Saunders said in his Cockney accent. "Let's see, two pallets side by side, twenty-two of them, so eleven in length times five feet. It would be fifty-five feet long. Bloody hell."

"Bloody hell indeed," Jenkins said. "You'll have a short window of time to find and destroy it. If you miss it, our economy won't be worth a toss."

"Aye. No pressure, eh, sir?"

"None at all. The bogus money is supposed to arrive in Bremerhaven on Thursday probably during the early hours after midnight. You'll take a sub from London as far up the river to Bremerhaven as the captain will take you. After you complete your mission, you'll escape on the same sub, which will wait on station for you."

Saunders thought about it for a moment. "I'm thinking it might be worthwhile to take a camera and get photos of the whole thing."

"Interesting idea," Jenkins said. "Do that."

"Very good, sir. Anything else?"

"No. Mallory will arrange your sub and let you know where to be and when."

"We'll tell the men and set up some training to get everyone ready for this one. Haven't blown up anything for a few weeks."

Jenkins laughed.

Saunders raised an eyebrow.

"That will be all, gentlemen."

The two men departed and once outside climbed in their staff car, Saunders driving. He didn't start the car and Barltrop looked over. The two friends regarded each other silently for a time with puzzled expressions.

Barltrop went first. "Something's up with the colonel."

"Aye. He actually laughed out loud. Heard anything on the grapevine?"

"Nothing except the usual whining."

Saunders chuckled. Someone was always complaining about something the colonel did or said, or perhaps even thought about doing or saying.

"Well, something's happening. He's not transferring out is he?"

Barltrop looked aghast. "Never happen. They'll haul him out by his boots."

"Aye, you're right. It's in his personal life. Does he have a lady friend?"

"I've . . . he's never shown the slightest inclination toward seeing anyone."

"Then I'm stumped."

Barltrop nodded. "Me, too."

Saunders shrugged. "If he wants us to know, he'll tell us. Let's get this show on the road."

With that, he started the car and aimed for their barracks.

7

Tom and Pamela Dunn's house
The Hardwicke Farm
5 miles south of Andover, England
26 November, 1415 Hours

Master Sergeant Tom Dunn, from Iowa, had become a relatively famous Ranger recently thanks to his receiving the Medal of Honor directly from President Roosevelt just over a month ago. Just two weeks ago, a reporter from the Andover newspaper had driven out to Dunn's and Pamela's house south of Andover. They lived on Pamela's parents' farm in an extra house built near the main house. Some people would call it a mother-in-law house, but Dunn and Pamela called it home. Whenever he was able to get off the base he drove out to be with her.

The story had been published the previous Sunday, the nineteenth. The alliterative headline screamed: Hubby Hero. It was an unexpectedly fair and complimentary article, playing up the angle of British-American cooperation, with a wry comment about Pamela's sacrifice in moving to the States after the war. It mentioned few details about Dunn and his work citing the Official Secrets Act, but did tell readers, a little breathlessly, that Dunn was the best Ranger in the outfit and his Medal of Honor had been for some action quite spectacular. The reporter promised to get a copy of the citation some day and print it for the readers in a follow up story. He had no way of knowing the citation was entirely fictional. You simply couldn't tell the public that Dunn had blown up the Nazis' atomic bomb laboratory. Panic would ensue.

Dunn's men, after hearing about the article, naturally got a copy, cut it out and stuck it on the barracks' bulletin board. One of the knuckleheads, so far unidentified, had drawn a Saunders' red handlebar mustache on Dunn's face.

Dunn wore his dress uniform, as he usually did on Sundays, but not his sidearm, his favorite 1911 Colt .45. Well, his new favorite. He'd lost his previous favorite when he'd been accidentally knocked into a dam reservoir in western Germany. The bomb he and his squad ultimately used to destroy Hitler's Dam had clipped him in the shoulder as it rolled down a ramp toward the water. The 6,000 pound beast gave him too big a hit to recover from. His best friend, Dave Cross, also his second in command, had jumped in and pulled him out with the help of the squad's big man, Bob Schneider. When they got him over the dam's ramparts and lying on his back, he wasn't breathing and had no pulse. Schneider, who'd become the squad's ad hoc medic, tried something his dad had told him about years ago: chest compressions. It had worked, a miracle as far as the men were concerned, and they had Dunn back. Dunn had suffered some temporary effects during the escape, not being quite as sharp and together as usual, but within a few days of returning home, he was back to normal.

Pamela and he had attended church with her parents earlier in the morning and eaten Sunday lunch at the Hardwicke's kitchen table.

"Hey, honey, I'm ready," Pamela's voice came from the living room. Dunn was washing up in the bathroom.

"Be right there!"

He finished up, and joined his wife at the front door.

Her two dogs, a black Labrador named Sammy, and a brown and white collie called Winston, waited at their feet, looking impatiently out the door, their tails wagging. She'd raised them from puppyhood and had trained them herself. They responded to her voice commands and hand signals. Not so much with Dunn, who they tended to either ignore or simply lick whenever he tried to get them to do something that didn't involve a treat.

"Is it still raining?"

"Just a mizzle."

Dunn laughed. Where he would have used the word "drizzle," Pamela and her parents used the other word, which meant the same thing. *Gotta love British English,* he thought.

Pamela wore a yellow, hooded rain slicker. Dunn slipped on his flat garrison cap, which would offer little protection. He figured he'd survive.

She flipped up the hood, but before opening the door, turned to him and looked up expectantly. Dunn, not being a knucklehead, leaned down and kissed her a good one.

She pulled back and said softly, "Wow, buster."

Dunn grinned. "Still got it, huh? Even though we're coming up on our four month anniversary?"

She laid a hand on his chest and murmured, "Oh, you still have it. How about me?"

"My toes are curled, my dear."

She laughed, a low, pleasant sound that Dunn had grown to love.

"Ready?" he asked.

"Yep." Where she would have said, "yeah" or "yes" she now said "yep," Dunn's Iowa usage rubbing off on her.

She opened the door and the dogs flew outside.

Pamela and Dunn stepped outside, Dunn closing the inner door.

He took her hand and they started their walk.

The sky was gray, an everyday occurrence lately, and it was cold, perhaps forty degrees Fahrenheit. They crossed the barnyard at a leisurely pace. Dunn let her set the speed. She was nearly four months pregnant. She'd suffered some problems while working as a nurse in France for the Queen Alexandra's Military Nursing Service. She'd fainted and there was spotting. Her supervisor sent her back to England right away, and her family doctor, Dr. Swails, examined her. Everything was fine, he'd said, but she had to stop working, and watch her physical activity. To make up for her need to help others, she volunteered at the Barton Stacey Hospital—which was where she'd previously worked and where she'd met Dunn earlier in the year—reading to the patients.

When they reached the west side of the barnyard, one of their favorite places, they looked west down over a misty field. Trees had changed to their golds, reds, oranges, and yellows, but now the leaves were gone. Visibility was poor, only about a hundred yards. The bottom, far end of the field was blanketed by the fog and invisible, as was the valley in the distance. They stood together, his arm wrapped around her shoulders.

The rain suddenly let up, but the air still felt damp.

"You feeling all right?"

"Maybe a bit tired, but otherwise, yes. Nothing to worry about."

"Anything you need? Something you'd like to buy?"

"I could use a thicker sweater for the house. I feel cold most of the time."

Dunn pulled out his wallet and asked, "How much?"

"No need, I have plenty in my old checking account."

She'd had the account since she'd returned to Andover in 1943 to be near her parents. They were still suffering the loss of her brother, Percy, their only other child, who'd been killed at Dunkirk in May 1940, fighting a delaying action that helped 330,000 British and French soldiers escape in the "Miracle of Dunkirk" as Prime Minister Churchill called it.

They'd decided she'd keep it until they left for the U.S.

"Is the weather like this in Iowa in the fall?"

"Yep. Almost identical, a little colder. Plus, we can get the first snowfall by the end of the first week of December, so that's probably on the way there."

"How much snow comes?"

"Any given storm can drop from an inch to a foot, give or take a bit. Thing is, once it snows, it typically stays until spring, with new snow piling on. I've seen a height of three feet of snow by the time we get to March."

The two dogs ran by, barking happily. Possibly searching for a squirrel to antagonize.

"Your dogs will love the deep snow, especially the Lab."

This made Pamela smile.

"So will Tom, Junior." They'd already picked out the name if the baby was a boy, and he would have Percy, Percival, as a middle name in honor of her brother. Dunn insisted the baby would be a boy. Pamela was building a girls' names list on the side, just in case.

"Sledding?"

"Oh, yep. All day. Finished off with hot chocolate and fresh baked chocolate chip cookies."

"Sounds wonderful."

"It sure is," he replied wistfully, lost in childhood memories.

Tires crunched on the gravel driveway and the dogs pointed and started their alarm barks.

A small black car drove tentatively into the barnyard and stopped a respectful twenty feet away from the couple. A young blond woman got out and looked around apparently perplexed. She seemed not to see them.

"Can we help you, miss?" Pamela called.

The woman jumped, surprised, and her head whipped around to face them. "Oh, dear, you startled me." She raised a hand to her mouth.

"I'm sorry," Pamela replied, noting the woman wore red fingernail polish.

The Dunns walked toward the woman. She wore a tan raincoat, but it didn't hide her curvaceous shape. Nicely-formed calves were visible below the hem of the coat. She had a blue scarf over her head and an umbrella in her hand, which she opened after a struggle with the mechanism. An expensive-looking camera hung from her neck.

The dogs ran over to the woman, their tails wagging. She held out a hand for them to sniff. When they were satisfied they'd captured all possible aromas from her they sat down off to the side.

Pamela held out her hand, which the woman shook. She had a firm grip.

"I'm Pamela Dunn and this is my husband, Tom."

"Pleased to meet you. Evelyn Harris." She shook Dunn's hand while staring into his brown eyes.

"I seem to be lost. I'm looking for St. Peter's Church. I'm a sucker for older architecture."

Pamela smiled. "That's our church and I can tell you how to get there. It's not far."

Evelyn reached out and touched Pamela on the arm. "Oh, thank you so much."

Pamela gave the directions and asked if they made sense.

Evelyn grinned and said, "They do. I know the road you mean. I drove right past it thinking it wasn't the right one. Silly me. Sorry to trouble you."

"It's no trouble at all. Would you like to come in and have some tea? Warm up before you get going?"

"You're so sweet, but no, thank you. I want to get to the church and take the best pictures I can get on a day like this."

"It's a lovely church. We were married there last July."

"Oh, my goodness, how wonderful." Evelyn glanced at her camera and then back at Pamela. "Would you mind if I took a picture of the two of you? It would go so well with the pictures of the church. You know, give people faces to associate with the church and connect with. I often sell my photos to newspapers, magazines, and book publishers who need them for a history of England sort of thing."

Pamela looked at Dunn, who shrugged.

"I'd be happy to send you a copy . . ."

"Okay, sure. Where do you want us?" Pamela said.

Evelyn looked around and her eyes settled on the barn, and the two houses. "The buildings will make a wonderful, authentic backdrop. How about right here?" She pointed at a spot.

"Of course."

Dunn and Pamela moved obediently to the place Evelyn had selected.

She positioned them so they faced her left, showing a part-frontal part-profile view of their faces. "Could you slip the hood off, Pamela?"

"Oh sure."

"Perfect!" Evelyn chirped.

She took a couple of shots, and had them turn to face her for a few more. The dogs, who Pamela had directed to sit quietly at their feet, watched everything Evelyn did.

She backed up and knelt about ten feet away.

"I'd like to get a couple with your dogs."

Pamela lowered a hand to Winston's head and scratched it absentmindedly.

Evelyn caught the motion and snapped the picture. She took another one of the dogs, rose and stepped closer.

"Thank you so much. These are going to turn out wonderfully and who knows, maybe you'll be in a magazine soon."

Pamela laughed.

"I must be on my way. Thanks again for all the help and the great photos. You two are great!"

She walked quickly back to her car and got in. As she turned around and drove away, she waved a hand out the open window.

"What a nice woman."

"Yep."

"Quite the looker, too."

"I hadn't noticed," Dunn said dryly.

"Uh huh. Good boy. Aren't you a good boy?"

The dogs' ears perked up at the sing-song voice Pamela used.

The couple resumed their walk, which led them north past the barn.

Evelyn glanced in her rearview mirror as she slowly departed the barnyard. The couple was now walking away toward the barn.

"God, I am *so* good," she chortled.

Getting the pictures of the targets at their home would be noted by her superiors and her credentials would climb within the Abwehr.

She recalled the dangerous intensity of Dunn's eyes and she lifted the lid to the tiny suitcase on the seat next to her. She glanced lovingly at the Luger inside.

Would her partner give her the pleasure of killing Dunn and the wife or take it for himself?

RONN MUNSTERMAN

8

Reichführer Heinrich Himmler's office
SS Headquarters
Berlin
26 November, 1530 Hours, Berlin time

Sturmbannführer, SS Major, Dedrick Förstner stood silently outside the closed door to Himmler's office. He raised his hand to knock, but paused with the knuckles a few centimeters from the wood. He was uncharacteristically nervous. This was his first one-on-one meeting with the *Reichführer*. When he'd received the order to appear in Himmler's office, he had, as would anyone with any sense, started running through his memory for mistakes he may have made. Nothing had come to mind, although Himmler may have simply decided he had done something wrong.

Förstner closed his eyes briefly, opened them, and knocked twice.

Through the door he clearly heard a faint, "Enter."

He opened the door and stepped through to the office. He walked across the room to a spot behind a single upholstered chair in front of Himmler's desk. He met Himmler's eyes noting how small and beady they looked through the thick glasses the *Reichführer* wore. Clicking his boot heels together, he gave Himmler the Nazi salute and said, "*Heil* Hitler!"

Himmler returned the salute and said, "*Heil* Hitler. Be seated, *Sturmbannführer* Förstner."

Förstner stepped around the chair and sat down.

Himmler sat perfectly upright in his large leather chair. As always, he wore his black SS uniform, as did Förstner. A small man, Himmler's dark hair was cut extremely close, especially along the sides where it was shaved off.

Himmler looked down at his desk and opened a dossier. He read a few passages and looked up at Förstner. "You were under the command of *Obersturmbannführer* Skorzeny for quite some time."

"Yes, sir. It was my distinct honor to serve under the lieutenant colonel."

"You were on the mission to rescue our friend Mussolini."

"Yes, sir."

Operation Oak was successfully executed on September 12th, the year before. Skorzeny's Waffen-SS unit flew in gliders to the mountaintop where the fascist leader was being held prisoner. He'd been removed from office by the Italian King, Victor Emmanuel III, the previous July. They'd waltzed in, grabbed the former dictator and shoved him into a small motorized plane. Although the plane was overloaded by his bulky presence, Skorzeny had insisted on accompanying the Italian dictator all the way to Munich. There he paraded the dictator in front of the cameras and created his own famous persona.

"*Obersturmbannführer* Skorzeny recommended you for this mission."

Concealing surprise that his former commander would bother, as he had so many more important things to do at this time, Förstner replied, "I'm honored."

Himmler nodded. Of course he was honored. "I understand your English is quite good."

"Yes, sir. My parents and I often visited England, and once America, when I was younger."

"Good. That will be very helpful. This mission is one of vengeance and to send a message to the American Rangers and

British Commandos stationed at a particular U.S. Army base in England. Both units have become an irritant for us and we intend to make one of them pay dearly for interfering with our right to conduct the war as we see fit."

Förstner nodded. "An execution."

"With additional penalties."

"Yes, sir."

"You'll fly in under cover of darkness and parachute down."

"Understood, *Reichführer*."

"We have a female operative in place. Her operations name is Evelyn Harris. She is in Andover, a small city about a hundred kilometers southwest of London. You will be her husband, Robert Harris. You'll meet her at the Star and Garter Hotel in Andover. She has been hunting for and has identified the main target. He is based at Camp Barton Stacey, but is known to leave the base frequently to stay with his wife and her family. Your assignment, with Evelyn's assistance, is to kill them all. As brutally as possible. Burn down the house as well.

"His name is Master Sergeant Thomas Dunn."

"With pleasure, sir."

RONN MUNSTERMAN

9

Camp Barton Stacey
27 November, 0655 Hours, 30 minutes before sunrise

Saunders directed half his squad to the right of the target while the other half stayed put to provide supporting fire for the advancing team. The target was a barn built around the turn of the previous century, which made it almost 150 years old. Its stone base reached ten feet high and the rest was wood construction. It had belonged to the widower farmer who sold his property to the U.S. Army to be included as part of the base. He'd moved into Andover, seemed to enjoy his life, and promptly died six months later, of boredom, people liked to say.

The sky was gray with clouds. An earlier rain had left everything wet. It was a cold twenty-five degrees Fahrenheit.

The squad members wore ponchos over their uniforms and their Brody helmets.

His two best demolition men, Chadwick and Dickinson, were on the team advancing on the barn. The five Commandos reached the southeast corner of the structure, and knelt, their suppressed Stens at the ready. On their backs they each carried fifty pounds of explosives. Two men also carried smaller packs of incendiary devices.

Chadwick glanced toward Saunders, who was a mere thirty yards away. Saunders lifted a hand and dropped it.

Chadwick raced toward the barn's wooden double door. He lifted the wood latch and pushed the right door open. Glancing inside, he made sure it was clear, then darted through the opening. The other four Commandos rushed in behind him and spread out, shucking off their packs of explosives. There were two main support posts, each a third the way across the length of the barn's open space. Above them the loft covered the entire length of the building. In the center were six pallets filled with stacks of old newspapers, the closest thing Saunders could find to represent millions of pounds of British money.

While three men began setting the explosive charges on the posts, and on the foot thick support beam, the two men with the incendiary devices placed them on the papers and set the timers.

Experienced men, setting the charges only took a few minutes. Chadwick checked to make sure everything was done, and led the men outside. Dickinson, the last man, pulled the door closed and latched it. They ran back along the side of the stone first floor, and took a sharp right to return to the rest of the squad. Once there, the entire squad took off and ran toward a small rise in the field. They dashed around to the side opposite the barn, and hit the wet ground.

Saunders and Barltrop, as was common, were side-by-side, peeking over the hillock. The rest of the squad was stretched out to their right. Everyone was prone on the soaking wet grass. Saunders lifted his left wrist and eyed his watch. The incendiaries would ignite first setting the pallets of paper on fire. Thirty seconds later, the explosives would go off. If they waited any longer, it was conceivable that the fire might consume the timers and detonators on the explosive packs. Low chance, but still possible. He'd instructed Tim Chadwick to make sure the packs were on the other side of the support beams. He shook his head to himself. That was why they were having a rehearsal in the first place, better to find problems here instead of in Germany.

His second hand ticked across the twelve. About fifteen seconds later, a small whooshing sound came from inside the barn. The fire. Right on time, the explosions rocked the roof, blowing a hole in the center, smoke and fire leaping upward, and the front doors blew off their hinges, flames shooting ten feet into the barnyard. The roof swayed to the right, settled back into place, shuddered, and collapsed straight down into the barn. The fire, receiving plenty of wood for fuel and air to live, erupted into the gray sky. Flames appeared to fill the barn from one end to the other, dancing in all directions according to the air flow and heat.

Saunders and the men could feel the heat from fifty yards away, and the roar of the fire filled the morning air. No one moved, captivated by the fire.

Ten minutes passed. Fifteen. Thirty. The flames began to diminish.

Saunders touched Barltrop on the shoulder and stood. His second in command joined him, and they marched toward the black, soot covered stone opening. When they reached a point about ten feet away, the radiant heat made them stop. If felt like they were standing in front of an open industrial oven.

Inside the barn everything was black. The roof and the fallen beams were still smoldering. All of the wood had the peculiar flaked look caused by extreme heat. There didn't appear to be any paper left.

The sky suddenly opened and it poured. When the raindrops struck the heated surfaces, steam formed adding to the clouds of smoke.

"The rain'll probably finish it off, Steve."

"Yeah. Looks like it worked the way we expected."

"Aye."

Saunders looked at his watch again and as he dipped his head, water ran off his Brody helmet, dripping to the ground. "Let's get back to the barracks and everyone can clean up. I'm ready for breakfast. We can go over the plan and review what just happened with the men at the mess hall."

"Sounds good. I'm starving."

By the time the squad of Commandos made it to the mess hall, it was eight-thirty. The hall was empty except for the workers on the food line. The men grabbed their food and coffee and settled in around two tables they pulled together.

Saunders sat opposite Barltrop.

He was twenty-six and married to Sadie since September twenty-third. He'd joined the British Army in late 1939, which had kept him from being caught up in the Dunkirk Miracle. He often felt guilty about not being on the continent to help out. His first combat was in North Africa under General Bernard Montgomery. It was there his actions drew the attention of his superiors and he and his new friend, Steve Barltrop, were selected for Commando School in Scotland, at Achnacarry House. Born in London's East End, he was a true Cockney, defined as being born within earshot of the Bow Bells of St. Mary-le-Bow.

As a teenager, he'd fallen in love with architecture and planned to start his own construction company after the war. With three older sisters, who had all married servicemen, he'd had a happy childhood, even though his father was a man of few words, and rarely expressed his feelings. That had taught Saunders to tell his family he loved them often. Even during the war, or perhaps because of it, he never said goodbye to family whether in person or on the phone without saying, "I love you."

Steve Barltrop was a year younger than Saunders. He'd grown up in Cheshunt, a small town about fifteen miles north of London. Saunders' wife, Sadie, was also from Cheshunt. Their wedding had been held at a local church there, which was where Barltrop met his current girl, Kathy. She was Sadie's cousin and worked in London for the Royal Navy's Staff Department. Barltrop had been best man for Saunders and had given an outstanding speech. He had brown hair and piercing blue eyes. A master mechanic, his dream was to work on the British Grand Prix team as Chief Mechanic. And add to that, marry Kathy.

He was the quintessential second in command. He anticipated Saunders' needs as well as the squad's, and in combat made lightning fast decisions to get the job done. His reaction time was extraordinary, like recently in Egypt when they were attacking a rebel outpost. One of the enemy soldiers had tossed a grenade. Barltrop snatched it up, and threw it back inside where it exploded taking out many of the rebels.

Newly promoted Sergeant Tim Chadwick was one of the squad's true demolitions experts. While they all were good at handling explosives, Chadwick had a golden touch and an eye for how much was needed for the task at hand. A fisherman's son from the northern English village of Amble, he could handle anything that floated. With swept-back blond hair and blue eyes, he could pass for German if only he could speak the language.

Christopher Dickinson, also a new sergeant, was Chadwick's best friend and their favorite thing to do together was blow things up. Growing up in Manchester had turned him at a young age into a United fan. Playing professional football was what every Manchester boy dreamed of doing as an adult, and Dickinson was no exception. His nose was crooked, the result of a misjudged header shot in his early teens.

A tough and reliable Commando, he inexplicably loved performing magic tricks, especially for kids. Everywhere he went, even into combat, he took a pack of magic cards, silk flowers, and other light-weight magic paraphernalia. Walking down the street in Andover, you'd likely spot him surrounded by a crowd of laughing kids.

Corporal Cyril Talbot was one of five replacements who'd arrived together not long after the squad, on its way to an Austrian castle, lost half the men during a night fighter attack. The shortest man in the squad at five-seven, he was likely one of the strongest with a wide, powerful body. From the central England city of Birmingham, he was a natural mimic and had taken over the late Geoffrey Kopp's role as the Saunders impersonator. He could move through any terrain like a cat, albeit a big one, without making a sound. He liked to sneak up on his squad mates during training exercises.

Lance Corporal Martin Alders, a twenty-four year old from London's affluent West End, was a thin man of five-nine with wiry strength. An accomplished chef, he'd had to talk his way out of being assigned to a cook's role. At Commando School, he'd proven himself by finishing first in his class. His face was narrow, matching his body type, and he had soft hazel eyes.

Lance Corporal Ira Myers was a big man, nearly as wide as Saunders in the shoulders, but narrower at the hips. He'd been raised on a farm near Sheffield, and his father had taught him to shoot well. So well that he became the squad's sniper using a scoped bolt-action Lee-Enfield .303. He reminded Saunders of one of Tom Dunn's men, Stanley Wickham, who was from Texas. Myers had the same sort of self-effacing manner.

Corporal Albert Holmes was a six-foot redhead, whose hair was even brighter than Saunders' and his face was speckled with freckles. He was quick to smile and people immediately took a liking to him. He spoke Egyptian Arabic like a native, which was more or less true as his father had been a member of the Diplomatic Corps in Cairo. Holmes had spent most of his childhood there. His skill had proven to be useful on the recent mission to Cairo.

Corporal Billy Forster was a handsome lad from Southampton. He had a strong jaw line and green eyes. Getting dates was not among his list of difficulties. Even though he loved ships due to growing up in a port city, he'd joined the army rather than the Royal Navy because his father had been a soldier in the Great War. He'd signed up for Commando School as soon as he'd finished recruit training.

The latest replacement, for Kopp, who had been killed during the mission to blow up Hitler's Dam, Corporal Ted Bentley, was twenty-three. Saunders had selected him because of his high scores in shooting and problem solving, the two things he valued the most. He was the squad's long distance runner and could outlast everyone. From Bristol on the west coast of England, his family owned a horse training facility. His father had trained a number of winners over the years. An accomplished rider, he often complained that it was a shame the army had seen fit to replace horses with tanks.

The men ate their breakfast quickly, the only way soldiers knew how to eat, but they managed to keep an easygoing banter alive.

Saunders double-tapped a knife against his coffee cup. Everyone looked his way.

"Well done today, lads. Later this morning, we'll take a look at the air recon photos of the warehouses in Bremerhaven. Get a feel for where the krauts might store the fake money."

Saunders and the squad discussed a few possible changes to the mission plan for about fifteen minutes. He broke up the meeting and everyone headed back to the barracks.

10

Gertrude Dunn arrived at her desk a few minutes late. Several of the other women had stopped her in the hallway to ask her what had happened and did she really disarm a knife-wielding robber? They were incredulous when she answered that she had indeed done all of that. While they said all the right and nice things about how brave she must have been, she could see in their eyes a couple of other things: fear that it might happen to them, and that she was entirely crazy to have done it, even if it had worked out. As the women walked away, she'd sighed. The reaction by the other women was irritating. It angered her that they seemed to think she should have just "let" the man take their purses and hard-earned money.

She removed her pink sweater and pulled her wooden, rolling chair out from underneath her desk, but didn't sit down. She leaned forward instead and picked up a piece of notebook paper. She held it up to read: Gertrude, see me immediately upon arrival. It was signed by her supervisor. Another sigh escaped her lips. *Now what?*

She picked up her notebook, the one the piece of paper had been torn from, a pencil, and headed toward Mrs. Cookson's office. It was in the back of the monstrous room where the analysts worked. Gertrude had only been there about seven weeks.

Cookson's door was open so Gertrude knocked on the door jam. Cookson waved a hand at her to come in without bothering to look up. As soon as Gertrude entered she saw two other people sitting in the office, to the side on a small sofa. She stifled her initial reaction to the woman, Alice Nicholson, officially her mentor. Unofficially, her tormentor, at least back in training in St. Louis, Missouri.

Gertrude didn't recognize the man sitting with Nicholson. He had one lanky leg crossed over the other. His face was thin and he had a pinched mouth. Gertrude took an instant disliking to him as his unfriendly dark eyes seemed to size her up.

Cookson looked up. "You already know Alice."

"Yes, ma'am."

"This is Mr. Price. He's from your OSS office in Washington, D.C."

Instead of standing and offering a hand, Price just nodded at Gertrude.

That steamed Gertrude, so she didn't acknowledge him.

"Have a seat," Cookson said.

Gertrude did, turning her chair so she could face Alice and Price.

"It's Mr. Price's show, so I'll turn it over to him," Cookson said.

Terrific, Gertrude thought, keeping her face a mask. She looked at him, waiting.

And waiting.

He seemed to enjoy making her wait.

Well, I can play his stupid game, too. She thought of the times she and her sister, Hazel, would play the staring contest game. First one to blink lost and had to do the other's chores for the day. One time, Hazel had tried to fight off a sneeze to no avail and she blinked as you always do. She received no mercy from her little sister.

Gertrude eyed Price, went to her calm place and continued to wait. Without blinking.

After about sixty seconds, Price broke eye contact. Gertrude allowed a tiny smile to cross her lips. When he looked back she was again in her frozen position.

He cleared his throat, an unpleasant high-pitched sound like fingernails on a chalkboard. "I understand you disarmed a man with a knife." His voice was high-pitched, too. It grated on Gertrude's ears.

"Yes," she replied. She almost lifted her hands to the "so what?" position.

"You said your, uh, brother, taught you how to do that."

"Yes."

"Why did he do that?"

Gertrude shrugged. "You'd have to ask him."

Price frowned. "I'm asking *you*."

"He just wanted me to know how to defend myself."

"Defend yourself? In Cedar Rapids , Iowa? Really? That's not exactly New York City, is it?"

"We have our problems," she replied, just to be contrary.

"Uh huh. Well, let's try something. Please stand up."

"Mr. Price, what are you doing?" Cookson interrupted, sounding alarmed.

"Bear with me, ma'am," Price answered in a condescending tone. He stood and stepped away from the sofa. "Please rise, Miss Dunn."

Gertrude jumped up and faced him. *Fine, asshole.* She still had her pink sweater in her left hand.

He reached inside his jacket and withdrew a knife from a sheath on his black belt.

"Take this knife away from me."

Gertrude's first thought was to look at Alice or Mrs. Cookson, but knew that would be a mistake. *Gee whiz, these guys and their tests.*

She took a fighter's stance and so did Price.

He took a tentative swing at her, which she avoided easily. *Trying to get me used to a slow attack, then he'll speed up.*

She let the sweater in her left hand unfold turning it into a matador's cape.

He suddenly charged, knife hand coming up for her throat.

She flicked the sweater over the top of his knife hand and grabbed the other end with her right hand. She rotated her hands so the sweater tightened around the hand and forearm like a noose as she spun to her left.

He tried to pull back the knife hand, but it was trapped in the cloth which was getting tighter by the second. She yanked him forward, completing her half turn.

His hand and arm were stretched out as far as they could go and he, overbalanced as he was, took an involuntary step forward with his left foot.

His leg collided with her right hip and he flipped over. He landed hard on his right side, his arm pinned by Gertrude's left foot.

She knelt on her right knee. She let go of the sweater with her left hand and short punched him in the jaw. His eyes rolled back and he went limp.

She rose and freed her sweater. Picking up the loose knife, she sat down on the sofa next to Alice.

Alice grinned at her. "Nice."

"Oh, dear," Cookson said as she rose and ran around to the downed man.

Price came awake with a start and stared around the room, obviously trying to figure out what had happened. He got up slowly with Cookson's help. He rubbed his jaw and looked at Gertrude.

She grabbed the tip of the knife blade and bent the knife into a u-shape.

He suddenly grinned. "Training knife. Lucky for me, I'd say." He sat down in Gertrude's chair and leaned on his bony knees. "Wow. That was some punch, lady. Your brother is obviously quite the teacher, but you have some serious skills."

Gertrude smiled. She leaned forward and held the rubber knife out to Price, handle first. He took it sheepishly and slid it back in the sheath.

"I get that this was a test. You and whomever else didn't believe I'd done what I told the police. Or . . . you thought it was a fluke. Right?"

"Uh, right, the latter," he said, surprised by her nailing it so quickly.

"So what was the test for?"

"The OSS recognizes that you're here because of your intellect and powers of deduction and codebreaking. These skills were uncovered rapidly in St. Louis. However, because of those skills, we stopped looking for others you might possess."

"What? Now you want me to become a fighter?"

He shook his head. "We prefer field agent. Or sometimes operative."

"*A field agent?* Working where?"

"I can't tell you that."

"Hm. No, of course not. Where's the training for that?"

"Somewhere not far from Washington, D.C."

"And if I say no?"

"Back to your desk and reading telegrams and letters. Day . . . after . . . day. Until the end of the war. You can do so much more."

Cookson, who had taken her seat again, frowned at his demeaning remark, but let it slide. Gertrude did, after all, work for the OSS and was only on loan to her department.

"How soon do you have to know?" Gertrude asked.

Price checked his watch. "Seventeen hundred. My flight, or our flight if you say 'yes,' is at seventeen-forty-five. Do you need some time?"

Gertrude glanced at Alice, who kept a blank expression on her face, obviously not wanting to influence Gertrude. Cookson looked much the same.

Looking back at Price, she said evenly, "I'd better go to my room and pack, don't you think, Mr. Price?"

RONN MUNSTERMAN

11

Dunn's barracks
Camp Barton Stacey
28 November, 0942 Hours, the next day

Dunn and Cross walked from their just-parked jeep toward the barracks through the pouring, cold rain. They wore ponchos to ward off the water, but their boots splashed through the many puddles of standing water along the gravel and mud walkway. All of the chairs the men liked to use to sit outside and smoke on a nice day had been grudgingly pulled back inside the barracks.

Dunn yanked open the door and entered the barracks. Half of the bunks were lined up on the right wall and the other half across from them. At the far end of the barracks stood the squad's armory, containing their Thompson .45 caliber submachine guns, M1911 Colt .45s, British suppressed Sten submachine guns, M1s, and one 1903 Springfield bolt-action scoped sniper rifle.

Most of the men were on their racks either reading a letter or writing one. Others were reading a book or a magazine. Two were playing chess over an ancient wood board and set. One was patiently teaching the other how to play.

The men stopped what they were doing to look at Dunn. In many squads, the arrival of the squad leader would cause the men to rise to a near-attention position. Dunn squelched that idea long ago. He didn't view it as important. For an officer yes, no question, but not for him. He knew for a certainty that he had his men's respect, and he didn't need a rule of behavior in place to prove it or stoke his ego.

"Morning, guys."

"Morning, Sarge," the group replied.

"Gonna need your attention. We just met with Colonel Kenton. Gather around Cross's bunk, we'll need his map holder."

Cross had long ago put up a pair of hooks at the head of his bunk to hold maps and other items to show the men during mission prep.

"Dave, need your map of Hamburg."

A murmur of excitement passed around the room. They'd been stuck on base for over a week and were starting to get antsy. The men got up and ambled over to Cross's bunk. Some sat down across from it, while the rest stood at the foot.

Dunn took off his helmet and poncho and put them on the floor. From his shirt pocket he pulled out a piece of paper with his notes from the meeting with Kenton.

Cross pulled out his wooden trunk from underneath the bunk and flipped the lid open. He rifled through the stack of maps until he found the one he wanted. He rose and attached the map to the hooks. It showed northwest Germany, and Hamburg in particular. The scale was good enough to see individual roads and streets. The Elbe River waterway coming in from the northwest and the city were clearly marked.

Dunn took a position next to the map, and faced his men. Cross stood on the other side of the bunk.

Staff Sergeant Alphonso (Al) Martelli had been with Dunn since early August. An Italian Bronx boy, whose parents owned a neighborhood grocery and lived upstairs, he carried his Bronx accent like a badge of honor. He spoke fluent Italian which was why Dunn selected him from another squad to go on a mission to Italy. Due to Martelli's excellent work, Dunn had made the temporary transfer permanent. A good looking young man, he had black swept-back black hair and brown eyes.

Corporal Hugh Kelly joined the squad in early October. He was from a seemingly unusual place for someone of Irish heritage, Greenville, Mississippi. He'd often taken offense to northerners making fun of his great-grandfather who'd served in the Confederate Army. One thing inevitably led to another and he'd end up losing a stripe or two for fighting. In spite of that, he'd signed up for and was approved to go to Ranger School in Scotland. One last fight there and harsh words from the commandant about being sent back to his unit finally taught him to dampen his easy-to-rile temper.

He scored extremely high in shooting and problem solving, which was what Dunn was looking for. Like Martelli, he had black hair, but his eyes were blue. While Martelli had fallen in love with an older Italian woman and planned to go back to marry her after the war, Kelly went out with a different girl every time.

Staff Sergeant David M. Jones, Jonesy, had been assigned the role of the squad's sniper. This happened on the firing range shortly after he'd arrived five months ago. He'd put on a shooting exhibition for Dunn and the squad, laying ten rounds inside a seven and a half inch circle from 600 yards with his late uncle's 1903 Springfield.

A Southside Chicago boy, he'd grown up blocks from Comiskey Park, and was of course a White Sox fan. An artist, he'd attended the School of the Art Institute of Chicago for two years just prior to signing up for the army. He drew caricatures of the men, who loved them, proudly hanging them above their bunks and sending them home to their families and girlfriends. Jonesy was a slender six-footer with a widow's peak and blue eyes.

Corporal Eugene Lindstrom's parents apparently had a wicked sense of humor because Lindstrom had been born in Eugene, Oregon. This had taught him not to take himself too seriously, and his dry wit cracked up the squad on occasion. He'd joined the squad at the same time as Jonesy, back in June. He'd been assigned as Jonesy's spotter and the two worked well together.

He'd just recently returned to the squad after several weeks in the hospital. He'd been shot in the thigh while on a mission in the freezing Arctic. He'd risen to legend status when he single-handedly frightened off a polar bear that'd had thoughts of making a meal out of the Ranger squad sleeping in their Arctic tents. About the same height as Jonesy, he was a little stockier, and he wore his brown hair short against the scalp, but not quite bald.

Corporal Chuck Higgins had such a gregarious nature that people just seemed to like him on the spot. His red-haired feistiness countered his relatively short height of five-eight. From Lincoln, Nebraska, where his father was an archeologist and professor at the university there, Higgins planned to follow his father's path. He'd gone on many summertime digs with his dad. His knowledge had been useful on the Arctic mission when the squad had rescued from an SS platoon a treasure trove of gold, silver, and other valuables, including a so-called mythical Sword of Ice that SS Commander Himmler wanted very badly.

Technical Sergeant Dave Cross had met his boss and best friend at Ranger School the year previous. Born in Winter Harbor, Maine, he was the son of a fisherman. He'd joined the army right after Pearl Harbor, like Dunn. For a time prior to Pearl Harbor, he'd lost interest in fishing and had left home for work in New York City. Three years later, he longed to return to the sea with his dad. A year younger than Dunn, he was a little heavier and wider. He had sandy hair and bright blue eyes. The two men worked well together and as the second in command, Cross often led half the squad. He'd been Dunn's best man back in July. He'd recently confessed to Dunn he had hopes for a girl in Winter Harbor who'd been a high school classmate he'd admired from afar. Not long ago, he'd sent her a letter and was waiting to see if anything would come from it.

Staff Sergeant Rob Goerdt was the only other man on the squad from Dunn's home state of Iowa. A farm boy raised near Dyersville, he was the youngest of ten kids. Like Dunn, he'd attended the University o f Iowa, but they'd never crossed paths.

Since joining the squad in early August, he'd earned the Silver Star for destroying seven tanks with a bazooka, and capturing three complete crews. He also won a Purple Heart for getting hit by a German grenade's shrapnel at the Battle of Cassino. Of German heritage, he'd spoken the language at home. It had come in handy on a few missions. His ethnicity showed up in his looks: light colored hair over blue eyes. A huge baseball fan he, like Dunn, loved the Cubs. His goal for after the war was to get into professional umpiring. His biggest dream was to work the plate in game seven of the World Series.

Sergeant Stanley Wickham, the second biggest man on the squad at six-three and two-twenty, had played high school football in East Texas where he'd set about every rushing record possible. Colleges were watching him his senior year. After graduating, he'd enlisted in June, 1942, earlier on the same day the United States Navy defeated the Imperial Japanese Navy at Midway. He spoke with a peculiar blended accent of British, which he'd picked up quickly, and Texan, which he, of course, was raised into. The curious sound of his voice mesmerized the local girls and he quite naturally took a liking to that. It didn't hurt that he was also movie-star handsome. He, along with Dunn and Cross, were the only survivors of the original squad that graduated together from Ranger School at Achnacarry House.

Sergeant Robert (Bob) Schneider II, a kind, compassionate soldier, had lived in many places in the States because his dad was U.S. Army. He was bigger than Wickham by an inch and twenty pounds. He'd developed into the squad's medic and had helped save Lindstrom in the Arctic, and Dunn when he'd been knocked into the reservoir of the dam they were getting ready to destroy. These events had started him thinking about, but not sharing with anyone, someday going to medical school, perhaps the famous and leading Johns Hopkins in Baltimore. His other main task was to slug around the squad's radio. That's what you got for being the biggest guy.

Under the leadership of Tom Dunn, this group of men from all over America had gelled into one of the fiercest small fighting units anywhere.

12

Dunn glanced at his notes once and was able to put them away thanks to his photographic memory. He touched Hamburg on the map with a pencil. "The Germans are storing liquid oxygen for their V2 rockets not far outside Hamburg. They mix the liquid oxygen with fuel. That mixture ignites and drives the rocket. It's located east of this large hill," he circled a spot with the pencil, "and it's covered with camouflage netting making it look like part of the hill and flat land from the air. We only know about it in the first place due to a spy in the city. He evidently followed a truck most of the way, and went back at night for a closer look. The fencing around the facility is chain link and there's a pasture with cattle on the east side of it. You can see it's close to a town called Buxetude, which is about seven miles from Hamburg's center.

"We're taking a sub to a point part way down the Elbe River waterway, and a dinghy to the western shore. From there it's about a six mile hike. There are six storage tanks. They're a little smaller than you'd see at a fuel depot, but still huge. There may be some guys there who do maintenance, even at night, but there's not much in the way of security beyond a few armed guards at the main gate and a few walking the perimeter. The road that feeds the facility runs east-west ending inside the fence. There's some kind of office, a small building set back about twenty-five yards from the gate. We don't know if anyone's in it at night. It seems logical that the maintenance workers might gather there for coffee or whatever.

"The fence is not electrified, which is good news, since we'll be cutting our way in from the north side. We're taking the maximum amount of explosives with us: fifty pounds each. Suppressed Stens and the usual other items." He looked at his sniper. "Jonesy, take your oh-three. Who knows if we'll need it or not."

Jonesy nodded. "Okay, Sarge." Even though Jonesy had a standing order to take the sniper rifle, Dunn usually remembered to say something about it in these pre-mission meetings.

"Schneider and Wickham will cut an opening in the fence for us. We'll pair up for setting the explosives. Colonel Kenton said he'd talked to a construction guy, who suggested targeting the valve pipe they use to fill the trucks that transport the liquid oxygen to the V2 launch sites. He said it would be slightly weaker there. He also told the colonel that we'd better be a half mile away when the shit goes up, his word, because the fireballs will be aggressive and enormous, and the shock waves will move with terrifying speed at ground level. You've all seen aerial film of our B-17 bombs hitting the ground in Germany?"

The men nodded. It was an awesome display of explosive power.

"Well, remember the circle of air and dirt that expands from each bomb? That's your pressure wave. It's so fast it could overtake an aircraft like the P-51 Mustang."

The men shook their heads.

"Sheee-it, indeed," muttered Wickham in his Brit-Tex accent.

"As I mentioned, to get there, we're taking a sub into the Elbe River waterway."

There were a few groans. Martelli held his hand up.

"Yes, Al?"

"How long is the trip?" Martelli's face gave away his dislike of submarines.

"Twenty hours or so."

"Oh, man . . ." Martelli said, his face pale.

"We'll leave the same way we came in and head for a rendezvous with the sub, which will wait for us."

"Oh, goody," Martelli quipped.

The men laughed.

Dunn held up his hand and they stopped.

"I estimate it'll take us no more than thirty minutes to get everything done and get out. Five to seven more to double-time to a tree-covered hilltop a half mile away. We'll hunker down and watch the facility to confirm its destruction."

"Any questions?"

No one had any, but then Martelli raised his hand again.

"Yes, Al?"

"So . . . we're really taking a sub?"

"What's the deal, Al? You've been on a sub before."

"Yeah, well, that was before I realized sometimes they go down but don't come back up."

"You've been watching war movies about the Pacific again haven't you?"

Al looked affronted. "Why do you say that?"

The room erupted in laughter and Dunn gave them their head. Eventually the chuckles died down.

"Anyone not Martelli have any questions?" Dunn stared at Martelli, daring him to ask another. The Bronx kid just grinned.

"If you think of any, you know where to find me. We need to leave here at oh three thirty tomorrow morning to make it to the sub in London on time. We'll meet this afternoon right after lunch to go over assignments. I'd like the weapons and explosive packs to be ready no later than seventeen hundred. Okay, that's all."

Dunn headed for his private quarters and the men began working on their weapons.

Ronn Munsterman

13

Eastern Shore of the Wadden Sea
5 miles northeast of Bremerhaven, Germany
30 November, 0043 Hours, Berlin time, 2 days later

Sergeant Steve Barltrop was the first to jump out of the black rubber boat the squad used to paddle ashore from the British submarine that carried them from London. It had been nearly an entire day and night of terror for Barltrop, no fan of the sea whether on top of the waves or underneath. He pulled hard on the rope towing the boat closer until it stopped against the sand.

Saunders and the rest of the men hopped out, their boots splashing. Chadwick and Alders helped Barltrop drag the boat farther across the sand to a point close to the grass growing on a small sand dune. They flipped the boat upside down and Chadwick got a tan camouflaged net out of his pack. They spread out the net over the boat. Next they scooped sand haphazardly onto the net. After that was done, Alders grabbed a handful of long blades of wild grass about two feet long and, walking backwards, started sweeping it across the boat's scrape marks in the sand. He waited until all of the men had climbed over the sand dune and he swept away their footprints, too. He tossed away the makeshift broom and joined the squad who'd taken a knee in a semicircle in front of Saunders.

Some of the men carried satchels filled with fifty pounds of explosives. Others carried incendiary devices they would use to burn the money. Chadwick and Dickinson carried an additional smaller pack filled with the timers and detonators. The men wore black grease on their faces. Everything they wore was black: instead of their usual uniforms they wore jackets over sweaters, and pants; rather than the Brody helmet, their heads were covered by a watch cap, pulled low almost to the eyebrows; knit gloves protected their hands from the cold air. They carried Sten guns with an integrated suppressor and combat knives.

The night sky was partially clear, revealing a full moon. This was fortunate weather for late November, otherwise travel would have been much more difficult with snow on the ground.

Saunders didn't want to waste any time. "Everybody okay?"

The men gave him a nod. "Right. Five miles. One hour for the first three, but we slow down as we get closer to the outskirts of the city. Our Bletchley information narrows the warehouse possibilities to three, all within a mile of each other, which is bloody lucky. The shipment is supposed to already be there. We'll set up in an abandoned building and send out a couple of scouts. Questions?"

No one had any.

"Holmes, you have point for the first hour. I'll take the rear."

"Right, Sarge."

"Good. Let's go, lads."

The men rose and formed up, Holmes taking his spot at the front and Saunders the last place. Holmes watched the men form a column. As soon as they were ready, he turned around and marched off to the southwest, toward Bremerhaven in the cold, clear moonlit German night.

14

Tree-covered hilltop
1/4 mile northeast of the liquid oxygen storage facility
7 miles northwest of Hamburg, Germany
30 November, 0105 Hours

The trip on the British submarine HMS *Sea Tiger* had taken the twenty hours Dunn had estimated for Martelli. A lot of time spent doing nothing. Reviewing the attack plan on the liquid oxygen storage facility only took a few hours. The captain had been accommodating to Dunn's choice of landing zone, which was at a place in the Elbe River waterway that was split by a narrow island five miles long. Both of the channels were quite deep, with adequate room for a submerged vessel. The entire waterway was very deep all the way to the Hamburg docks. Undoubtedly one of the reasons Hamburg had always been a thriving port city. Well, except for the repeated Allied bombings.

They'd bypassed the small town of Jork, which was near the water, on the way. Dunn and his men were kneeling, looking to the southwest. All they could see was a pasture with a few dark shapes standing around, presumably sleeping cows, and another hilltop.

But they knew the facility was there; intelligence said it was in spite of what their eyes told them.

"Let's go," Dunn ordered.

He took point himself and the men formed a column behind him. They were carrying their fifty pounds of explosives, timers and detonators, and their 9mm Sten guns with integrated suppressors and 32-round magazines. They wore their night operations clothing, identical to what Saunders' Commandos were wearing.

The air was clear, the sky cloudless and the full moon shed more than enough light for the men to see well. The ground was covered with moisture that was in the process of crystallizing into frost. Luckily, it wasn't crunchy under their boots yet. A north wind worked its unpleasant magic on their faces.

Dunn kept his eyes in constant motion, sweeping the landscape in front of him from side to side. He confirmed that the dark forms were indeed cattle, apparently so asleep they had no idea there were ten dangerous men passing by. Dunn idly hoped there wasn't a bull among the group, although he knew, from experience on his friend Paul's family farm, that bulls were segregated from the herd to prevent unauthorized bull-cow hanky-panky.

Straight ahead he spotted a tree and marched toward it. As he got closer, he realized he'd been hoodwinked by the clever camouflage net mentioned in the intelligence report. The netting was staked to the ground and went straight up forming a wall, yet the tree looked real from a distance. He reached the net. It went to his left and right at least a quarter of a mile. It was the biggest piece of deception he'd ever seen. He dropped to a knee, lifted the edge of the netting a couple of feet, and peeked inside.

Fifty yards away, the north chain link fence ran from his left to his right. He was at a slight angle to the facility and could see all six of the storage tanks. The gate on the other side and the small office were blocked from view by the massive storage tanks. He examined the areas next to the chain link fence.

Still holding up the netting, he waved at his men to come forward. As Cross came by, first in line, Dunn whispered, "Have the men get on their bellies. You keep an eye out for guards by the fence. None are in sight now."

"Will do, Sarge."

The men crawled under the net quickly, and Dunn slipped through after them, lowering the net back to the ground.

Dunn joined Cross on the damp ground glad to have the heavier jacket on. He checked his watch in the light of the moon, which while sufficient to see okay, was dimmer under the netting. He sighed.

"Now we wait."

"Ayup," Cross whispered.

Twelve minutes passed. Two guards appeared around the northwest corner of the chain link fence. They walked slowly. Dunn thought they were obviously going through the boring motions of being a sentry at a location where nothing happened. Ever. *Well, surprise, guys. Tonight's your unlucky night.*

It took the sentries five minutes to mosey along the length of the northern boundary. They never once looked toward Dunn's position.

"Jeez, they're slow," muttered Cross.

"Maybe they'll take a coffee break."

"Hope the hell so."

After the Germans disappeared, Dunn waited two minutes.

He rose and said, "Let's go."

The squad rose and Dunn took off with the men right behind him. When they reached the closest point of the fence, Dunn checked it at the top and the bottom, looking for any tell-tale signs it was actually electrified; can't take chances on that. It was safe.

Wickham and Schneider each pulled a pair of heavy-duty wire cutters from their jacket pockets and went to work on the chain link fence. Schneider made the horizontal cut about four feet off the ground, while Wickham made a vertical cut on the right. When they finished, Schneider stepped aside and Wickham pulled the fence open to the left like a door.

Dunn waved the men through. He went last and pulled the fence back into place. He tied it together at one point with a piece of black string. Hopefully it wouldn't catch the eyes of the sentries on their next pass.

The squad reached its demarcation line and smoothly split into five groups of two. Each group ran toward its assigned storage tank. One pair, Martelli and Higgins, was assigned to blow up two tanks, so they would use only one fifty pound satchel of explosives on each instead of two like everyone else was doing. They had the one in the middle of each line of three. The hope was that the explosions of the tanks on either side would contribute to their destruction.

Martelli knelt beside the valve of the first tank. He shrugged off his satchel and laid it on the ground. The valve happened to be positioned on the shaded side of the tank, receiving no moonlight. He opened the satchel and removed, by feel, the detonator and timer. He handed the timer to Higgins and nodded toward the area on their right, which was in the moonlight.

Higgins nodded and ran to the shadow's edge. He dropped to his knees, held the timer in the moonlight, and set it.

Meanwhile, Martelli lifted the satchel and hung its shoulder straps over the valve's two foot long, four-inch diameter pipe, which was about three feet off the ground.

Higgins returned and held out the timer. Martelli connected the detonator's wire to the timer, tightening the brass thumbwheel. He gently pushed the detonator into the top explosive block. Taking the timer from Higgins, he gently laid it back inside the satchel, tucking the wire inside. He made sure it wasn't crinkled and was still secured to the timer. He closed the satchel's flap.

"Time for the next one."

He rose and took off with Higgins on his heels.

The rest of the pairs finished with their assigned tanks and headed back to the demarcation line.

Dunn said to Cross, "Almost there."

"Ayup."

"Did you see anyone in the office?"

Cross had been on the east side of the tanks and had a view of the office. Dunn had been on the west side and his sightline had been blocked.

"No lights on. I could see the two guards at the gate and spotted the sentries stopping to chat for a minute before continuing on their round. They should be passing our gate soon."

"Let's hope they're still bored to tears."

Dunn turned to look toward the fence. He spotted the sentries, who were approaching the cut fence position. He held his breath. The men passed the opening and kept going. He released his breath.

"They missed it."

"Good."

A couple of minutes passed.

The night air carried new and unwelcome sounds.

Dunn looked at Cross. "Are those truck engines?"

RONN MUNSTERMAN

15

Downtown
Bremerhaven, Germany
30 November, 0130 Hours

Chadwick exited the building through a transom-style window and lowered himself to the alley outside. Dickinson followed immediately after. The two men ducked and ran south along the alley, careful to dodge the many crates and garbage cans strewn about. Chadwick reached the end of the alley and stopped. He peeked around the corner and the street there was clear. He took off again at a full run toward a dark building right in front of him. Someone on the inside opened the door and he and Dickinson bolted through. Albert Holmes closed the door quietly and joined the rest of the Commandos, who were resting on the floor in the abandoned building's main area.

There was just enough moonlight sneaking in the warehouse through the windows that the Commando squad could see each other pretty well. Saunders and Barltrop formed an odd lump on the floor. They'd employed the old trick of squatting under a poncho, in this case two, to be able to use a torch. They were examining a ten-year-old map of the city, on which intelligence had helpfully marked three locations where the forged wealth might be stored.

Chadwick walked up to the lump and whispered, "Hey Sarge, that building's a bust. Nothing there."

"Right. Okay, thanks." Saunders' voice was muffled by the ponchos.

Inside the poncho, Saunders drew an X across the mark for the building Chadwick was talking about. He used his fingers to measure the distance from their location to the next possible treasure spot. "Quarter mile."

"Right. I'll get Chadwick in here."

Saunders turned off the torch while Barltrop and Chadwick smoothly changed places. Once Chadwick was settled in, Saunders flicked the light back on, aiming it at the map on the dusty floor. The reflected light gave each man a ghostly appearance, the same way kids did by holding the torch under their chins around Halloween.

Saunders eyed his ghoulish partner. His nose wrinkled and he sniffed lightly. "What the bloody hell did you step in, Chadwick?"

Chadwick sniffed and his nose wrinkled up, too. "Oh, bugger all. Must've been the garbage cans we had to dodge. Here, just a sec."

He rearranged himself so his boots were outside the ponchos. "Better?" he asked.

Saunders took a tentative sniff. "Loads. Thanks."

He pointed at the map with his pencil stub. There's the second one. Four blocks. May have the name 'Bauer' on it."

Chadwick looked closely, memorizing the location. "Got it, Sarge."

Saunders pointed to another spot on the map. "Here's number three. It looks to be about six blocks south of the second one."

Chadwick noted the location. "Be back as soon as."

"Be fooking careful, mate."

Chadwick grinned, looking even more like a ghoul than before. "Always am, Sarge."

"Aye, but still."

Chadwick eyed his squad leader and friend. He nodded solemnly. "We will."

"Right. Off with you then." Saunders clicked off the torch and pocketed it. The men stood up and untangled themselves from the ponchos, letting them fall to the concrete floor.

Chadwick grabbed Dickinson by the arm and pulled him toward the door they'd just barreled in through.

"Two blocks east, two blocks south. Big building on the southwest corner. Might have the name 'Bauer' painted on it somewhere."

"Right. Lead the way."

Chadwick opened the door an inch or so and peeked out onto the alley. Seeing nothing to worry about, he pushed the door open a little farther and looked around the door's edge. Nothing there either.

"Let's go," he said.

The men slipped quickly, but quietly, south down the dark alley.

At the street, Chadwick, still in the lead, took a look. Clear. He went around the corner to the left, heading east. Dickinson followed in his silent footsteps. With numerous stops and starts, they reached the corner just north of the target warehouse. Chadwick knelt and Dickinson laid a hand on his left shoulder. Both of them eyed the building across the street. The expected name Bauer was painted on the bricks in white letters near the roof. It had three floors. The assumption was that the money would be stored on the first floor, wherever it was, but they couldn't count on that to be true and they might have to clear all three floors, like they did in the first building.

Chadwick closed his eyes and listened intently for a moment. He opened them, satisfied there were no footsteps or vehicle sounds.

"Ready?"

"Yeah."

Chadwick rose and the two Commandos darted across the street. They stopped in front of the recessed wooden front door. Dickinson slipped a two foot long pry bar from his pack and jammed the slender, curved end between the door and the jam right above the lock. Chadwick scooted over to make room. Working carefully to maintain as much silence as possible, Dickinson slowly leaned his weight into the pry bar, pushing the end in his hand toward the jam. This caused the slender end to leverage in the opposite direction, into the door. The only sound was a little creaking of the wood as it complained about the pressure. Suddenly, the lock's brass tongue was free and the door slipped open. Dickinson pulled the door the rest of the way and the two men rushed in. Chadwick closed the door behind him, but the damage to the wood around the lock kept it from latching in place.

He ripped off a long strip of the American's new miracle multi-purpose olive drab duck tape. Someone on the squad, possibly Dickinson, had heard about it from someone in Dunn's squad and asked for a roll. Soon every Commando in the squad had "appropriated" a roll from a friendly American soldier. He wrapped a length of it around the interior doorknob and stuck the other end across the wood jam. It held the door in place. It would work for a while, which was all they needed.

They looked around the large office and spotted another door, which had to lead to the warehouse. They crossed the room and opened that door, which was unlocked. They were greeted by a fairly long hallway, perhaps twenty feet. A couple of doors were situated on one side. They checked each room. One was a supply closet and the other a bathroom, both vacant. Moving on they reached the end of the hallway and found themselves in front of a door with a big glass pane in it filling the upper half.

They ducked down as soon as they saw a moving light. Someone was walking around with a torch. A single low-wattage lightbulb hung from a wood beam in the ceiling, shedding meager light on the enormous room. *It's about as bright as a half-moon in there,* thought Chadwick.

He raised his head enough to see in. The light bobbed and swayed as the person walked along. It seemed to be at the far end of the storage space, which was about fifty feet square. Chadwick realized the first floor must be subdivided into separate rooms. He was about to tell Dickinson it was going to take a long time to clear the building when the night watchman, as he'd come to think of the person, came into view. The light from the torch swung around to Chadwick's right and illuminated three long rows of large crates on pallets. He did a quick count of the row he could see most clearly; seven pallets. Times three. Twenty-one. Close to the twenty-two Saunders thought there'd be. Of course, he thought, one of the other rows might have eight.

"I think this might be it. I see at least twenty-one crates the right size," he whispered over his shoulder. "But there's someone in there with a torch."

"Right," Dickinson replied.

The night watchman came into view. He seemed to be an old man, based on the way he walked, stooped over slightly and with a shuffling gait. He slowly made his way to the crates. He shone his light up and down the rows of crates. He seemed to be counting. Apparently satisfied they were all still there, he turned and walked away, headed directly toward the door Chadwick and Dickinson were behind. He carried a black holster with what might be an old revolver. Hanging from his chest pocket was a silver whistle.

"Blimey!" Chadwick whispered. "Back to the office! Quick!"

Dickinson didn't bother asking "why?" He took off at full speed. Soon, the two were back in the office. Chadwick closed the door behind them. They looked around the room. Dickinson pointed.

They scooted across the room and knelt behind a four-drawer file cabinet that was five feet tall.

A moment later, they heard the door at the far end of the hall close. Footsteps grew louder and louder.

Chadwick, who had the position to see the back door, raised his suppressed Sten gun. He hated to have to kill an old man, but he might have to.

The footsteps stopped. A door opened and closed a few seconds later.

A full three barely-endurable minutes passed when suddenly came the sound of a toilet flushing.

Chadwick stifled a chuckle. Dickinson patted him on the back.

The bathroom door closed again and the footsteps faded. The warehouse door closed.

The Commandos made their way back to the warehouse door. Chadwick peeked. The watchman was nowhere to be seen. Where had he gone? He studied the room. Finally, at the far left corner he spotted another door. Perhaps to another storage room. On the right, beyond the lines of crates was a loading dock door, the kind that lifted up like a garage door.

"Quick. Let's get in there and check the crates."

The men stood. Chadwick pulled the door open carefully, not wanting to make a sound. Once through, Dickinson closed it. They ran to the first wooden crate. Dickinson got out his pry bar again. He eyed the end of the lid. He found a small gap and jammed in the slender end. Slowly he applied pressure. In a short time, he had loosened the lid enough so they could get their fingers underneath. Together they lifted. The nails squeaked as they were pulled from the wood below them, but the men didn't stop. When the lid was open a foot, Chadwick held it in place while Dickinson dipped a hand inside. He grasped something hard and lifted it out. They knelt behind the crate.

Chadwick flicked on his small torch, which had tape across the lens so only a tiny sliver of light shone out. He aimed it at the object in Dickinson's hand.

"That's it, Chris."

Dickinson held a pack of five-pound notes worth five hundred pounds.

He shone the light into the crate. "God, almighty. Help me close this thing."

Dickinson set the money on the floor and together they got the lid closed tight enough that no one could tell it'd been opened. Dickinson picked up the package of fivers. Chadwick turned off the light and the men ran to the storage room's door and slipped into the hallway. Chadwick took a few steps and stopped.

"What is it, Tim?" Dickinson asked pulling up beside his friend. "Hear something?"

"No, that's not it. Would you leave that money in the hands of an old security guard?"

"Ah. Good point. Maybe we should go around and check the back?"

"Yeah."

They made it to the front door and Chadwick cut off the tape holding the door closed and stuck it in a pocket. After checking to make sure it was clear outside, they went out. Chadwick closed the door and while Dickinson leaned into it, he slapped duck tape on it at the bottom to keep it shut.

"Let's go," he said. They stayed close to the building, in the shadows, sliding along. At the corner, Chadwick peeked down at the street, which faced the storage room where the money was located. Next to the building, a large German transport truck and a staff car sat dark and threatening. Two soldiers with rifles slung on their shoulders stood next to the building where the loading dock door would be. The red glow of a cigarette came from the car's driver's side.

"Bloody hell," he said as he pulled back. "Found the real security."

He leaned against the front of the building. "Probably an entire squad in a truck. A staff car with at least one inside."

Dickinson nodded. "Best tell Sarge."

"Yeah."

They ran the four blocks, stopping where prudent, and entered the warehouse where the rest of the squad was waiting.

Saunders and Barltrop met them at the door.

"Found it, Sarge," Chadwick began, "but there's a problem."

"Isn't there always?" Saunders replied.

RONN MUNSTERMAN

16

German liquid oxygen storage facility
7 miles northwest of Hamburg, Germany
30 November, 0140 Hours

Cross nodded. "Yeah, those are truck engines. Shit."

"Well, we can't risk them trying to connect their truck hoses to the tanks and discover the satchels." Dunn rose and called to the men, "Change of plans, boys. Stay in your pairs. We've got to take care of those trucks."

The men jumped to their feet and Dunn ran off toward the tanks. The squad fell in behind him. He led the men down the space between the two rows of tanks. At the end, he stopped and edged close to the tank on his left. He peeked around it. Three fuel trucks were lined up at the gate waiting as the guards checked their IDs and bill of lading papers. At least Dunn figured that's what they were doing.

He checked the office. Still no lights. That meant the only problems to handle were the two guards at the gate, the pair walking sentry duty around the perimeter, and the truck drivers. He gauged the distance to the trucks to be forty yards, well within the Sten guns' range. He formed a mental picture of the attack he wanted to make. He explained this process to others as being like a movie in his head of what was going to happen, and who would do what. It was like predicting the future.

He swung around and gathered the men close. He described his attack movie and gave everyone their assignments. He checked his watch. "A reminder, men, twenty-five minutes to reach the safe point. Gotta be damn quick here."

His men nodded their acknowledgement of being on the clock. A deadline, no pun intended.

Dunn waved his hand forward. Three teams went back around the north side of the tank and took up positions in its shadow, aiming at the gate-truck targets. Jonesy sighted on the third truck's windshield, the driver's side. He couldn't see inside, and actually barely had a shot because of the angle and the truck in front of it, which almost blocked the entire windshield. He would have to lay five shots into the target and hope one got the driver.

Dunn and Cross, plus Goerdt and Kelly, took up prone positions to the right of the storage tank. Dunn checked his watch. When its hands hit the appointed time, he said, "Fire!"

The *pffft* sounds of the Stens firing at a rate of 600 rounds a minute, and the louder metallic clacking of the bolt snapping back and forth filled the night air.

The two guards were hit first and collapsed to the ground.

Jonesy's five shots peppered the windshield on the driver's side, causing spider web cracks to form. He changed magazines and fired five more times. The glass shattered revealing a man with dark stains on his chest slumped over against the door.

The second truck took a lot of rounds, some of which hit the truck's gas tank. It ruptured, spilling gas on the ground. A spark from another round striking against metal flew into the gas. Blue and yellow flames shot upward and the gas burned in a line all the way back to the source. There was a *whump* of the explosion. Red hot pieces of the truck flew in all directions. Some hit the fuel tank of the first truck and it blew up as if in sympathy to its dying friend. The third truck simply caught fire.

Dunn was about to give the order to depart when motion to his right caught his attention. The two sentries were running back toward the burning pyre of trucks. Dunn tapped Cross on the shoulder and pointed. The two marksmen raised their weapons and fired a couple of short bursts. The sentries flopped to the ground and lay still.

Dunn checked his watch. They had twenty minutes to get to safety. He stood and whistled three times. Cross and he took off running back the way they'd come. Goerdt and Kelly were right behind them. As they passed the north side of the storage tank, the other three teams joined the column. No one wanted to stay here too long.

At the chain link fence, Dunn kicked the door flap and tore the little string. He leaned over to go through and push it all the way open. As each man ducked and ran through Dunn grabbed him by the jacket and yanked hard to get him through faster. When the last man was through, Dunn checked his watch: eighteen minutes. Even though his head told him his men could cover almost two miles in that time, and that they were only going a half mile, the fear of getting caught in the pressure wave was still rearing its ugly head.

He glanced back. The dark ominous shapes of the tanks were bathed in the back glow of the trucks' fires, which seemed to be dimming. Black pillars of smoke threatened to block out the moon.

Six minutes later, and at last, it seemed to Dunn, the men reached the safety of the tree-covered hilltop and they settled in behind some of the larger trees. Dunn and Cross shared a large oak. They were both breathing hard after all the excitement and running.

Cross leaned over and whispered, "I'm not sure, Tom, but we might be getting too old for this shit."

Dunn chuckled. "Yep. Don't tell anyone."

"Right. These young pups would run right over you and happily leave their boot prints on your back."

The two best friends laughed knowing that was so far from the truth it was merely hyperbole. They knew each and every one of the other eight men in the squad adored Dunn, respected him more like an older brother, and would do anything for him, including die. Part of that love was due to knowing in return that Dunn would do exactly the same thing for them.

Dunn thought about the two men he'd known the longest, Cross and Wickham. The bond they'd forged under fire was quite unbreakable. The bonus was simply that they liked each other. The other, newer, younger men in terms of time in the squad, also shared the same under-fire bond. No other event in a man's life created a connection as strong as the one born from sharing combat together. Each of the men had proven himself time after time. Dunn felt honored to serve with them. He suddenly realized that while he often spoke to them about how good they were and how much he appreciated them, he'd never actually told them it was an honor to serve with them. He vowed then and there to do that as soon as possible.

Cross nudged him with an elbow, drawing him out of his thoughts.

"One minute to go."

"Ah, okay. Thanks." He got to his feet and called out, "Men! If you want to watch the show, make sure you close one eye to save some night vision. As soon as the explosions go off, get back behind the tree in case the pressure wave reaches us. I'm not kidding. It's faster than sound waves and could be here in less than five seconds. Open your mouths and cover your ears. Close your eyes."

Dunn sat down and rolled over onto his stomach to watch. He decided not to do a countdown, opting for the surprise instead. He closed one eye.

An enormous, bright light looking like a miniature sun ignited. Dunn thought it had a diameter of at least two hundred yards. The clock in his head hit four.

"Everyone get behind the trees!" he shouted.

He heard the rustling sounds of the men following his order as he ducked back behind the oak. Cross was already there, mouth open, hands over his ears, eyes closed. Dunn did the same.

A roaring sound approached the hilltop. Dunn could hear it through his protective hands. He had time to think, *Oh Lord . . .*

The pressure wave struck the trees and burst through the open spaces picking up leaves and fallen branches from the ground like a tornado, driving them forward. Dunn's oak shook, but held. Leaves fell from above.

A teeth-jarring, chest-rattling *boom* hit them like the rolling thunder from a too-close lightning strike. It seemed to go on and on and on. Dunn found himself moaning as if in tune with the explosion. The sound echoed across the river valley. The pressure wave was gone.

Dunn opened his eyes and dropped his hands. He rolled over and looked. The men did the same.

An ugly fireball was still climbing into the moonlit night. Dunn thought it had expanded to five hundred yards. It was difficult to determine just how high it was because there were no human scale reference points. Nevertheless, he guessed it had to be a thousand feet. It made him think of the Pillar of Fire from the Old Testament.

"Everyone okay?" he shouted. "Sound off for me!"

Each man yelled back that he was okay, or some variation of that. Dunn sighed in relief.

As he watched the fireball roiling in the air, he noticed a less bright line of fire climbing a hill in the distance. He frowned. Then he realized the remnants of the gigantic camouflage netting were on fire.

"Wow, look at the fire on the hill, Dave."

"I see it. Pretty swell."

"Yep. Wish I had a camera."

"Ayup. Me, too."

As they watched, the fireball began to change colors. The orange yellow was giving way to black as the fire burned out, leaving behind only thick, probably deadly, smoke. Soon the Pillar of Fire converted to the Pillar of Smoke.

Dunn lifted his binoculars and zoomed in on the spot where the tanks had been. Even though the smoke was still rising from there, he was able to determine that the tanks and the building were gone, destroyed in the fireball. It looked like a crater of gigantic proportions covered the entire area.

"Wow. Check it out." He handed the glasses to Cross.

Cross looked and whistled. "Wow is right." He gave Dunn the glasses back.

"I think it's safe to say the show's over. Let's get the men up and head back to the sub."

"Excellent idea," Cross said, rising to his feet. "Holy shit. Look at this."

Dunn got up and looked where Cross was pointing. At a spot six feet off the ground, an inch thick tree limb had been driven into a tree behind them like a spear.

The rest of the men had gotten to their feet and they all stared at the spear. They exchanged uneasy glances, then looked at Dunn.

Schneider spoke up for all of them, "Sarge, thanks for making us stay behind the trees."

Dunn smiled grimly. He was so glad he'd been tough about it. He nodded. "You're welcome."

The men appreciated him not saying "I told you so," which he never did.

"Everyone ready for the safety of a nice metal tube under water?"

He got a chorus of "hell, yes!" Even submarine-phobic Martelli joined in.

"Off we go. Wickham, lead us back."

"Righto, Sarge," Wickham replied in his Brit-Tex accent.

17

**Downtown
Bremerhaven
30 November, 0300 Hours**

Chadwick had point and led the squad of Commandos down the dark street toward the target warehouse. Their shadowy forms moved like smoke along the sidewalk close to each building they passed. It was cold and their breath created rising clouds of steam. Moonlight touched the street, but not the sidewalk. No one else was out. It was the middle of night after all. They passed a grocery store with a delivery van parked out front, and a men's clothing store.

When Chadwick reached the front of the warehouse, he knelt and cut off the tape that was holding the door closed. Rising, he opened the door and stepped into the dark office. Nothing had changed since he and Dickinson had left. He waved an arm in the doorway and the rest of the men ran quietly inside. Dickinson, who was last, taped the door closed from the inside.

Chadwick looked at Saunders, who nodded. He ran across the office floor and opened the door to the hallway. He took a quick peek and, seeing it was clear, moved into the hallway, the men following right behind him. Pointing at the two doors Dickinson and he had checked earlier, he moved on ahead. Myers opened the door for the bathroom and found it empty while Talbot checked the supply closet, also clear. The squad moved to catch up with Chadwick, who had just reached the door to the storage room itself.

Chadwick examined the storage room where he and Dickinson had found the horde of forged money. The same lightbulb burned near the ceiling, throwing its dim light across the huge room. He didn't see the night watchman.

Saunders had moved up right behind him. "Crates still there?"

"Yeah, Sarge. Ready to go in?"

"Aye."

Chadwick opened the door, backing up to make room for its swing into the hallway.

As the squad filed in they dispersed to cover the room from different vantage points. Chadwick and Saunders ran to the door on the far side and stopped, each on one side of it. Chadwick tried the doorknob. It turned, but when he tried to pull the door open, found it to be locked. The watchman had locked it behind himself.

Chadwick had talked with Saunders before they departed for the target warehouse about what to do with the watchman, since he was just an old man doing his job. Saunders had simply said that if he showed up before they ignited the money and tried to interfere, they'd have no choice but to kill the man, civilian or not. For some reason this troubled Chadwick. Perhaps he kept thinking of the old man as being someone's grandfather.

"Locked," he whispered.

Saunders patted him on the arm and they ran to the crates. Saunders waved at his men. Forster and Holmes stayed put to keep an eye out for trouble. They handed their packs to Alders and Myers, who along with the others, joined Saunders and Chadwick. The men shrugged off their packs. They paired up and began using their pry bars to get the lids of the crates off. It was slow tedious work because they had to keep noise to the minimum. As each pair finally pried the lid free, they set it quietly on the floor.

Every single one of the men except Chadwick and Dickinson, who'd already seen the huge stash, gasped at the sight of so much money in one place, fake or not. Then they recovered and began laying the incendiary devices one each on top of the stacks of money, in the center.

Dickinson grabbed up a bundle of tens and twenties to add to the fivers they'd already taken to return to England for examination.

When that was done, each team grabbed the remaining satchels, which had the plastic explosives in them. Dickinson pointed at various vertical wooden support beams and each assigned team set about placing their satchel against the base of the beam, which was a foot square in size. The intent was to bring down the entire warehouse, at least the part over the money, which should have already burned to nothing more than charred bits.

By 3:20, everything was ready. The incendiaries would ignite at 3:25 and the plastic explosives satchels at 3:35, giving plenty of time to burn the money.

Saunders checked his watch and said to Barltrop, who was nearby, "Steve, let's get the men on the move. I'll stay with Chadwick by the door to the office to make sure the money burns up. Wait for us in that office. When we come running, we all hit the road."

"Right, Mac."

Barltrop went off to gather the men. He spoke to Chadwick and pointed toward Saunders. Chadwick nodded and ran over to Saunders. The squad exited the storage room and headed toward the office to wait.

Saunders and Chadwick took a kneeling position next to the door to the escape hallway. Saunders checked his watch again: 3:18. "Two minutes, Tim."

"Right."

At 3:19 the far door opened and the old watchman entered the storage room, his torch bobbing as before. He walked along, slowly swinging his beam, as before, to and fro across the floor and the walls. He made it to the larger open area where the crates sat. The open crates.

He evidently didn't notice anything amiss right away, but when he got to about ten feet from the nearest crate he pulled up short. He pulled his revolver and looked around the room, swinging the flashlight around wildly. He missed Saunders and Chadwick, who had quietly opened the hallway door and slipped through. They watched him through the window in the door.

"Bloody hell," Saunders muttered.

The watchman shuffled over to the first crate and aimed his torch inside. He backed up suddenly and looked around as if trying to find an escape. He seemed to calm down after a little while, still standing near the crates. He stood completely still as if trying to decide what to do. He holstered his weapon.

"Sarge, let me go get him out of there. We can gag and tie him up and leave him somewhere on the way."

"Are you fooking kidding?"

"Come on, Sarge, he's probably someone's granddad."

"Oh for crying . . ." Saunders began. "Oh, all right. Hurry."

Chadwick opened the door and ran on his silent rubber-soled boots toward the watchman, who had his back to his attacker. Something made a noise on Chadwick, whether it was a too loud boot fall, or something with his Sten gun, he never figured out. But the watchman turned with surprising quickness and aimed his torch right at Chadwick, who was bearing down on him.

"Halt!"

Chadwick continued running. He fully expected the man to draw his gun, but instead he reached up with his left hand, unhooked his silver whistle, put it to his lips, and drew the initiating deep breath.

Having no choice now, Chadwick fired two rounds which struck the man in the upper chest.

As Chadwick watched, the old man seemed to crumble in slow motion to the floor. He kept the whistle between his lips.

A shrill sound came from it, echoing in the huge room. The man crashed to the floor. He took another deep breath.

Chadwick was one step away.

Another sharp whistle blow rocked the room.

Chadwick yanked the whistle away from the man and took his revolver, which he tossed some distance away.

Chadwick looked at the old man, who stared up with the glassy eyes of a dead man.

"Shite!" he whispered to himself. He glanced at Saunders over his shoulder. Saunders was waving his arm madly.

Saunders ran to the office to get the squad.

A clanking sound came from the dock door.

Chadwick glanced at the rising door, seeing German boots and legs underneath. He checked his watch. He looked at the crates quickly, and ran toward the hallway door. He fired several bursts at the legs under the door, which was already almost two feet off the floor.

A man fell to the ground hands grasping his damaged legs.

The incendiary devices ignited with a giant flash that brightened the room as if the sun had stopped by.

By the time Chadwick got half way to the hallway door several things happened at once:

Saunders and the men arrived.

The crates flared and burned, the flames going high enough to lick against the wooden support beams above them. Chadwick could feel the heat on his back.

The dock door reached its highest point.

RONN MUNSTERMAN

18

Gertrude Dunn, who'd turned just nineteen the previous month, stepped out of the black company car and looked around in the rising full moon's light. A monster of a two-story farm house stood to her right and a massive barn was across the barnyard to her left. The car was parked by the gate in the fence surrounding the house, which was also encircled by old, naked trees that acted as sentinels. They threw dark, sharp-lined criss-crossed shadows across the ground. The air was cold, and a strong north wind tore through her thin Bermuda-strength jacket. She hugged herself for warmth and walked to the rear of the car.

The driver, a man of about fifty, who had said nothing to her on the drive from Washington, D.C.'s airport, already had the trunk open. He reached in and lifted out her one and only suitcase. He held it out for her and she took it, having to regrettably unwrap her warming arms from her body.

"Knock on the door. Someone'll answer and let you in. If you're hungry, they'll show you where the kitchen is."

"Okay, thank you. Thanks for the ride."

She offered her hand, which seemed to surprise the man. He grasped her hand and shook it.

"Good night, miss."

"Good night, sir."

He closed the trunk with a clunk and got into the car. He started the engine, drove in a wide left half-circle, and back down the extremely long driveway to the county road.

Gertrude turned, opened the gate, and walked through, closing it behind her. As she walked across the yard toward the house a rustling sound came from her right, deep in the shadows of the house. She wondered if it was a cat prowling about for a late mouse snack.

When she was a few steps from the porch stairs, the sound of running feet came from her right. A woman wearing a white nightgown screamed as she ran around the corner of the house. Startled, Gertrude stared at the woman's ghostlike appearance. In a flash, the screaming woman ran past Gertrude. As she did, she yelled, "Help me!" Gertrude's gaze followed the terrified woman, who was now heading toward the barn.

Heavier footsteps caused Gertrude to turn around. A dark form streaked around the same corner of the house right toward Gertrude. It changed directions to go past her toward the barn and the other woman. She spotted something in the form's right hand.

Gertrude spun to her left, hefting the suitcase, still in her left hand. The suitcase flew in an arc and crashed into the stomach of the dark form, who screeched in pain and went down. It dropped the object in its right hand and rolled over onto its side holding its stomach with both hands.

Gertrude snatched up the object, a short-barreled revolver, and pointed it at the person on the ground.

Bright lights blazed on from the porch and the barn. She kept the gun aimed at the person on the ground. Several people burst through the front door and down the steps. The one in the lead, a tall, athletically built man in his thirties arrived first. He knelt beside the person on the ground and helped it sit up. He pulled off the watch cap and the woman's blond hair fell to her shoulders.

Tears of pain streaked down her cheeks and glistened in the bright lights.

Gertrude lowered the weapon so it dangled near her thigh. She set down her suitcase.

Another person, a young woman with brown hair, knelt to help. The man stood and faced Gertrude.

She tried to make out his expression, but it was dead pan.

He held out his hand and looked pointedly at the revolver.

Gertrude backed up, but left the revolver dangling at her side. "An explanation first."

"You'll do as you're told. Give me the gun," the man ordered.

"Not 'til you explain who you are and why I should listen to you at all."

The man raised his hands. "All is well. I'm David Walker. I'm in charge of training here."

"Uh huh." Gertrude looked around: the woman on the ground, glaring up at her now; the other woman helping the injured one; the intended victim, who had run back to join the group, standing there with an amused look on her face as she shivered in the cold.

Gertrude looked at the pistol for a moment, opened the cylinder and upended the gun, letting the shells fall out into her hand. She glanced down at the brass and chuckled as she closed the cylinder. She flipped the weapon over onto its back using her trigger finger as the pivot point and held it out to Walker butt first.

He took the proffered weapon and jammed it into his waistband. He held out his hand again.

Gertrude smiled. "You want these expended shells? Didn't even use blanks, huh?"

"Didn't want anyone to get hurt. You know, blanks can cause damage."

Gertrude nodded sagely and handed over the empty shells. "Yes. So can suitcases."

The injured woman got to her feet and took a step toward Gertrude. Walker stepped in front of her. "Forget it, Mildred. You knew this could turn out this way."

"Stupid girl!" Mildred turned and stomped up the stairs. She slammed the door behind her hard enough to make the glass panes rattle.

"I see I've made a friend."

Walker frowned. "Don't be a smart ass, young lady."

"Don't be a smart ass?" Gertrude snorted. "Well, you should have thought of that before you recruited me, Mr. Walker. Where's the kitchen? I'm starved."

The ghostlike victim walked over to Gertrude and offered an arm. "I'm Louise. Come with me. I'll show you to the kitchen and your room, as well as act as a buffer between you and Mildred."

Gertrude started to say something about not needing a buffer for anyone, but realized the woman was just trying to help. She would need friends here, so why not accept the offer?

She slipped her arm through Louise's. "I'm right with you, Louise."

Gertrude retrieved her suitcase and the two walked up the stairs and into the house. A wide foyer greeted them. The stairs to the second floor were ahead and on the right, while a hallway took up the left half of the space. To the right was the living room with several stuffed chairs and a sofa. The dining room was to the left. The table had ten chairs around it. Louise disengaged her arm from Gertrude's so they could walk single file down the hallway.

The kitchen was enormous, of a typical farm house style with another table as big as the one in the dining room. Louise walked around the table and gestured to Gertrude.

"Have a seat. What sounds good? I can rustle up some scrambled eggs, bacon, toast, and there's always coffee on." She pointed at a silver pot on the stove, the flame underneath on low. "Cups in left cabinet."

"That sounds wonderful." Gertrude set down her suitcase and walked over to the coffee pot. She opened the cabinet door and found the cups.

"Coffee for you?"

"Yeah, please."

While Gertrude poured the coffee, Louise set about getting the fixings for the late night breakfast out of the fridge and laying it all out on the counter by the six-burner gas stove.

Gertrude took the coffee cups to the table and sat down on the side closest to the stove. She watched her new friend beat the eggs with a fork. She'd already lit a burner and set a heavy cast iron skillet on it.

While Gertrude watched Louise prepare breakfast, she admired the woman's efficient movements. She was shorter than Gertrude, probably standing five-three. She was fit with a body shape that made you think of a dancer. Her brown hair reached her shoulders and when she glanced at Gertrude, it was with brown eyes. She smiled and turned back to the food.

Gertrude took a grateful sip of the hot coffee, black.

Just then, David Walker came into the kitchen. He took in what the two ladies were doing and simply sat down at the table directly across from the new arrival. He frowned at Gertrude.

She just stared at him over her coffee cup. She raised an eyebrow to see if she could entice him to actually say something.

It worked.

"Welcome to The Farm." He stood and leaned over the table to offer his hand.

She set down the coffee cup and shook hands without rising.

"Thanks. Are all your welcomes like mine?"

He smiled for the first time. "Yeah. Or some variation of it. Mildred has recovered from your shot to the belly, in case you were wondering."

Gertrude smiled. It was a shark's smile. "I wasn't."

"She was just doing her job."

Gertrude nodded in agreement. "Yes. Sometimes that can be painful."

He sat back in his chair, apparently more than mystified by Gertrude's attitude. "You don't seem to feel guilty at all for hurting a teammate." He frowned again to emphasize his disapproval.

"You're kidding, right?" She sat forward, both hands flat on the table. "Here's what I saw: a screaming woman being chased by some unidentified person, gender unknown, with an object, a weapon, in hand." She sat back and crossed her arms. "I stopped an attack. The fact that it was your idea of a training exercise for me indicates to me that I passed the test. Your efforts here to make me feel guilty are really just a waste of time. Yours and mine. Now do you mind if I eat my late breakfast?"

Walker grinned. "Yes, you passed. Yes, I was trying to make you feel guilty, which is, as you said, a waste of our time." He pointed at her suitcase on the floor. "I'll need to take that. Didn't anyone tell you to come with no belongings?"

"No, no one told me. What are you going to do with my suitcase?"

"I'll arrange to have it shipped to your home. You can write a short note explaining its arrival, if you think it's necessary."

"I see. Yes, I'd like to send a note. I assume a censor will read it?"

Walker smiled. "Of course."

Gertrude opened the suitcase after laying it on its side. She pulled out a piece of stationary and an envelope, and a pencil. She closed the suitcase and latched it. She wrote a quick note to her parents, a P.S. to her sister Hazel, and put it in the envelope. She left it unsealed and handed it to Walker.

"Thank you. By the way, did anyone mention that you'd have a new name here?"

Gertrude stared at him briefly. "Looks like someone keeps dropping the ball."

"Welcome to The Farm, Peggy."

"Peggy, huh?"

"Yes."

Gertrude shrugged. "Fine. I'll be Peggy."

"Good." He stood. "Wake up time is oh five-thirty hours. See you here at this table for," he grinned again, "another breakfast at oh six hundred. Good night, Peggy, Louise."

He picked up her suitcase and left.

Louise turned and grinned at Gertrude. "Nicely handled. You did well. A word of advice, though. The training here is hard. Very hard. You won't always do it right. Just learn from mistakes and never, ever repeat one."

Gertrude nodded. "Thanks for the advice."

"Let's eat."

Soon Gertrude was shoveling eggs, bacon, and toast in her mouth as fast as possible, but not before asking for the catsup. Something else she'd learned from her older brother, Tom Dunn.

19

Forged Money Warehouse
Downtown Bremerhaven
30 November, 0322 Hours, Berlin time

Saunders returned with the rest of the squad and burst through the hallway door into the storeroom. He spotted Chadwick running toward him.

Several German soldiers stepped forward at the dock door and raised their rifles, searching for targets. Saunders could clearly see their faces in the light from the fire.

He frantically motioned for Chadwick to get down.

Chadwick dove to the floor and so did Saunders.

The Germans fired a volley, the bullets passing through the air where Chadwick had been running, and where Saunders had been standing.

Saunders fired a burst, but he missed. He crawled to his right and fired again. Several of his men knelt at the hallway door and fired.

The Germans ducked and ran to the right side of the open door. Once there, they resumed firing, some kneeling, others leaning and firing over their comrades' heads.

Saunders knew he was in a tight spot. He had to hold the Germans at bay until just before the explosives went off. He checked the crates holding the forged money. As he watched, several of the sides simply fell over like a tree that had been felled. He could see the dwindling mound of cash. It was burning on all sides. It wouldn't be much longer before nothing would be left but ashes.

The Germans seemed to be stymied because they could find no targets.

Saunders waved at the men in the doorway behind him.

The squad split up, half crossing to the left and the others sliding down the right side of the burning storeroom past Saunders.

Barltrop yelled instructions and the men on the right side laid down heavy suppressing fire.

The other group advanced along the far wall through the smoke. When they were only ten feet from the enemy, the Commandos opened fire. Dickinson, who was leading the group, saw all the enemy soldiers go down. He ran to the door and looked outside.

Another truckload of soldiers pulled up, the brakes squealing in protest. An officer was standing in the street yelling at them and waving his pistol as they jumped down.

Dickinson motioned to Barltrop, who nodded and led his group to the door. Once there they began firing, along with Dickinson and his men.

The Germans dashed back behind their truck.

Saunders and Chadwick jumped up and ran toward the dock door.

Barltrop examined the garage-style door. It seemed intact. He reached up and pulled on a rope dangling from the bottom edge.

The door started down.

Several Germans leaned out from behind the truck and fired.

A supersonic bullet struck Chadwick in the upper left chest. He spun in a half circle from the force of the bullet, toppled over onto his side, and lay still, two feet from Saunders.

"No! Tim!" Saunders shouted as his men unleashed another firestorm of Sten gun 9mm rounds at the enemy soldiers by the truck.

Just as Barltrop almost had the door all the way down something heavy clunked against the metal door and fell to the ground outside. He had just enough time to see it.

The door closed.

"Grenade!" He shouted as he seated the latch. He dove to his right.

Everyone else hit the floor as far to the side of the door as possible, scrambling behind some of the ceiling support beams.

Saunders ran over to a barely conscious Chadwick and grabbed him by his jacket. He dragged him to the side and draped his body over the wounded man.

The explosion tore through the bottom of the door, shredding the metal inward forming razor sharp edges. Shrapnel from the grenade itself and pieces of the door pinged across the room, slamming into the wood beams and walls.

Smoke began to fill the now closed room.

Saunders got to his feet and shouted, "Everyone out!" He bent over and picked up Chadwick. He carried his downed soldier over his shoulder and ran to the hallway door.

The rest of the squad was right behind him.

The squad ran down the hallway, and across the office. Saunders stopped at the door while Barltrop checked the street. He nodded to Saunders. Barltrop shouldered the door open, ripping the duck tape off, and led the way out. The squad turned right and ran down the street. Saunders was next to last, with Dickinson just behind him.

At the corner, the squad paused long enough to check to make sure the cross street was clear. Barltrop checked his watch and stopped running. He motioned for the men to hit the deck, which he did, too.

The explosion in the warehouse sounded incredibly loud in the early morning air. The shockwave shot down the street like a tsunami, shattering windows along the way.

The German soldiers by the storeroom door, the truck, and the staff car were thrown across the street and through the large windows in the building directly across, and against the brick facing. Their bodies left bloody smears on the bricks and the window frames. No one survived.

Flames engulfed the warehouse. Ash from the forged money floated away.

Saunders, who had as gently as possible laid Chadwick down, had again covered his friend's body. Now, he got to his knees and examined the wounded commando. Barltrop got up and ran over. The rest of the men huddled around.

Saunders tore open Chadwick's jacket and shirt, exposing the bloody wound. It was located two inches up and toward the man's neck from the left nipple. As Chadwick breathed, bubbles frothed in the wound.

"Oh, Tim," Saunders moaned. "Someone get their first-aid kit open."

Dickinson, whose face was crestfallen at the sight of the bubbles, acted first, opening a gauze pack, and holding some out for Saunders.

Saunders grabbed the gauze from Dickinson and wiped the area around the wound, cleaning the skin of the blood as best he could for it was still seeping and bubbling. He threw aside the gauze and grabbed another. He dabbed the wound itself, pressing hard for a minute.

Chadwick groaned.

Meanwhile, Barltrop got his kit out and tore open a sulfa pack and handed it over.

"Start tearing off strips of adhesive tape, Chris," Saunders instructed.

He tossed the bloody gauze away and poured the sulfa in and around the wound while Dickinson was tearing off strips of adhesive tape. He took a piece of tape from Dickinson and laid it right across the wound and pressed hard.

Chadwick groaned again.

He repeated with several strips forming an asterisk across the wound.

"Give me strips of duck tape."

Dickinson dug out his roll of duck tape. He began tearing six-inch strips to give to Saunders.

Saunders made a large rectangular bandage cover with the tape, creating a makeshift airtight seal. Barltrop handed him a bandage and he taped that over the duck tape seal, and pressed hard again.

Chadwick groaned once more and fainted.

Saunders buttoned up Chadwick's shirt and zipped the jacket closed. He took off his own jacket and covered the wounded man's upper body. Hopefully, it would prevent him from falling deeper into shock.

He glanced at his watch, and looked up at Barltrop. Saunders tipped his head a little sideways and frowned. Barltrop understood immediately. He was thinking the same thing: for Chadwick to have any chance at all of surviving his wound, he had to be treated by a doctor. The closest friendly doctor was on the HMS *Sea Spray*, almost two hours away by foot and dinghy. Far too much time.

Barltrop nodded, gave his friend a thumbs up, and turned around. He started north on the street and ran about a block. The grocery store's van was still parked out front. He let go of his Sten gun, letting it dangle on its shoulder strap. He looked around the street quickly. Empty of people.

Off in the distance, sirens pierced the night.

He opened the driver's door and got in. He pulled a pocketknife from his pants pocket, something he always carried. His combat knife would have been too unwieldy working under the steering column. He put the gearbox in neutral and in less than thirty seconds, he hotwired the engine and it rumbled to life.

He put the truck in first gear and did a U-turn. He soared down the street to his men and completed another U-turn, pulling up right alongside them.

Dickinson and Saunders carefully loaded Chadwick into the back of the van. They jumped up to be with him. The rest of the men crowded into the back, except for Myers, who joined Barltrop in the cab. The cab area and cargo space made up one large open interior space. Saunders patted the back of Barltrop's seat.

The sirens were getting closer.

"Go!"

Barltrop floored it and the delivery van screamed down the street.

Because they'd marched into the city they'd taken a different route than the one he'd have to drive to get to the beach where their boat was hidden. Hopefully, it was still where they left it.

"How long, Steve?" Saunders asked.

"It's five miles. Maybe ten minutes."

"No, gotta be faster."

"Right." Barltrop stomped on the pedal and the van accelerated. He reached seventy-five kilometers per hour on the speedometer, which he calculated to be a just over forty-five miles an hour. Reluctantly, he switched on the headlights. He had to be able to see farther ahead at this speed. With the lights on, although they had the blackout zone covers on that only allowed a thin stripe of light out, he increased speed again until he reached ninety-five, which was almost sixty miles an hour . . . on a city street.

They burst out of the city, traveling along a narrow, but well-paved road going northwest, the right direction

Motion caught his eye and he checked his outside left mirror.

About a half-mile back, a German troop truck raced after them.

20

Eastern Shore of the Wadden Sea
5 miles northeast of Bremerhaven
30 November, 0337 Hours

Barltrop pushed the gas pedal to the floor, trying to squeeze out a few more miles per hour. The chasing truck, heavier and probably loaded with the same number of men, had trouble keeping pace, especially on the curves. Barltrop, even though primarily a mechanic in his own mind, understood perfectly well the physics of taking a corner as fast as possible, yet maintaining control of the vehicle. For the right-hand curves, he swept left before the curve taking a shallower, much faster line as he guided the van to the far inside of the curve, tires screaming and nearly touching the right edge of the pavement. Each curve gained him twenty to thirty yards on the truck whose driver just didn't have the required skill, or nerve that Barltrop did.

Myers, who had been acting as navigator, shouted, "Beach turn off one hundred yards on the left." He pointed, but Barltrop's eyes were already on the road leading to the beach.

"Hang on tight, lads!" he shouted.

He slowed, downshifted, cruised to the right and braked hard just before the turn off to the beach. He turned the wheel and the rear of the van drifted to the right. He whipped the wheel back to the right to control the slide through the curve. He shot out of the curve and straightened the wheel. He up-shifted and glanced in the mirror. No enemy truck.

The dirt road led straight west and was slightly downhill. Tall grasses lined the road as did several large weeping willow trees, their thin, nearly leafless dangling branches touching the ground. Barltrop slowed for the last curve ahead, and downshifted just before turning the wheel to the right. The road ran parallel to the water, which was about fifty yards away across the sand. Barltrop's eyes were in constant motion, checking the mirror, the road, and the grassy sand dune ahead to the left. He was looking for his landmark, a tall shrub of some sort that they had passed to get to the road. He felt that the enemy truck was about a mile behind, but that distance only translated into about two minutes at the speed he figured the truck was moving.

"There's the shrub, Sarge!" Myers yelled, pointing.

Barltrop braked hard, but not enough to lock things up and go into a skid. He downshifted once more into first gear and the engine revved in response. He spotted a narrow gap in the sand dune, noting it would barely be wide enough for them. Slowing almost to a stop, he cranked the wheel hard left and guided the left tire against the left edge of the gap. The right tires ran up over the dune itself, lifting that side of the van a good two feet. He ran the vehicle slowly forward until they reached the sand of the beach. The right side returned to normal and he turned sharply to the right. After a few more yards, he stopped. He stayed put, leaving the engine running for the next job for the van.

"Everyone out!" Saunders bellowed.

The men jumped down. Saunders, Dickinson, and Holmes hurriedly but gently carried Chadwick off the van. Saunders and Dickinson teamed up and carried the wounded Commando across the sand to the boat.

At the same time, Barltrop turned the van around and drove back into the gap. He moved slowly along and aimed the left tire for the ridge of the sand dune. When the front and rear left tires were elevated the two feet, he flung open the door. He climbed out on the running board while holding onto the wheel with his right hand and the door frame with his left, his hip keeping the door open.

In coordinated moves, he yanked the wheel left, flexed his thigh muscles, and jumped off the van. He landed hard on both feet, not unlike a parachute landing, and kept his balance.

The van, trying to climb up onto the sand dune, was overmatched by the physics of inertia and force vectors. It overbalanced to the right and tipped over onto its side, completely blocking the gap. The engine ran a little longer, but died when the right rear tire bit into the ground underneath most of the van's weight.

Barltrop ran back to the men, who had already set the dinghy upright. Holmes and Myers dragged the boat to the water's edge while Saunders and Dickinson carried Chadwick. They carefully loaded him into the bottom of the black boat.

Saunders stood up and said to Dickinson, "You three get him to the sub. The rest of us will stay here and take care of the Germans. We'd never get far enough away to be out of their range otherwise. Plus, I don't want anyone to spot the sub."

"Understood."

"Tell the doctor he's got a sucking wound and needs help ASAP."

"Will do, Sarge," Dickinson said, his expression grim.

Saunders nodded and patted him on the arm. "Off with you, lads."

The men quickly pulled the boat into deeper water and climbed in. Myers and Holmes unshipped the oars and began rowing, while Dickinson sat on his knees next to Chadwick. He put a hand on Chadwick's right shoulder and squeezed gently. He leaned close to his friend's ear.

"You're going to be okay, Tim, I promise. We'll take care of you, but you're going to have to fight. Can you do that for me, mate? I need you to come back."

Chadwick regained consciousness for a moment. Long enough to whisper, "See you soon, Chris." He closed his eyes and passed out again.

Dickinson closed his eyes and said a little prayer to himself.

Tears leaked down his cheeks.

Saunders and Barltrop positioned the remaining men behind the sand dune's ridge about ten yards north of the gap. Barltrop was closest to the narrow opening and Saunders was at the opposite end of the line. Over the sound of the gentle surf they could hear the approaching truck's engine. Saunders tapped Martin Alders on the shoulder, who in turn tapped Billy Forster. They both looked at their squad leader, who held up three fingers and started a 3-2-1 countdown. When he lowered the last finger, the three men rose to a combat crouch and climbed over the ridge. They ran forward until they were at a point ten yards past the overturned van. There, they dropped prone and disappeared in the tall grasses to wait.

The German truck came into view over the crest in the dirt road. The driver evidently spotted Barltrop's tipped over parking job and stopped his truck. After a few seconds, it edged forward slowly. When it was about even with Saunders and his men, it stopped again. The driver got out and ran to the back of the truck. The tailgate clanged open and one soldier peered around the rear corner of the truck, his MP40 submachine gun at the ready. He scanned the area carefully. Unable to spot anything, he waved his hand. Three men ran around the truck to the front and they knelt there, waiting and searching.

Saunders watched and waited. With only four Germans in view, he had to wonder where the others had gone. It seemed unlikely these were all there was.

Motion over the hood, on the other side bore out his suspicions; three helmets bobbed along and stopped. Seven. Roughly one-to-one odds. However, it typically required a three-to-one odds for the attacker to win. Although that tended to be for a "well-defended" position. A sand dune ridge could hardly be called well defended. In a split second he examined the layout of the upcoming firefight and determined what would happen. Barltrop and his men would wait for Saunders to start the fight, unless circumstances gave them an opening.

Saunders glanced back at the man at the rear of the truck. Huh. Just as he'd expected, the German had raised his weapon and sighted at a point about five yards to Saunders right. The enemy soldier was good enough to expect an ambush and had nearly targeted Saunders' men spot on. *Not bad,* thought Saunders. *But not good enough.*

Keeping his eyes on the man at the rear, he whispered to Alders, "I have the bloke at the rear. You take number three and Forster, the second. I'll come back and get number one. Fire when I do."

Saunders laid out each man's primary target so they didn't waste time and rounds firing at the same one.

"Yes, Sarge," came a whispered reply.

Alders leaned over and passed on the message to Forster.

The men slowly raised their Sten guns and acquired their individual targets. Saunders sighted over his weapon. His target seemed to be waiting for something. Better not to let him go first.

He squeezed his trigger. The suppressed Sten made its funny *click-clack* sound caused by the bolt sliding back and forth. Flame erupted from the barrel. His target got hit three times in the upper body and dropped straight down.

Alders' and Foster's weapons flared and their targets collapsed.

The man first in line by their targets looked over his shoulder at the sound of bullets hitting the bodies of his comrades. A few rounds had hit the truck's fender making loud clanging sounds.

Saunders, who had pivoted to the right, fired a round that knocked the man down. He looked over the truck's hood. The helmets on that side had disappeared.

MP40s began firing from the other side of the truck.

Saunders knew they were firing at Barltrop's group.

He unclipped a grenade from his jacket and pulled the pin. It would require a precise throw for an imprecise kind of weapon. He gauged the distance and positioned himself for the toss.

"Stay down, lads," he whispered to his two men.

He threw the grenade toward the truck. It had a high arc, more like a mortar round. It hit the peak of the arc and started downward. He watched it in much the same way a golfer does a shot toward the green, trying to discern exactly where it will land. If the grenade fell short and hit the hood, it might bounce far enough away to have no effect on the enemy.

The grenade disappeared from sight. It missed the hood. Had it traveled too far?

It went off with a loud bang and a bright flash. Shrapnel pinged against the truck.

Screams of pain rose to shrieks but, mercifully, stopped in mid-screech.

Saunders ducked and yanked his walkie-talkie off his belt.

"Saunders to Barltrop."

"Barltrop, here."

"Everything all right there?"

"Affirmative. Enemy seems to be down."

"Understood. Hold fire. We're going to check it out."

"Roger. Hold fire confirmed. Out."

"Out."

He clipped the five pound device back on his belt. Tapping Alders, he pointed toward the rear of the truck.

The three men rose to a crouch and they ran through the tall grasses to a point past the rear of the truck. Saunders could see into the cargo area. Empty. He ran forward toward the truck, eyes never leaving it. He stopped a few yards away. The soldier he'd shot first lay in a crumpled heap, weapon away from the body.

Saunders edged more to the left and forward so he was squarely behind the truck. He raised his Sten and with his left hand waved Alders forward.

Alders and Forster crept forward to join Saunders. He gave them a "wait here" sign and ran forward to the left rear and peeked.

All three enemy soldiers on that side were down.

He turned to Alders. "You lads check the two at the front. Be careful."

"Yes, Sarge."

Saunders walked around the corner, his weapon aimed downward at the bodies before him. They were a bloody mess. It looked like the grenade had landed between number two and number three. The two in the front had been blown forward and the one behind toward the rear, landing on his back. Sightless eyes stared up at the dark sky. The two men closest to the weapon were in worse condition, and their uniforms were still smoldering from being lit on fire.

He stood up and looked across the hood.

"Clear over here," he said. "How's it over there, Alders?"

"Got a survivor, Sarge."

Saunders couldn't believe it. He ran around the front of the truck.

Alders was kneeling beside a German who lay on his left side. He was breathing hard and fast.

The German opened his eyes and realized he was surrounded by British soldiers. He tried to roll over and crawl away, but passed out.

Saunders walked around and looked at his face.

"God Almighty. He's just a kid."

"Yeah. Maybe fifteen or sixteen, I'd say."

"Bloody hell."

Saunders shook his head and took a deep breath. "Okay. You guys pick him up. Let's get back to the other side of the ridge with the others."

"Right, Sarge."

When the men were back together, Alders and Forster laid the enemy soldier on the sand, on his left side. They set to work with their first aid kits. The boy had been shot once in the lower right side, just above the belt.

Saunders stepped over by Barltrop.

"Good work, Mac."

"Aye."

"That was quite a grenade toss."

"One for the books, for sure." Saunders checked his watch, and looked out at the dark water. He saw a long thin shape riding the surface. Or was it wishful thinking?

"Is that our ride?" he pointed.

Barltrop eyed the water. "Yeah, looks like."

"Hope someone comes back soon. Don't like being exposed out here."

"Me, either."

Saunders realized that only fifteen minutes had passed since Dickinson and crew had departed the beach. With a full boat and everyone rowing, it was a good five minutes to the pickup point. With only two rowers, maybe ten to fifteen. Five to unload. Another ten to get back. Forty to forty-five minutes.

"I figure we have at least twenty-five minutes to wait for a retrieval."

"Ah, boy."

"Aye. Let's set up an outer perimeter ten yards past the far truck."

"Right."

"Nice driving by the way."

Barltrop grinned, his teeth bright white in the moonlight.

"Sure you want to work in the pits?"

"Pretty sure, yeah."

"Just wondering, is all."

"Yeah."

Barltrop left to assign Myers and Talbot the task of guarding the perimeter.

Saunders stood with his arms folded across his massive chest and his head bowed. *Mission accomplished, Colonel Jenkins. Oh, by the way, I might lose one of the best men I've ever had the privilege to serve with.*

He grit his teeth and fought a losing battle with tears.

21

Eastern Shore of the Wadden Sea
5 miles northeast of Bremerhaven
30 November, 0413 Hours

Alders and Forster had done the best they could with the young German's wounds. The bleeding had stopped and he was breathing more or less normally. He'd awakened, and watched them work with wary, frightened eyes, but had grown sleepy, probably from blood loss and his eyes closed again. The two Commandos stood nearby, checking on him periodically.

"Good job, lads," Saunders had said on one of his passes as he paced up and down the beach, his eyes toward the water, and on his watch in equal parts. He stopped moving suddenly and turned to face the water. He raised a pair of binoculars to his eyes.

"Oh, thank God."

He dropped the field glasses, letting them dangle from his neck. He turned around and ran back to the men. "Boat's coming, lads. Let's get down to the water. Alders, Forster, you okay with carrying the young lad?"

"Sure, Sarge," Alders replied.

Barltrop went to get the two men guarding the perimeter.

By the time the men arrived at the lapping water, the boat was a mere ten yards off shore. A wave lifted it and pushed it closer. Four sailors were rowing

The boat ran aground and the Commandos helped drag it closer, but not all the way up onto the beach.

"Glad to see you," Saunders said.

"You, too, Sarge," replied one of the sailors in the front of the boat. "Climb aboard."

"Right. On you get, lads."

The men waited until Alders and Forster loaded the wounded German, then got in. Everyone grabbed a paddle and began pushing the boat toward the submarine.

Saunders looked over his shoulder every so often to make sure more Germans hadn't arrived. Nothing yet.

The men were wet from splashing through the cold water while they boarded. The wind picked up adding to their miserable state. It was strong enough they'd had to change directions to compensate. The waves whipped up and the boat bounced hard enough on each one to jar their teeth.

After a particularly hard slam, Barltrop muttered, "Bloody hell." No one replied. Their teeth were chattering.

The long black form of the sub appeared to grow and grow. When they finally reached it, the men were exhausted. Sailors on deck threw ropes to the two sailors in front to tie it off. A rope ladder unfurled and the end landed in the middle. One of the sailors on the dinghy yelled up to toss a rope for a wounded man. When that rope came down, Alders and the sailor tied a loop around his chest, under the armpits and cinched it tight between his shoulder blades.

The sailor gave a wave and the men above began pulling the wounded German up. Soon they had him over the boat's gunwale and onto the deck. Two sailors picked him up and carried him to the nearest open hatch. One climbed down the ladder. Together, they lowered the German aboard.

The Commandos began climbing the rope ladder. Barltrop and Saunders went last. When Barltrop got aboard, he immediately turned and held out a hand for his best friend. Saunders grabbed it and climbed up onto the deck.

The four sailors who'd rowed out to get them climbed aboard. Saunders thanked each one and shook his hand solemnly. As Saunders turned away to go to the hatch, the sailors brought aboard the dinghy and lashed it to the conning tower. Saunders idly wondered whether it would stay there when they went under the surface.

Once he was below deck, Saunders headed for the infirmary. He burst into the doctor's domain and looked around. He spotted Chadwick on a table, a sheet drawn up close under his chin and a blanket on top of that. The doctor stood nearby with a concerned look on his face. When the doctor saw Saunders he walked over to him and guided him back out into the passageway, closing the door behind him.

The doctor was an older man, perhaps in his fifties, with the attendant gray hair. His eyes, though, held a combination of compassion and honesty. Although submarines typically carried an orderly instead of a doctor, Colonel Jenkins always arranged for a doctor to go along on Commando unit missions. In expectation of serious emergencies, the doctor carried with him each Commando's basic medical information. If he wasn't needed, great, but if he was needed and wasn't there, someone would die. Too much time and money had been spent on creating a Commando to allow that to happen unnecessarily.

Saunders looked at the doctor and discovered he couldn't bring himself to ask the question.

The doctor sensed this and spoke first.

"I got the bullet out, but his lung was punctured. You gents already knew this."

Saunders nodded glumly.

"I did what I could with the puncture, and amazingly the lung did not collapse. The adhesive and duck tape seal may have prevented that from happening. Be sure to tell whoever did that they did a great job."

"Aye, yes, sir, I will." He didn't want to bother taking credit for it.

"He will need further surgery when we get back." The doctor's eyebrows knitted. "Not to alarm you, but that's not a certainty for him."

Saunders rubbed a hand over his face, kneading his forehead. He dropped his hand.

"He lost a lot of blood and he has a rare blood type, A-negative. We've already given him what we have aboard, but he should have some more soon. I see from your records you're the same type."

"I am," Saunders said quickly. He took off his wet jacket and rolled up his sleeves. "Show me where."

The doctor nodded.

"After we get you started, I'll check the crew for others."

"Yes, sir."

The doctor led him to another room next door to the infirmary. He opened the door and they went in. An orderly was working on some equipment on a table across the tiny room. A single cot sat against the wall on the right.

"Mr. Johnson, this is Sergeant Saunders. He's going to give you a unit of blood."

"Make it two, sir."

The doctor gave a wan smile. "No good, Sergeant. One is the max. You know this already."

"I want to."

"I know, but I can't risk your health or life by overstepping the safety rules. No."

Saunders looked angry, but dropped it. *Doctors.*

"I'll leave you with Mr. Johnson."

Saunders nodded. "Thank you, sir. I appreciate what you've done."

"You're welcome."

The doctor turned to leave.

"Doctor, how's the German kid?"

The doctor looked over his shoulder. "We're prepping him for surgery right now. Too soon to say anything until I get in there and see the damage."

"I think he's only fifteen or so, sir."

The doctor pressed his lips together. "I understand."

He left the room and the door clicked closed behind him.

"Have a lie down here, Sergeant."

Saunders did as he was told and the cot creaked in complaint when it took the full brunt of his weight.

The orderly raised an eyebrow and gave a tiny smile.

"Don't say a word."

The orderly's smile broadened. "Wouldn't think of it."

"Aye, right you are."

The orderly got an empty sterile bottle and tube ready. The bottle was secured to a small, low table so it would be below Saunders' arm. He deftly tied a rubber strap around the Commando's upper arm and tied it off.

"Make a fist."

Saunders obeyed.

He grasped Saunders' arm gently and straightened it. He checked the inside of the elbow, tapping softly.

"Excellent veins."

"I'm so proud."

This drew a chuckle from the orderly. He swabbed the area with an alcohol-soaked cotton ball and tossed it in the trash bin. He readied the needle. "Here we go."

He inserted the needle. "Relax your hand."

Saunders opened his fist.

Johnson attached the tube to the needle and pulled the plunger. Blood flowed through the tube and began to fill the bottle.

The orderly taped the needle in place and rose.

"Be sure to lie still. Don't want to knock the needle loose."

"Right."

"I'll just be over here working on stuff. I'll keep an eye on the bottle. You can rest if you like.

"I just might do."

Two hours later, Saunders sat quietly next to the cot where Chadwick lay. The young man looked pale from shock and loss of blood. Saunders' half empty blood bottle hung from a hook above Chadwick and fed his right arm.

Barltrop entered the room and joined Saunders.

"Any news?"

Saunders shook his head. "Doc says all we can do is wait. His blood pressure is low, but seems to be rising since they attached my bottle to him."

'That's good to hear."

"Aye. Doctor tracked down a mechanic aboard who has the same blood type in case Tim needs another one."

"That's good news. What about the German kid?"

"Got lucky. Bullet missed important stuff. Gave him some blood. Should make it. They shackled him to his cot and put an armed guard with him."

Dickinson walked in, his face ashen with worry.

Saunders told him the same thing he'd just told Barltrop.

Dickinson closed his eyes and seemed to sway. Barltrop grabbed his arm to steady him. Saunders got up.

"Here, lad. I need to stretch my legs, why don't you take over for me?"

Dickinson smiled at the thoughtful lie.

"Thanks, Sarge."

"We'll check back in a bit."

"Okay."

Saunders patted Dickinson on the shoulder. He and Barltrop left.

Dickinson laid a hand on Chadwick's shoulder, closed his eyes, and bowed his head. He said a prayer out loud.

When he finished, he opened his eyes and looked at his friend.

"Time to stop lying around doing nothing, mate. How about you wake up and we'll go get something to eat. Are you hungry? I'm starving. I would kill for a few biscuits, wouldn't you?"

He kept up an ongoing chatter, but Chadwick didn't respond.

22

Aboard the HMS *Sea Tiger*
In the Elbe River waterway south channel
30 November, 0435 Hours

"Welcome back," the submarine captain said.

"Thank you, sir. Mission accomplished."

Dunn and the mid-forties Captain Bartlett were seated in the captain's quarters. Dunn glanced around the tiny room. It was painted gray, and felt oppressive. Like his own quarters, it had the basics: a bed that was more like a cot, a postage stamp desk that folded down from the wall, and a lightbulb screwed into the wall just high enough so you couldn't hit it with your head, although it did have a metal framework around it just in case you inexplicably decided to jump into it.

"I saw all your men returned, and no one appeared to be hurt? Correct?"

"Yes, sir. No injuries. Went mostly to plan." Dunn explained about the trucks arriving at an inopportune moment and the sentries, and what he'd done about them.

Captain Bartlett nodded. "Sounds like you handled it just right."

"Thanks. We're looking forward to the ride home."

The captain's eyes shifted slightly, inadvertently betraying that he had something to tell Dunn.

Dunn raised an eyebrow. "What is it, sir?"

"After you left, maybe an hour or so, we received a coded message from your Colonel Kenton. It was marked Top Secret, so I had my radioman, who, just so you're aware, has clearance, go ahead and decode it for you." He pulled a folded piece of paper from his shirt pocket and handed it to Dunn.

"I read it, so I would know if we needed to make any special preparations. Turns out we don't. Anyway, read it and I'll await your comments."

Dunn took the paper and opened it. "Thank you, sir."

It was a long message and it covered the entire page.

When he was finished he muttered, "Damn Germans."

"I'm sorry. It seems so bizarre. Why would they create such a thing?"

Dunn gave the captain a sad look and shook his head. "They're desperate, sir. They'll do anything they can do to win a lost war. Plus, they're just crazy."

The captain stared at Dunn for some time, not saying anything. He seemed to realize Dunn was telling him something he officially couldn't tell him. This wasn't the first bizarre thing the Germans had built. "Yes, I see. They must be crazy."

He stood and Dunn rose. "Let me know what you need me to do. I received a message, too, from my superior officer. I'm instructed to assist you in any way necessary."

Dunn nodded. "Thank you, sir. For starters, could I have private use of the wardroom for a mission meeting? Perhaps in five minutes? We'll be done before breakfast."

"Certainly, I'll let the cook know first, and the men."

"Thank you, sir. Oh, do you happen to have a camera aboard we could use?"

Bartlett nodded. "We do. I'll have it delivered to you."

"Thanks again, sir."

Dunn and his men gathered in the wardroom. The men eyed him warily, knowing intuitively that plans had changed.

He told them exactly that first, and said, "Hamburg. We've been ordered to Hamburg. The mission is going to be of a different sort from the kind we're used to, and certainly different from the one we just finished. It's going to be all stealth, no engagement with the enemy at all unless unavoidable, like to protect ourselves."

A murmur went around the men. No engagement? They weren't really built like that.

Dunn acknowledged the sounds. "I understand fully how you feel. I felt the same way when I read Colonel Kenton's message." He held up the paper for the men to see.

"So here it is. The crazy krauts are up to no good. Again. You know very well how they keep trying to deploy some kind of deadly weapon designed to kill thousands. Just think of our recent mission with the ground up uranium they were going to spread over the front line. Think of how many Americans they would have killed. But most of you have experienced only weapons aimed somewhere over here. This new one is targeting the States!"

The wardroom erupted in shouts of anger and quite a few four-letter words describing Hitler.

Dunn patiently waited while the men's angry fire cooled down to a high simmer.

He took a deep breath. He was about to go into uncharted territory. "For some relevant background, the colonel gave me permission to tell you about a mission that Dave, Stan, and I went on back in June. It's top secret and has never been released for public consumption, and never will be. Well, at least for fifty years, when it can be unclassified." He paused to look around the wardroom. The door was securely closed.

"Men, you cannot discuss what I'm about to tell you with anyone, ever. That means family, friends, anyone. If you do and it gets found out, and it always does, you go to prison. You don't pass go and you don't get two hundred dollars."

He looked at each man in turn and received a tiny, nervous nod.

"In June, we attacked the Nazis' atomic bomb laboratory near Stuttgart."

He was greeted by several blank stares.

"For those of you who might not know, the atomic bomb is a type of bomb that uses uranium to generate an unbelievable explosion. One weapon would be like dropping thirty thousand, one-thousand pound bombs."

Silence greeted this information. Those who'd had the blank stares swallowed heavily, trying to imagine a bomb like that.

"With the help of the German scientist in charge of the lab, we were able to explode their uranium just like an atomic bomb. It destroyed the lab completely and the Germans lost any capability to create a new one.

"There were only seven of us. In later action we lost three, and one lost his leg, Squeaky Hanson, who some of you knew."

A few nodded. They'd liked Hanson. He was home working at his dad's Western Auto store.

"The Germans were going to fly the atomic bomb to the states, probably New York or D.C. Our friend Sergeant Saunders and an American pilot stole the jet bomber right from under the krauts' noses, and that put an end to the possibility the Germans could attack us directly.

"That's changed . . ." he paused because Jonesy held up his hand.

"Jonesy."

"That's what you got the Medal of Honor for, isn't it?"

Dunn nodded. "Yes."

"He didn't want to accept it. Thought the whole squad should have gotten it," Cross said. "But Colonel Kenton said it was already decided, and it had to be one guy."

"Let me get this straight," Martelli said. "You set off an atomic bomb that no one knew existed, and destroyed the Nazis' only hope to use one of those things against our civilians?"

Dunn's cheeks colored. He cleared his throat, suddenly nervous. He nodded.

"Sarge, you saved thousands of lives, probably including my family's. No one else can say that."

The men burst into applause and were grinning ear to ear.

"Ah, come on now, guys . . ."

Cross caught Dunn's eyes and shook his head. "For once, Tom, for one damn time, accept the applause. Take the credit."

Dunn felt himself about to tear up and he swallowed the sizable lump in his throat. It was one thing to have the President of the United States hang a medal around your neck, and quite another for the men who depended on you to keep them alive, and who would do anything to save your life, to give you accolades.

The applause settled down, but the men were looking at Dunn as if expecting a speech.

He pressed his lips together for a moment, trying to calm himself.

"Thank you, guys. That means a lot to me. But you know I was just doing my job. Any of you would have done the same thing."

Gentle laughter greeted this.

"Sarge," Martelli said shaking his head, "you know damn well not one of us would have figured that out. Jeez, you're impossible."

Dunn grinned. "That's what Pamela tells me most days."

This was worthy of uproarious laughter.

Dunn held up his hand and the men quieted down.

"Okay. Thanks. I appreciate it very much. I have one more thing to say before I tell you more about the mission." He had to stop for a moment to gather himself. The men waited patiently.

"I just wanted to say that it is my profound honor and privilege to serve with you. I am so proud of each and every one of you. I will remember our time together for the rest of my life."

The men all came to attention without prompting from anyone. Even though it wasn't protocol, each man raised a slow motion salute to Dunn.

This time Dunn's eyes did tear up.

He returned the salute.

"Thank you, men."

The squad nodded at Dunn.

Dunn cleared his throat. "Back to our mission."

The men shifted on their feet a little showing their readiness.

"Bletchley Park picked up messages describing yet another new weapon. You'll have to bear with me, because it seems insane, but I've been assured it will, in fact, work.

"You're all aware of the V2 rockets that have plagued England over the past few months."

Everyone nodded, their expressions both wary and worried.

"Their damn engineers have figured out a way to tow three V2 rockets by submarine *under water* all the way across the Atlantic. They'll be able to park three hundred miles off shore and launch their rockets. They could destroy huge sections of any seaboard city they choose. Then when the shitheads are done, they go back to Germany, reload and repeat."

The room erupted again.

Dunn stood silently by as the men colorfully vented their anger.

When the men returned their attention to him, he said, "Bletchley says they can tell from the daily messages that the Germans are in the production process, and close to finished, but we don't know exactly where the submersible rocket carriers are actually being constructed.

"Our job is straightforward: find out where the sons of bitches are building these things and get word back so our bombers can blow them all to hell and back."

"You mean we're doing a recon job?" Wickham asked.

"Yep. Quiet in, quiet out."

Wickham nodded. "Oh, okay. Sounds kinda boring."

"You never know, Stan."

Wickham shrugged. "Uh, okay. Whatever you say."

Dunn looked around at the men. A small smile touched his lips. "What, no complaints?"

"Whatever you need done, Sarge," Schneider said.

He unfolded a map on the table and produced a piece of paper from his trousers pocket. "Sergeant Cross brought along the map of Hamburg and Colonel Kenton gave us the addresses of the main shipbuilders there, only two of them actually. While Cross and I work on the plan, you guys start preparing by cleaning your weapons and checking the magazines. Refill as many magazines as possible from our extra supplies.

"Okay, men, let's get to it."

The men dispersed. Dunn nodded at Cross and they went to Dunn's quarters. He'd been given a single-bunk room, much like the captain's. Perhaps this one belonged to the executive officer. Dunn turned on the metal-framed lightbulb and the men sat down at the tiny desk opposite each other. Dunn pulled close a notepad and laid a pencil on it. He glanced up at his best friend.

"Ready?"

"Ayup," the fisherman's son replied in his best Nor'easter accent.

The men started working on the mission, knowing it would be of a different type than usual, and therefore perhaps more challenging.

RONN MUNSTERMAN

23

London
30 November, 1800 Hours, London time

Colonel Rupert Jenkins closed the door of his staff car and stood
still, looking at the estate's home. The house was massive, rising
threes stories with the front spanning almost two hundred feet. The
stone was square cut and light tan. Windows were spaced evenly
on each floor. The front door had two wide steps. The one-way
gravel driveway was bordered by trees and in the other seasons,
one would have seen flowers everywhere. Exiting the tree-lined
area, the space in front of the house opened up. The drive expanded
so that it was a good fifty feet wide, providing ample room for
many cars to park. Tonight, Jenkins' car was the only one. To the
left, a wide formal English garden with short, perfectly trimmed
hedges occupied the area between the inbound and outbound
driveways.

He'd driven himself, worrying the entire trip about what he was
going to say to this woman. The one he hadn't seen in twenty years.
That she had indeed ringed him back gave him hope. When he
asked if he could visit her, she'd said yes surprisingly fast. He'd

fully expected either an outright "no" or a lengthy dissertation on his failure as a beau those many years ago. He frowned to himself. Perhaps she was saving the lambaste for the face-to-face meeting.

The front door opened.

He'd expected the butler to be there, but no, it was her. Lady Alice Clayton herself. A gasp escaped his lips.

As he walked toward her, his legs felt wooden. He wondered whether she would laugh if he just collapsed, unable to walk any farther. Somehow he made it to the first step and stopped. His eyes had never left hers.

Her long red hair draped her shoulders. Her blue eyes seemed to be on fire, and she had smooth fair skin. She wore a captivating dark blue evening gown. It accented her still youthful form. Her slender hands were clasped together in front of her. Even though Jenkins wore his dress uniform, he felt underdressed in comparison. He had to fight off the urge to grasp the bottom of his jacket and snap it, and to check his tie.

"Hello, Rupie." Her voice was soft, husky, and gave off a warmth that had been missing on the phone.

"Hello, Alice. Lady Alice, I mean." Jenkins flushed at his misstep.

"Oh, please, it's just Alice between us."

"Right. Alice."

"Won't you come in?" She smiled radiantly.

Jenkins' heart almost stopped.

He almost flew up the remaining step and held out his left arm. She slid her arm through. They walked inside through the wide door.

The foyer was as he remembered. Huge. Wide, high, and long, with the stairs leading up straight ahead. She led him into the sitting room, which was on the right. He knew the dining room would be just off that room. The room's color theme was red. Carpet, furniture, and walls were various shades of red. He'd never liked it. Too bloodlike for a man who'd seen combat. But he wisely kept his own counsel on this topic.

They sat on a long, plush sofa. He'd expected her to take a seat on another sofa or chair, but there she was right next to him. His heart began to race. He wondered if he'd have a heart attack right there and then. How embarrassing that would be for her. Great headline: Beau returns from the past. Kicks off.

They sat quietly, closely examining the other's face.

Jenkins tried to speak, but his throat closed up.

She smiled and helped him out. "You're looking well, Rupie."

He swallowed. "Thank you. You look . . . incredible. Beautiful. It's so good to see you."

"As smooth as ever, aren't you?" She said it lightly, to take out any sting.

"Not trying to be smooth. Just honest."

"Finally."

He nodded. She was right. Honest he hadn't been when he'd led her to believe he could marry her and give up the army.

"Yes, finally. I'm so very sorry."

Her eyes teared up, surprised he would, could admit the betrayal.

He pulled a handkerchief from his pocket and handed it to her.

She took it gratefully and dabbed her eyes carefully.

"Is there some chance, even a small one that we could see each other regularly?"

She handed him the handkerchief and rose.

"I believe dinner is ready. Shall we?"

Jenkins stifled a sigh. So that was how it was going to be. Well, what could he have expected? He stood as well and took her arm again.

They entered the dining room, which had a table the size of a football field. High-backed chairs surrounded the table. Jenkins checked quickly and was relieved to see that place settings were located across from each other at one end of the table and not one on each of the ends. Intimate dinner.

They walked to the table and Jenkins pulled the intricately carved, heavy wooden chair out for her.

She sat, murmuring, "Thank you, Colonel."

Jenkins went around to the other side and seated himself. He stared at her for a moment, a smile touching his lips.

The servant's door opened and the butler led a staff of three into the room. A young lady of about eighteen, with her brown hair tied up in a bun under her white hat, carried a silver tray with a cover. She placed it gently on the long serving table behind

Jenkins. A man in his sixties carried another large silver tray on which were several serving bowls. He set it down on the table and stepped to the side. He wore a tuxedo and white gloves, as did the butler. The third person, an older woman with gray hair and a round, pleasant face bore a basket of hot, fresh rolls. She put it on the table and moved away.

The butler, the stern unfriendly man Jenkins had spoken to on the phone, looked at Lady Alice questioningly.

She nodded.

The staff immediately began serving, Lady Alice first, of course.

Jenkins watched with some admiration their smooth, coordinated movements, not unlike a choreographed dance or a well-trained army unit on dress parade. He looked down at the plump quail on his plate. Next to it were a large baked potato and uncut, but trimmed green beans cooked with bacon.

The butler poured a small amount of wine, a 1937 bottle of Pinot Noir, into Jenkins' glass. He waited for the colonel to sniff, take a sip and swirl the wine around on his tongue. Jenkins smiled at Lady Alice and nodded to the butler, who partially filled his glass first—so any bits of cork would end up in his glass and not the lady's—and went around the table to fill Lady Alice's. He came back to Jenkins and finished filling his glass.

The butler put the bottle on the table near Jenkins, and led the staff out of the room. Normally, the staff would stand by during dinner to help, but Jenkins surmised Lady Alice had given them instructions to leave so they could speak freely. He appreciated her thoughtfulness.

He lifted his wine glass and she followed suit. "To a new beginning, Lady Alice."

She smiled. "To a new beginning, Rupert. And it's just Alice, please."

"Alice."

They sipped from their glasses and set them down.

Lady Alice took the first bite, as was the custom, and Jenkins dove into his plate with gusto. It was far better than the base mess hall.

"How long have you been at the American army base?"

Surprised, Jenkins raised an eyebrow. "How?"

She grinned. "I have friends in many places."

"You checked up on me?"

"Same as you did."

"Are you still angry about that?"

"Oh, Rupert, I was never angry about that."

"But . . ." he spread his hands out in bewilderment, recalling quite clearly her anger on the phone.

Lady Alice laid down her fork. "All right, if you must know, yes, I was angry. But it was because you suddenly decided it was time to ring me and set things to right."

Her cheeks flared pink.

"You really did break my heart. It hurt then, and it hurts now."

Jenkins lowered his eyes, unable to withstand her glare.

"I am so deeply, truly sorry for hurting you. I know I did. I'm hoping you can forgive me." He raised his gaze. She was stunningly beautiful and seeing her like this took him back twenty years. His heart nearly burst.

"I know now I made a mistake. A tragic mistake."

He rose and walked around the table. She watched him with an expression similar to a cat eyeing a mouse on the floor. Play with it or kill it? Or both? She turned in her chair as he approached her. He knelt and took her hand.

"I love you, Alice. I love you so very much." He dipped his head.

She put her free hand behind his head and caressed the white hair.

He looked up at her, hope burning in his eyes.

"To your question from earlier: my answer is 'yes.' I want to give ourselves a second chance."

She stood and they fell into an embrace so tight Jenkins thought he might not be able to breathe. But he realized he could never live another moment and have breath without her.

She rested her head on his shoulder.

"I love you, Rupert. I always have."

They kissed.

And they were once again but twenty-two years old.

RONN MUNSTERMAN

24

Tree-covered hilltop
1/4 mile south of shipyards
Hamburg, Germany
1 December, 0231 Hours, the next day

Dunn and his men lay prone at the edge of a large grove of trees situated on a hilltop facing the shipyards of Hamburg. Higgins and Kelly were behind them facing the other way at the opposite side of the grove to provide rear security.

As Dunn watched the dark city, it was impossible not to see the remnants of fires on the northern side of the city, where smoke trails still headed skyward. One area just across the water from the shipyards still had flames shooting into the air, which reflected on the still water.

He'd been warned by Colonel Kenton to stay away from that side of the city due to a planned air raid. Obviously, the British, who bombed at night, had arrived. Whether they actually hit their targets was impossible to tell. That helped Dunn choose the south shore of the river, which provided a more direct approach to the excellent lookout point where they were hiding.

The distance from their landing zone to the hilltop had been a slow six miles, and it had taken close to three hours to get there due to the nature of stealth, which boiled down to one thing: not wanting to get captured.

Dunn had his field glasses to his eyes, but to get a better look at everything, they'd have to sit tight, make sure no one wandered into them, and wait and see what they could see. Sunrise would arrive in about five hours. With the early gray light that preceded actual sunrise, they'd have decent visibility around seven forty-five.

The squad was traveling light, for them. Their packs contained no explosives, just the extra K-rations they'd brought along on the liquid oxygen mission just in case it dragged on. Their extra magazines for the Sten guns were on their equipment belts. They wore the same dark clothes as the night before. Freshly applied black grease covered their exposed facial skin.

Cross was to Dunn's left and also had his binoculars up. He lowered them in frustration. "I don't see anything useful." He had whispered, but still managed to make it sound whiny.

"Relax. We've been here two minutes," Dunn whispered back.

Cross sighed deeply and Dunn patted him on the shoulder.

"It'll be a really long day if you can't relax."

"I know."

"Just a thought."

"Ayup."

Jonesy was on Dunn's right. Eugene Lindstrom, Jonesy's spotter, was next to Jonesy.

The sniper was scanning the wharf through his suppressed 1903 Springfield's sniper scope. An evil looking foot-long suppressor was screwed onto the barrel.

"Movement along the wharf," Jonesy said.

"Where?" Dunn asked immediately.

"See the three canals running southeast from the main channel to our left?"

Dunn tracked his field glasses to the area Jonesy had described. "Got the canals."

"Sweep right a little. Almost right in front of us."

"I see them."

"Me, too," chimed in Cross.

In the back light of the fires, a woman was walking fast and looking over her shoulder. Dunn imagined he could hear the *clickety-clack* of her shoes on the cobblestone street. Two men were following her and gaining in spite of her hurried pace. She glanced over her shoulder once more and started running. The men pursued.

They caught her before she reached the end of the block in front of a warehouse. They grabbed her and pulled her into an alley. There were trash containers and wooden crates lying around up and down the alley.

One man tore her coat off and threw it on the ground. He ripped off the blouse next.

"Ah shit," Jonesy muttered. He quickly tested the wind and lined up a shot on the attacker. The second man was obscured by the woman's body.

"I can take the shot, Sarge."

Dunn knew Jonesy could take the shot. He'd proven himself over and over again. But should he? Would it somehow give them away? As he watched the men struggle with the woman, she wriggled and fought and turned her head. Dunn could clearly see her terrified face in the moonlight which lit the alley.

"Take the shot."

Jonesy took a breath, let it out and waited for the moment between heartbeats, when his body would be perfectly still. His crosshairs were centered on the man's chest, the best target under the circumstances. He squeezed the trigger gently. The rifle spit and bucked back into his shoulder. In just over four tenths of a second, the supersonic round struck the man, knocking him back a couple of steps before he toppled over backwards.

The second man looked at the woman wildly, obviously thinking she had done something to his friend. He reached behind his back.

Jonesy smoothly worked the bolt and lined up shot number two.

The woman was still in the way. She struggled to get out of the man's grasp. Her feet slipped and she went down.

A knife appeared in the man's hand.

Jonesy fired.

The man dropped the knife and collapsed on the woman.

She fought to get free and got to her feet.

She looked around trying to figure out what had happened to her attackers. She rolled the man over on his back. She evidently saw the blood stained shirt. She backed up, her hands going to her mouth.

She looked around again, but of course, saw no one.

Suddenly she took a quick step forward and kicked the dead man in the face. She kicked him again. And again.

"Jesus, I don't blame her," Cross said.

She grabbed her blouse and coat off the ground. She slipped the torn blouse on and then the coat, wrapping it around herself tightly. She stood there for several minutes staring at her attackers, first one then the other. She raised her head and looked around the alley with her hands on her hips.

"What the hell?" Jonesy muttered.

She evidently had decided to do something. She walked over to the wall on her right and looked at the various crates and trash cans. She moved several crates by pulling one end out away from the wall. Then she used her right hip to nudge a trash can, about the size of a fifty-five gallon drum, to the side. She looked at the space she'd created next to the wall and at the two bodies lying crumpled on the ground, gauging and comparing. She pulled one more crate out of the way and stopped.

Turning, she went to the first man Jonesy shot and rolled him onto his back. Grabbing his ankles she slowly dragged his body across the ground and into the space she'd created. She rolled him onto his face, perhaps so she couldn't see it. Returning for the second attacker, she had more difficulty with him because he must have been heavier. She got him half way and had to drop his ankles and bend over at the knees to catch her breath. After a short rest, she resumed her grisly task. Soon the second body was lying next to the first one, also on his face.

With determination evident on her face, she pushed the crates back into position. She managed to pick one up and carry it a few feet before stacking it on top of one on the ground. She repeated that with one more. She hipped the trash can back in place, snug against one end of the stacked crates. She stepped back and examined her handiwork. She walked away and then back as if she was just traveling through the alley for the first time. She stared at the crates as she moved past. Once past them, she turned around and made a second pass from the other direction. She must have been satisfied because she walked back to the street. She stopped to look both ways, then walked to her right, back the way from which she'd come. A minute later, she was out of sight.

"Good lord, she must be a tough cookie," Dunn said.

"Pretty calm looking under the circumstances," Cross said.

"What about the blood? She didn't clean it up," Jonesy said.

"Maybe she figured if no one saw the bodies from the street, no one was likely to walk down the alley," Dunn said.

"Or she forgot," Cross said.

"Or she forgot," Dunn replied. He turned. "Nice shooting, Jonesy." Dunn reached over and patted the sniper on the shoulder. "Excellent, in fact."

Jonesy still had the rifle up, but his head was bowed, facing the ground.

"You okay?" Dunn asked, concern in his voice.

"She was so afraid, Sarge." He raised his head to look at his boss.

'Yes, and you saved her. Don't ever forget that."

Jonesy shook his head. "I won't. Not ever."

Dunn's eyes scrunched up. "You're not having a problem with killing those two are you?"

Jonesy shook his head emphatically. "Not one damn bit, Sarge. They had it coming."

"Okay. Just wanted to make sure since they weren't combatants."

"Technically."

Dunn smiled at Jonesy. "Maybe you should be a lawyer."

"Nah, can't stand them."

Dunn chuckled.

"What now, Tom?" Cross asked.

"We settle in. And wait for something to show up telling us where they're building the V2 rocket platforms."

Cross sighed.

"Relax."

"I am relaxed. I'm just gonna be bored."

The two Rangers eyed the buildings at the wharf.

"Any idea which one?" Cross asked.

"It should be the big one there." Dunn pointed at a long shape. "We'll have to watch all day. Maybe we'll get lucky and see something useful that proves it's the one. Otherwise we'll have to go down after sunset for a look. I'm not exactly thrilled at that prospect, but what can you do?"

"Yeah, not much. When is sunset?"

Dunn had asked the Barton Stacey weatherman about that for the first mission. "About sixteen hundred. Probably need to wait longer to get to full on dark."

"Going to make a long day of waiting."

"Yep. Let's leave Jonesy and Eugene on this side with me, and we'll keep Higgins and Kelly on the other. Two hour shifts. The rest, including the bored Dave Cross, will try to sleep deeper in the trees."

"Gee, what makes you think I'd be bored?"

Dunn punched Cross in the shoulder. "I don't see how a guy who grew up sitting around fishing can claim to be bored."

"Oh, well, see that's different."

Dunn sighed and gave up.

"Pass the word your way, and I'll do it mine.

"Okay."

"Will you tell Higgins and Kelly?"

"Sure."

"Thanks."

Soon, half of the Rangers were stretched out on their backs under the trees trying to get some shut eye.

Two hours later at four forty-five, the Rangers' shift changed. Cross, Martelli, and Schneider joined Dunn facing the wharf. Jonesy and Lindstrom sacked out as did Higgins and Kelly. Goerdt and Wickham drew guard duty on the west side of the grove.

"Anything?" Cross asked.

"Nothing."

"Okay."

An hour later, a small boat fired up its engine and crept along the river until it was out of sight.

"That's not a submarine," Cross offered helpfully.

Dunn heard Martelli chuckle lightly.

"Good to know."

At six a.m., Cross said, "Look there." He pointed to the left.

A group of about thirty workers, some carrying what looked like heavy toolboxes, walked from left to right along the wharf abutting the three canals Jonesy had pointed out earlier. While the Rangers watched, the workers kept moving toward the right, the east. Dunn moved his glasses farther to the right to see if he could determine where the men might be going. About fifty yards from the men was the huge building Dunn had pointed out to Cross. It was three stories tall and the length of a football field, perhaps a little longer and perpendicular to the water. It looked like the far end ran right up to the water's edge. This made Dunn think it was a shipbuilding facility and the boats were launched down an interior ramp to enter the water for the first time. A couple of minutes later, the men disappeared into a door on the west side of the building. He examined the building just to the east of it. It was much smaller, possibly used for storage. Even though it was smaller in overall size, it was a floor taller.

"If we have to go down there tonight, that looks like as good a place to start as any," Dunn said to Cross. "The big one. Maybe we can take a peek inside."

"Ayup."

At six forty-five, the next shift change, Dunn decided to take a break and crawled back inside the grove and slept.

25

Tree-covered hilltop
1/4 mile south of shipyards
Hamburg, Germany
1 December, 1108 Hours

Lindstrom woke Dunn up by calling his name several times. Best not to awaken a Ranger by shaking him.

Dunn opened his eyes to bright sunshine filtering through the trees' mostly empty limbs.

"What time is it?"

Lindstrom told him. "Sergeant Cross says you'll want to see this."

Cross had stayed awake rather than sleep, so Dunn could get some extra shut eye.

Dunn crawled up next to Cross.

"What's going on?"

Cross pointed toward the huge building they'd noted in the dark hours of the morning. "There've been a lot of staff cars pulling up to that building. Unloaded a bunch of high up navy brass, and some guys in suits. About twelve all together. They seemed excited. Figured something was about to happen. Started about ten minutes ago."

"Thanks for letting me sleep and thanks for waking me up for this."

"Sure."

"Any cops show up in that alley?"

"Nope. No one else has walked down the alley either."

"Good."

Dunn glanced around him. Jonesy and Lindstrom were together a few yards to the right. The rest of the men were awake and, except for Martelli and Goerdt acting as rear guard, were spaced out to Dunn's left.

Dunn asked about the two and Cross said they were on the west side of the grove.

About ten minutes passed.

A couple of smaller boats traveled in from the sea and moved farther to the east, out of sight, presumably to tie up at a pier.

Cross pointed with his left hand toward some vessels tied up at a pier farther to the north. "Lookit those E-boats, Tom."

Dunn looked where Cross was pointing. Three long boats were tied up in a row.

"They look like our torpedo boats."

"Ayup. But lots bigger. Over a hundred feet. Most of ours are around eighty."

"I bet you'd love to drive one."

"Pilot," Cross corrected automatically. "Yeah, sure would."

Motion as the west door of the building burst open caught their eyes. About a dozen men walked out at a fast pace. There were high ranking naval officers, and some wore suits as Cross had said. They turned right and marched quickly toward the water. At the water's edge, they stopped. All stared to the right, where the far end of the building would be.

"Shouldn't be too long," Cross said.

"Hm, yeah," Dunn replied.

Five more minutes went by. The Germans were shifting their weight from foot to foot.

Dunn laughed. "They look like little boys who need to go to the bathroom."

Cross chortled softly in return. "You crack me up, Tom."

"Heh heh."

The Germans stopped moving and turned as one, staring at something to their right.

"Here it comes," Cross said.

The large sharp nose of a submarine appeared. The boat was about fifty yards from the wharf and moving west at a crawl. It slowly revealed more of itself with a good fifty feet of boat visible.

"Jeez, that's huge," Cross said. "I can't wait to see the sail."

Dunn frowned at the term. "Sail? On a sub?"

Cross grinned. "Not a canvas one. You'd know it as the conning tower."

"Ah, well thanks."

"Ayup."

The boat continued to slide by the wharf. The conning tower finally appeared.

"What the hell? Look at that tower. It's huge," Dunn said.

The conning tower seemed larger and sleeker than any he had seen before. The boat was painted German gray and bore the identification number of U-2508, painted in white on the conning tower. When the boat was clear of the building, it coasted to a stop. Its fantail was right in front of the men on the wharf. The conning tower was located two-thirds the way back from the evil looking snout.

"It's hard to say for sure, but that thing looks to be at least a quarter again bigger than the *Sea Tiger*. How long is our sub?"

"It's a good two hundred feet," Cross answered.

"So this thing is about two-fifty?"

"Yeah."

He looked at the conning tower through his binoculars. He could make out two men there, facing the crowd. The taller of the two raised a salute.

One of the men on the wharf returned it.

"Well, now we know who's in charge down there. Wish we could see him clearly," Dunn said.

The men on the wharf looked right again.

"Something else is coming," Cross said.

A gray tugboat appeared. It puttered along carefully until it was just to the north of the sub's huge fantail, touching the sub with its rubber bumpers. Four sailors aboard the sub popped out of the aft hatch and ran to the fantail. A man on the tug tossed a line. A couple of the sailors caught it and tied it off.

"It has to be the V2 rocket platform," Dunn said.

Cross turned on his side and rummaged around in his pack. He pulled out the small camera Captain Bartlett of the *Sea Tiger* had loaned them. He readied it and aimed at the sub. He took a couple of shots of the sub, and lowered it, waiting for whatever was coming.

Two men on the tug were working on something on its fantail. Dunn focused his field glasses.

It was a thick cable connected to a metal ring. While one man worked to disconnect it, the other held the cable in gloved hands. As soon as it was loose, the one who'd disconnected it attached a smaller diameter rope to the connector. The other man threw the free end of the rope to the men on the sub. Quickly and smoothly, the sailors pulled the rope and cable to the sub. They knelt and attached the cable to a large metal tow ring positioned just below the deck. They stood when they were done and backed away. One of them lifted a small radio off his belt and spoke into it.

Dunn shifted his focus to the conning tower. The shorter of the two men also held a radio to his ear. He waved at the aft. The sailors untied the tug's anchoring rope and tossed it back aboard the tiny boat. The pilot gave it a little power and cranked the wheel to the right. It putt-putted away, moving in a semicircle to head back the way it had come.

Dunn lowered the glasses.

The sub began to move forward slowly.

The four sailors stood some distance away from the cable, but watched it intently. The slack was taken up by the sub's movement and the cable grew taut. It made Dunn think of a guitar string that had just been tightened. The sub continued forward.

Just as Dunn was wondering how long the cable would be, a strange looking object floated into view.

"It looks like a giant torpedo," Dunn said. "Look at the fins."

The object was indeed torpedo shaped and floated with half of its mass above water, showing one vertical fin and the two horizontal ones. Dunn assumed there was another vertical one under water.

"That's a little less than half of the sub, so what, a hundred, hundred and twenty feet?"

"Yes, I'd say so," Cross replied.

"Colonel Kenton said they could tow three of these things."

Cross took some more pictures, framing the sub and platform in each.

"You can't tell whether the rocket is aboard that thing."

"Yes, you can. If you look close, you can see a darker gray line painted above the midpoint. That's probably the line that shows them the rocket is loaded. If you can't see the line, it's loaded, like the red paint on merchant ships that sinks under the water when fully loaded."

"Okay, that's good to know. You sure, though?"

"Ayup."

"Okay."

While they watched, Dunn noticed that the Germans on the wharf were applauding.

He grimaced and said, "Go ahead and clap you assholes, it's never gonna fly."

"You tell 'em, boss."

The sub continued moving and seemed to be picking up speed; Dunn noticed the bow wave was growing higher. The platform passed the wharf and they waited for several minutes, but another one didn't appear.

Dunn gave a sigh of relief. "Looks like maybe they're doing sea trials."

"Ayup. I bet they'll be gone the whole afternoon."

The German spectators went back inside the building.

"Might as well eat something while we wait."

Dunn told the men to do that. Everyone except Dunn and Cross, and Martelli and Goerdt worked their way deeper inside the grove and broke out their K-rations. The two friends scooted back into the trees enough so they could sit with their legs crossed and eat their lunch, but still see the waterfront. Martelli and Goerdt ate while guarding the west side of the squad.

To their surprise, the submarine returned about an hour later, still towing the platform. The sub maneuvered in a wide circle in the river. It crept to a stop at the same point where Dunn and Cross had watched them attach the platform.

The man who was likely the tall captain they'd seen on the conning tower and a half dozen sailors appeared on the sub's rear deck, watching something behind the boat.

The spectators returned to watch the proceedings.

The tall officer on the conning tower raised a pair of binoculars to watch whatever was happening.

"I wonder if they're attaching the other two platforms," Cross mused.

"Makes sense. Hey, do you have enough film to take more pics?"

Cross glanced down at his camera. "Huh. Only one left on this roll. Here look at me."

Dunn turned to his friend. He hadn't shaved so he had a dark shadow along his jaw, chin, and upper lip. He still wore the black grease paint and the black watch cap.

"Smile dumbass, this is for Pamela."

Dunn lifted one side of his lips, as if he knew something funny that you didn't. The slight smile did, however, reach all the way to his eyes, which were crinkled in delight as he thought of his wife.

Cross snapped the picture.

"That should turn out real good."

"Thanks."

Cross busied himself with rewinding the film in the camera, and replaced it with a fresh one he'd pulled from his pocket. He put the used roll in a round watertight aluminum container exactly the right size for one roll; Captain Bartlett had given him a few. It was similar to an item you could buy at the hardware store to keep kitchen matches dry for camping or fishing. He pocketed this.

After a half hour, the men had finished eating. They crawled back to join Dunn and Cross, who had returned to their position at the edge of the woods.

"What's happening?" Jonesy asked.

"Sub came back. They might be hooking up the other platforms for another sea trial."

Jonesy nodded and raised his rifle. He sighted on the men on the wharf, centering on the officer who had returned the sub captain's salute. The man had turned around to talk to the other men around him. He was grinning. Jonesy didn't know the German navy's rank insignias, but he had a lot of stuff on his shoulders and braid on the bill of his hat. An Iron Cross hung below his throat. He was an older man, probably in his early fifties. Jonesy eyed the man's face.

"Huh. Isn't that officer Admiral Dönitz?"

Dunn took a look through his binoculars. The men routinely memorized the faces of well-known Nazis.

"Yeah. That is."

"Pretty easy shot, Sarge."

"No. I know it's tempting, but we're just here to observe and report back."

Jonesy sighed his disappointment, but lowered the weapon. "Yes, Sarge."

Soon, the sailors disappeared down the aft hatch, one of them closing and locking it.

About fifteen more minutes passed with nothing happening, and then the sub moved forward. The platform came into view. Dunn noted the gray line Cross had mentioned. It was still clearly visible above the water. As soon as the platform moved off to the left, another one appeared. It was identical to the first and its gray line was also visible. A third one passed by, also empty. The sub and its train of V2 rocket platforms eventually picked up speed and floated out of sight.

"I wonder if this trial will take longer." Dunn said.

"It might. They may want to do more maneuvering around with the entire set attached," Cross replied.

"That makes sense."

Dunn checked his watch: 13:45. They'd been on this hilltop for almost twelve hours. With much more to come.

RONN MUNSTERMAN

26

Star & Garter Hotel Restaurant
Andover, England
1 December, 1257 Hours, London time

Pamela Dunn, Tom Dunn's wife of four months, and Sadie
Saunders, the Commando's wife of just over two months, were
seated at a table near a window. It was Pamela's and Dunn's
favorite table because it was where they'd had their first, albeit
abbreviated, date. The table still had the same style of tablecloth,
a red and white checkered pattern. The window faced the usually
busy High Street on which the hotel's front door with the Doric
columns was located.

The two women sat across from each other in the chairs closest
to the window. Their husbands had become close friends and as a
consequence, so had they. Though the same age, Pamela was the
only one who had work experience.

Sadie had lived at home until marrying Saunders in late
September. She'd moved into a nice second floor flat in Andover,
not far from the Star & Garter. Pamela and Dunn had pitched in
with Saunders to get her situated. Pamela took her under her wing

since she was new to the town. They tried to meet weekly for a meal together.

"So Tom is off somewhere?"

"He is."

Sadie was a brunette with a beautiful face, slightly marred by a barely visible scar that ran from her right eyebrow to a point near her upper lip. It was carefully hidden by some makeup Pamela had recently given to her. It was the result of being struck by shrapnel from a Nazi buzz bomb back in mid-July. She had been shopping for a new dress to surprise Saunders when the bomb crashed and exploded near the clothing store. It had broken her right leg in several places and she'd had to undergo excruciatingly painful physical therapy. She'd done it so her father could walk her down the aisle, which he did.

Also pregnant, Sadie's due date was, at the moment, the fourth of July. This had pleased Dunn considerably when he found out, but he hadn't razzed Saunders about it yet. He was making him wait for the other shoe to drop. Pamela was due in mid-May, and that had remained constant throughout.

"Sometimes I wish Mac could tell me where he's going so I'd at least know where he is."

Sadie's eyes flitted to the window and back to Pamela.

"But other times, you're glad you don't know?"

Sadie's eyes misted over. She pulled a handkerchief from her purse and dabbed her eyes. She nodded. "I don't know how to explain it, but yes, I don't want to know."

Pamela reached across the table and patted her friend's hand. "I understand perfectly."

Sadie gripped Pamela's hand tightly.

"How do you stand it? I'm so afraid, all the time when he's gone."

"I pray a lot. My mum and dad help a lot, just being there to listen. I have friends from the hospital, and others I knew growing up."

"I appreciate your friendship, Pamela, but I wonder if I should move back home with my parents. I feel like I need their comforting presence."

"Sure. Have you made some other friends here? Perhaps at church?"

"Well, yes, a few. They're nice and all, but you're the only one I feel close to. They aren't married or involved with anyone in the military."

"So they have no clue?"

Sadie smiled for the first time. "Yes, that's it exactly. No clue whatsoever. No common ground at all."

"If you like I could introduce you to some other army wives I know. They married Americans like I did, and they truly understand."

"I'd like that."

Sadie glanced out the window. A mother and young boy of about seven walked by, hand in hand. She carried a small parcel from one of the stores on High Street. The boy helpfully carried a smaller package tucked under his free arm.

Sadie smiled at the sight and Pamela looked over, too, and smiled.

"That'll be us, won't it?" Sadie asked softly.

"It sure will be."

"I wish the war was over. I just want to return to a normal life."

"Me, too."

Pamela looked down at her plate. She'd eaten all of the chicken and potatoes.

"I'm stuffed. I hope I can waddle back to the truck."

Sadie giggled. Pamela was glad to hear her do that.

"Want me to give you a lift home?"

"No. I'm stuffed, too. I better walk it off."

"Me, too. I'll walk the dogs."

Sadie nodded. "I wish we could have pets in the flat."

"Have you asked the landlord?"

"No, but he made a point of it when we rented the place."

"Wouldn't hurt to ask. All he can do is say no again."

Sadie's face brightened. She shrugged. "Right. Why not?"

Pamela glanced around the restaurant and spotted the waitress who'd served them. She gave her a little wave.

The waitress, an older woman in her fifties, brought the check. Before she set it down, she asked, "Would you ladies like some dessert? We have baked apples." She winked and lowered her voice, "with cinnamon."

Pamela and Sadie both waved that idea away with a laugh.

"No more room, I'm afraid," Pamela said cheerfully.

"It was nice seeing you both again." The waitress laid the check down.

Pamela picked it up. They took turns paying. She dug in her purse to get a few coins out for a nice tip and put them on the table.

"Ready?" she asked.

"Yes."

Both rose and stretched. They slipped into their overcoats and put on hats.

"Meet you outside?" Pamela asked.

"Yes."

While Sadie went out the restaurant door to the hotel lobby, Pamela paid the check at the bar.

"See you next time, Mrs. Dunn," the old bartender said.

"Thank you, Mr. Goff."

Standing under the balcony supported by the Doric columns, the two young women hugged.

"Sure you don't want a ride?"

"I'm sure, thanks."

Pamela took one of Sadie's hands in hers. "You call me if you need to talk. Anytime. I mean it."

"I know you do. I will."

Sadie left, heading down High Street toward her flat.

Pamela stepped to the curb, looked to the right for oncoming traffic in the near lane, then the other way. It was clear and she walked across the street to her dad's lorry, which she'd borrowed to come into town.

She got in and set her purse on the passenger seat. She started the engine, stepped on the clutch pedal and slid the cranky floor gearshift into first gear. Easing out the clutch she gave it some gas and pulled away from the curb. Being a farm girl, she'd learned to drive at the young age of twelve.

She up-shifted to second and gave it more gas. When she reached the end of the block she turned right to get to the main road leading south out of town.

Behind her, a black car pulled away from the curb and drove down High Street, turning right onto the same road. Two people were in the front seat, a man and a woman, the man driving.

Pamela drove at fifty miles an hour, a safe enough speed for the 1938 Bedford WS drop side lorry. It rattled and clunked on the road which was a little rough in places.

As she neared the farm, the road curved to the east. She slowed entering the curve to prepare for the turn into the driveway.

The black car, two hundred yards back, slowed in response.

Pamela drove up the driveway after downshifting to first gear to make it up the hill.

The black car drove slowly by the end of the driveway, and sped up. It traveled another hundred yards and the driver pulled off the side of the road.

The man turned off the engine and the pair got out. The man, Waffen SS Major Dedrick Förstner, looked up and down the road, which was empty of other vehicles. He wore a dark shirt and pants, work boots, and a black flat newsboy cap. They walked to the car's boot, which he opened. He reached in and grabbed a pair of binoculars. He handed it to Evelyn Harris, who also wore a dark outfit and boots. Next he lifted a small camera and looped the strap around his neck. It was just for show in case they were caught out by someone on the farm. Their story would be they were novice birdwatchers. If they ran into the wife, who would likely remember Evelyn as the photographer looking for her church, they would say she remembered the farm.

"Ready?" she asked in German.

"Ja."

They set out, going north across the road and into the woods on the hill. They walked through the woods stopping every so often to listen. Hearing nothing worrisome, they advanced farther. They reached the top of the hill and turned west. The trees were a mix of leafless deciduous, and evergreens. They walked slowly and carefully across any places where there might be twigs to snap.

They found an open space just ahead and stopped to observe and listen. Satisfied, they moved forward slowly, Förstner leading, Evelyn walking in his footsteps. He stopped next to a three foot diameter oak. He leaned against it and looked ahead.

The rear of an old two-story stone farm house was just twenty meters away. To the north of the house, another, smaller, one floor house stood, facing south. Beyond that, he could see the top of the barn.

He stepped forward to the right and stood behind a birch tree, watching the front of the smaller house. A minute passed.

The door burst open and two dogs, a collie and a black Labrador sprinted toward the barnyard. The man held his breath. Dogs could be serious trouble. There was only one way to handle them. Pamela Dunn, wearing a heavy coat and what looked like work pants and boots stepped through the door, shutting it behind her. She followed the dogs. She whistled once and they romped back and ran around her, looking up at her with their tongues lolling.

"How sweet," Evelyn said dryly.

"Quiet!' he whispered.

Förstner led Evelyn around the back of the main farm house, noting the back door in the center of the rear wall. He stopped at the front northwest corner and knelt. The comfortable and reassuring weight of his Luger rested on his right hip. He'd first carried this particular weapon when he'd parachuted in with Skorzeny to rescue Mussolini.

He could see Pamela Dunn and her two dogs on the far side of the barn walking west at a good clip. He peeked around the corner to see the front door. It was closed. Pamela and her companions moved out of sight as they started downhill.

Evelyn's clever photos of the target and his wife had captured the layout of all the buildings and they matched what Förstner saw as he examined the barnyard, the barn, and the two houses. The barn's loft doors were open, but the one at ground level was closed. Barn's usually had a rear entrance, but he wanted to make sure.

"Stay here and out of sight."

"Where are you going?"

He didn't bother answering. He ran around the back of the smaller house and to the rear of the barn. A quick look was all he needed. One ground level door, closed, and one for the loft, open. An extended and swiveling support beam above the loft door was pushed to the right, toward him, with a pulley and rope dangling from it. Typical equipment for lifting items to the loft. He went to the door and put his ear close. He heard no animals moving around.

Satisfied he knew the farm's layout, he ran back to Evelyn.

"Let's go." He grabbed her arm.

She snatched her arm away. "Don't do that."

"Fine."

"Isn't there anything else you need to do?"

He gave her an incredulous look. "Like what?"

She shrugged. "Like going in the house to get the layout."

He shook his head slowly as if marveling at her stupidity. "Too risky. Her parents are probably home. Come on."

She gave up and followed, but stayed out of his reach.

They wound through the woods and, before crossing the road, checked for traffic. Clear. They dashed across the pavement and climbed in the car. A minute later, the car did a U-turn and headed back to Andover.

27

The shipyards
Hamburg, Germany
1 December, 2022 Hours, Berlin time

Under cover of darkness, Dunn and his men slipped down the front of the hilltop and reached the flat ground leading to the wharf. No police had come with sirens to the alley where the two dead attempted rapists were hidden.

The submarine had returned about three hours after leaving with all three platforms still attached. It performed what must have been a tricky maneuver going to the farthest point on the east side of the river, and moving in a half circle. The platforms followed like faithful puppies and the sub stopped about where it had started from hours prior.

The men who had been watching the sub when it departed had left, but returned to watch its arrival. The captain of the sub came ashore on a tug boat and after salutes were exchanged, received pats on the back and glad handshakes. The entire group of men disappeared back into the large building.

Dunn and Cross discussed Dunn's plan for their next task and fine-tuned it. It was time to execute it flawlessly.

The men traveled in groups of two side by side, with an interval of about five steps. The wharf had grown quiet after the shift change occurred, which had been hours earlier, around four p.m. Dunn had point and was paired with Jonesy. The sniper carried his Springfield on his back with the sling over his right shoulder and the weapon's stock behind his left hip. Like everyone else, he carried his Sten gun in his hands.

They advanced steadily along the west wall of the building just to the east of the very large facility Dunn wanted to target. The full moon had just risen a bit earlier and shone its light on the street they were using, casting long shadows behind the men. Dunn spotted what he was looking for on his left, and moved toward it. When he reached a point below the iron fire escape, he stopped and turned around. He waved at his men. They picked up the pace and soon were gathered near him. He pointed toward the shadow of the structure and they all took a knee there. Dunn pointed at Higgins, who was last, twirled his finger in the air, and pointed back the way they'd come.

Higgins nodded and turned around to act as rear guard, his weapon raised.

Dunn turned back around. He let his Sten gun dangle from its cross-shoulder strap. He laced his fingers together for Jonesy at knee height. Jonesy also let go of his Sten gun and lifted a boot, sliding it onto Dunn's handmade step.

"Ready?" Dunn whispered.

"Yes."

Dunn lifted and Jonesy reached for the bottom of the fire escape's sliding ladder. He wrapped his fingers around it and pulled down. It moved surprisingly smoothly and quietly. Evidently the Germans took fire safety seriously. The ladder finished its descent and stopped with the first rung about two feet off the ground. Jonesy leaped onto it and began climbing. Above him the winding iron staircase went all the way to the roof. Their goal.

Dunn jumped onto the ladder and began his ascent. He was about a half a floor behind Jonesy. The rest of the men would stay put. Jonesy reached the roof and peeked over the wall. It was clear, so he climbed over the low wall and stepped onto the flat roof. There was nothing on the roof at all, not unexpected, except a shed-like structure with a door. It was obviously the roof access from inside the building. The building to the south, which was the one a floor taller, blocked any view in that direction.

He waited for Dunn, who climbed over the wall and stood next him. Dunn took everything in at once and pointed at the structure. Jonesy ran over and checked the door. Unlocked, he signaled to Dunn. Dunn ran over and examined the structure. It was about ten feet square. *Perfect,* he thought, *if this is the right place.*

Jonesy stood to the left of the door, the side with the doorknob. He raised his Sten and nodded.

Dunn opened the door a couple of inches.

Jonesy peered inside. He could see nothing. Pulling his tiny flashlight from his belt and aiming it at the floor inside, he switched it on. A sliver of light revealed descending concrete steps and a hand rail on the right. Holding the lens against his thigh to block its light, he nodded to Dunn.

Dunn opened the door fully.

Jonesy stepped inside and aimed the light at the floor again. He started down the stairs. Dunn followed.

The two descended one floor and found another door in the same relative position as the first one. Jonesy turned off his light and opened the door a few inches. Bright light came from within. He peeked. He pulled back and beckoned Dunn. They traded places so Dunn could see inside.

The cavernous interior was brightly lit, but from outside you couldn't have known it due to the thick blackout paint on all the windows. Workmen were busy using arc welders on a new V2 rocket platform's fins. It was nearly complete. Two others were farther away in different stages of completion. Dunn gently closed the door. He pulled Cross's borrowed camera from his coat pocket. He opened the door and began taking pictures of the platform assembly line. Finished, he closed the door quietly again

Jonesy turned his light back on and pointed upwards, a questioning expression on his face.

Dunn nodded.

The sniper led the way back to the roof, turning off the light at the top.

They stepped out on the roof and closed the door. Dunn nodded to Jonesy, who returned the favor with his laced hands. A moment later, Dunn was squatting on top of the structure. Like the roof, it had a dark waterproof surface. *Perfect,* he thought again.

Jonesy knelt beside the door. He held his Sten at the ready.

Dunn knelt and shrugged his pack off. He rummaged around inside and pulled out two wide rolls of beige masking tape the *Sea Tiger's* chief mechanic had given him. He got his bearings and began laying down strips of tape from the east edge of the roof to the west edge. After completing the twelfth two-inch wide strip he stopped. He had created a number one. He moved to the right a few feet and laid down strips going left to right. This batch he made about four feet in length. He ran out of the first roll after three strips and started on the second roll. After finishing the left to right bar, he started on the vertical bar of the number seven. He ran it at a slight angle since we don't make sevens with a right angle of the two bars.

He rose to a crouch and examined his number 17 on the top of the structure. It was for the B-17s that would hopefully be coming soon to obliterate the building and any platforms still under construction. He raised each boot and wiped its sole clean with his gloved hands. Next, still crouching, he duck-walked carefully over the tape to help adhere it to the roof. If it had been raining, he would have had to think of some other method, perhaps some paint from the HMS *Sea Tiger's* maintenance store. He was extremely grateful it wasn't snowing. He hadn't figured out how to mark the building in that circumstance. He hoped the number 17 in light beige would stand out like a beacon for the lead bombardier. If the Germans found it for some bizarre and lucky reason, the bombardier would have to rely on Dunn's description and location of the building.

He put the empty and partial roll of tape in his pack and slipped it back on. He moved to the edge of the roof where he'd climbed up. He knelt, sat down, rolled over and let his legs dangle while grasping the roof with his hands. Jonesy grasped his lower legs and helped him down.

"A-okay, Sarge?"

"Yep. Ready to go."

Jonesy ran back to the spot where the fire escape was located. He knelt and swept his gaze across the roof. All clear.

Dunn slipped over the edge and started down the fire escape. Jonesy followed close behind.

They landed on the ground, their rubber-soled boots making little noise.

Jonesy turned and pushed up on the ladder. It smoothly rose to its original position.

Cross looked at Dunn expectantly.

"We confirmed they're building the platforms inside this building. Got pictures. All done with marking the top of a small building on the roof for the stairs up. We're clear to get out of here," Dunn said.

"Great, I'm all for that."

"You take point. Got the pathway figured out?"

"Ayup."

Cross ran to the opposite end of the squad, and waved at the men when he was ready. Dunn took Jonesy along, who became tail-end Charlie with Dunn right in front of him. This time, the men would move in close formation with a couple of steps between them. Cross led them carefully to the corner of the first block and stopped the line. He peered out. Clear. They continued advancing block by block and were only one from the relative safety of the woods.

Cross turned and led the men into an alley, the same one where the woman had hidden the two bodies.

Dunn was thinking they were doing well.

He should have known better.

RONN MUNSTERMAN

28

The shipyards
Hamburg, Germany
1 December, 2100 Hours

Two police cars pulled up at the far end of the alley. Four policemen jumped out, their flashlights sweeping the ground in front of them. Unknowingly, they were headed right at the Rangers.

Cross stopped the column and everyone knelt and leaned into the shadows. The spot where the bodies were buried behind crates was ahead about fifty feet. Dunn worked his way to the front and squatted beside Cross.

"What do you think?" he asked

Cross shook his head. "Someone must have found the bodies, or else the woman had an attack of guilty conscious and called them."

"Well, shit."

The police officers found the stacked crates. Two of them lifted off the top two and set them aside. They leaned in and shouted something. In a flurry of activity, they moved the other two crates and leaned over the bodies, rolling them over and checking to make sure they were indeed dead. They stood up and looked at one of the other two policemen, the boss. They shook their heads. The boss nodded and ran back to the cars. He slid inside one and to Dunn it looked like he was using a radio.

Dunn glanced over his shoulder. The end of the alley where they'd entered was a good sixty feet away. They were trapped. Thinking quickly he arrived at only one conclusion. One that bothered him to some degree. Maybe there was another way. He looked behind himself and saw Goerdt right there.

"Rob, come with me."

"Dave, give us cover fire if necessary."

"Will do, Tom."

Dunn pulled Goerdt close and told him what he wanted to do. Goerdt nodded.

Dunn rose slowly to his feet and started walking toward the three officers, who were actually looking the other way.

Although the moon had advanced across the night sky toward the south, there was still quite a bit of light in the alley. When he was about fifteen feet away, almost to the right point, one of the cops decided to turn around, perhaps to look at the bodies more closely. As he turned, his flashlight beam swept across Dunn's chest and continued on a bit.

Surprised, the officer swept the beam back and stared for a moment before deciding what to do.

Dunn raised his Sten.

Goerdt shouted, "Gestapo! Freeze!" in German.

It didn't work.

Each officer grabbed for a holstered pistol.

Dunn and Goerdt fired.

All three officers were struck and started to fall to the ground, but one managed to clear his weapon from the holster and fire a shot. It struck the ground at Dunn's feet with a spark, ricocheting off down the alley. It was incredibly loud in the narrow space and the sound echoed off the buildings.

All three officers were down and lay still, even the one who fired the shot.

Dunn turned and whistled at Cross, waving his hand to get the men moving. He ran toward the police cars.

The policeman in the car looked down the alley from inside the car, shock evident on his face. He started to get out of the car, but saw a bunch of dark shadows running his way. He slammed the door shut, started the car and drove off, tires screeching and smoking.

Dunn reached the end of the alley and raised his weapon, but the car's red taillights were already three blocks away. The rest of the squad caught up with him and milled about.

"Damn it!" he muttered. He looked at the men.

"We've got to move fast to get out of here before he comes back with reinforcements. Dave, take point again. Let's stick with the escape route we had in mind. I'm hoping the cop thinks we're some local criminal gang, not enemy soldiers."

"Okay."

Cross took the lead and the men raced across the last street and into the woods. He led them southwest for about a hundred yards until they were safely deep in the trees. Then he turned west. He carefully picked his way through the forest until they were a half mile west of the alley. Turning north to get closer to the river, he led the men to the edge of the trees and stopped. Dunn joined him.

They looked out at a main road leading west with a long pier and the river about three hundred yards away. The road was empty of vehicles.

"Follow the trees, Tom?"

"Yep."

Cross turned away and continuing to march westward, just inside the tree line, paralleling the waterway.

After about five minutes, they heard the sound of large trucks, possibly two or three.

Cross stopped the column and leaned against a tree. The rest of the men moved closer to the open space, being careful to stay behind the trees. Dunn stood next to his second in command. Three dark vans zoomed by. A small white sign on each roof read *Polizei*.

"Looks like we started a little police party," Cross said.

"Yeah. As long as they stay over there, I'm fine with that."

They continued their march west. Another five minutes passed. Dunn heard footsteps behind him and turned that way.

Jonesy sidled up next to him. He had run along the column of Rangers to reach Dunn.

"What is it, Jonesy?"

"The sub is moving again and it's towing those platforms. This time they're deeper in the water. Sarge, I think they loaded the rockets on them."

29

The Farm, Area B-2
In Maryland, 70 miles northwest of Washington, D.C.
1 December, 1515 Hours, U.S. Eastern Standard Time

Gertrude wore a pair of loose fitting black slacks, a waist-length khaki jacket over a tan short sleeve work shirt, and on her feet, ankle-high brown boots. She had tied her brown hair into a frizzy ponytail.

She and nine other young women, all brand new recruits, were lined up ten yards outside the woods that surrounded their main compound. Straight ahead was an opening that was the start of a two and a half mile long hiking trail.

The compound and all the land around it that was acquired by the United States government amounted to nearly 10,000 acres, or almost four miles by four miles. Part of the Catoctin Recreational Demonstration Area, the OSS opened the camp in April, 1942. In addition to the house where Gertrude had spent her first night, there were twenty rustic cabins constructed of local chestnut wood. Three large buildings formed a huge U: a long mess hall, a headquarters, and a structure which doubled as a recreation center and classrooms. Gertrude and everyone else had moved from the farmhouse to the cabins the day after she arrived to begin training.

The spot where Gertrude waited was two hundred yards west of the open end of the U-shaped commons.

The instructor, a forty or so year old man with a buzz cut and a loud voice stood at the end of the line of women. He wore black everything including a derby. Even his Errol Flynn mustache was black. Next to him stood Louise, the woman who'd played the victim for Gertrude's little arrival exercise. She carried a pencil and a clipboard.

He eyed the women, making sure they were standing behind the start-finish line. Raising a Colt .45 loaded with blanks—no tiny starter pistols for the OSS—he said, "Ready . . . set . . ."

Bang!

The shot echoed across the open space behind the runners.

The women surged forward. As they neared the woods, they began to jostle each other, no one wanting to give ground to another. Gertrude was third and as she went by number two, she shouldered the shorter woman who was forced to side-step to keep her balance, losing a step.

"Hey!"

"See ya!" Gertrude shouted back.

The woman in the lead settled into what Gertrude thought was an excellent pace. It felt like about an eight minute mile. They ran through the woods, the trees never more than a few yards away. All the leaves had fallen and in places the running trail was completely covered. Their feet crunched through the leaves. The air was cold, about thirty-five degrees, and the sky was covered with gray clouds. *Welcome to December,* she thought.

When she was stationed at Bermuda, she'd started running again, pounding out three miles a day on the wonderful sand on the beach. She'd started running in the first place because of her brother, Tom. After he'd signed up the day following Pearl Harbor, he'd started running three miles every morning. He finished his semester at the University of Iowa, and had come home to Cedar Rapids for the winter and to wait for the time to go to boot camp. One morning a week before Christmas, Gertrude, then only fifteen years old, met him by the front door at six a.m. They ran together every morning thereafter until he left, including Christmas and

New Year's Day. He'd slowed his pace for her and egged her on when she began to tire the first day after two miles. She'd made it the whole distance and vowed to herself to continue even after he shipped out to the army. And she had. Running gave her time to think, and to quiet her mind at the same time, even if that seemed contradictory. Her longest distance was eight miles, which she tried to do about once a week. In Bermuda, she'd stayed with the three miles as a way to remember the times with her brother, whom she missed terribly.

The trail ran roughly straight in a westerly direction, with some convolutions due to the terrain. The woman in the lead maintained a steady machine-like pace. Gertrude was happy to stay one step behind her. She planned to hold that position until they were a hundred yards from the finish line. A sprint over that distance was doable and she should be able to pass the woman.

Although it was cold out, a sheen of sweat formed on her brow. She refused to wipe it away, for fear of disrupting her rhythm. She wished she's worn a hat.

The terrain started uphill just before the turnaround point, but the woman still kept her pace. Gertrude smiled to herself as her legs acted like pistons, her arms swinging in perfect rhythm. A large clearing appeared. An oak tree had been cut off at about six feet. A white sign with red letters had been nailed to the east side of it. It read:

Half way! 2 1/2 miles.

Go around me.

A red arrow pointed right. The lead runner went around the right side, leaning into the curve to the left. Gertrude stayed with her. Just as Gertrude was about to pass face-to-face the shorter woman she'd bumped, the woman threw her left leg into Gertrude's path.

Possessing excellent reflexes, she simply hurdled the leg without breaking stride.

Without looking over her shoulder, she shouted, "Have to do better than that!"

She glanced at the runner ahead. Was she a little farther ahead? Yes.

She sped up and reclaimed her position one step behind. They passed face-to-face the rest of the field one by one, some of the slower runners casting dark looks at the two leaders so far ahead of them.

They had been prohibited from wearing watches, but she was still certain they were on an eight-minute-mile pace. Not her fastest ever, but still good.

They passed a marker, a wooden placard on the right side of the trail nailed to a small post. Also white with red letters, it read:

200 yards to go

She looked over the leader's shoulder. The exit to the woods was visible, a narrow gap between the trees with brown grass in the distance. She measured the distance remaining and picked her spot.

Just as they passed that spot, a hundred yards from the finish line, Gertrude upped the gas. She closed on the leader, frizzy ponytail flying in the wind.

The leader evidently heard Gertrude's boot steps and sped up, too, resuming her one step lead.

Gertrude bore down,

So did the leader.

No matter how hard she pumped, the leader stayed one pace ahead.

They neared the finish line, two fast runners sprinting, panting.

The leader crossed the line.

The instructor called out the times he read from a silver stopwatch hanging on a strap around his neck:

"Thirty-nine and forty."

Gertrude passed the line.

"Thirty-nine and forty-one."

Gertrude smiled to herself. It had been an eight minute mile pace after all. The sprint at the end helped them beat forty minutes by a hair.

Louise wrote the times down on her clipboard.

Both women slowed and coasted to the side. They bent over at the waist, hands on knees, gasping.

The short woman crossed the line and joined them.

The leader walked a few paces to a wooden table where a stack of white towels sat. She plucked up three and carried them back. She handed one to Gertrude and the other to the short woman.

"Thanks," both women said, in between deep breaths.

All three stood there wiping the sweat and grime from their faces and necks as they watched the remainder of the field finally cross the line. Soon, there was a gaggle of hot, tired, and sweaty women around the table toweling off.

The instructor walked over to them carrying the clipboard. His Colt was holstered safely away.

His Farm name was Rick. No one used their real names and no one knew their real names, except for Walker, the man in charge. The past did not exist here. Whatever accomplishments they may have had meant nothing. The only things that did matter were the skills they brought with them, their ability to learn and adapt faster than average, and their ability to persevere.

Gertrude was getting used to being called Peggy. The winning runner's name was Ruby and the third place finisher was Edna.

"Listen up, gals!" Rick said.

The women faced him.

"Listen carefully for your order of finish. I don't like repeating myself." He looked around the semicircle they'd formed around him. They seemed to be paying attention.

He read off the names giving their finishing position right after the name.

"Now, we determine who is paired with whom for a two-girl team. Listen up!" As he started to read off the names of the team pairs, it was obvious after the second one, he was putting the first place finisher with the last place woman, and so on. Gertrude was paired with number nine.

Edna started to complain to Gertrude and Ruby, but Gertrude shushed her. "Never complain. He'll just make you a target." Edna looked at Gertrude uncomprehendingly. "Don't draw negative attention to yourself, ever. He'll make it harder on you."

The light bulb went off in Edna's eyes. She looked at Rick with a wary expression.

"All right, girls, pair up with your new partner."

The women did that.

"When we add the times for each partner, we have the new order of finish for the run. Listen closely." He read off the fifth and fourth place teams. In third place were Ruby and her partner. Ruby looked unhappy for a moment, but hid it quickly. Gertrude and her partner got second, with Edna and her partner winning first.

Gertrude's expression didn't change, but she seethed inside. She glanced over at Edna who caught her looking. Edna gave her an overly sweet smile and put her arm around her partner.

"We're going to the Trainazium next!" Rick shouted happily. "Line up in your teams in order of finish."

There was some general grumbling about the Trainazium. It was made up of physically challenging structures. After the women followed instructions, Rick set off at a fast jog. He smiled in anticipation as he ran.

They arrived at the first Trainazium challenge. It was designed to teach trainees how to walk and maneuver in tight spaces. It also improved their dexterity and strength.

It was a fifteen by fifteen feet square structure made up of sixteen oak tree poles sunk into the ground. Each was about a foot and a half in diameter and ten feet tall. The gap between them was three feet. It required painstaking movements just to step or jump from one to another. A slip and fall landed you in a safety net. A built-in ladder was set in place to climb to the top of the first pole.

The women stared at it in disbelief and groaned. They'd just run five miles. Their muscles were tired and shaky like they get after carrying something very heavy too far. Completing the course across the Trainazium would be horrendously difficult.

Only Gertrude didn't complain. Instead, she said, "Swell. Can I go first?" She raised her hand.

Rick smothered a smile as he looked at Gertrude. He shook his head. "No, Peggy, you'll go last today."

Gertrude kept her face impassive but frowned on the inside. *So that's how this place is going to be. Fine. I can do it.*

30

**The shipyards
Hamburg, Germany
1 December, 2135 Hours, Berlin time**

Dunn looked east and spotted the submarine's evil snout gliding through the black waters. Behind it he could see three long humps. Jonesy was right, they were floating deeper in the water, therefore they had to be loaded with the V2 rockets. He figured it would take them about an hour to get back aboard their own sub, another ten minutes to explain things well enough to convince the British captain to pursue the German sub, and possibly another five to ten minutes to actually get underway; almost an hour and a half lead is what the German sub would have. And once it submerged was there any realistic way for the HMS *Sea Tiger* to catch it and sink it with torpedoes?

He tapped Cross on the shoulder and asked that question. Cross shook his head.

"Be close to impossible."

Dunn looked back at the sub, which was less than a half mile away. The bow wave seemed larger. It was gaining speed.

"Damn it, Dave. Can we stop it somehow?"

"Not with our weapons. We could steal a small boat and try to detach the cable, but that's hardly the best option."

Dunn looked around at the boats tied up along the pier. He raised his hand and pointed.

"What about one of those?"

The three E-boats Cross had pointed out earlier were still docked in a row.

Cross followed the point. "Jeez, Tom. You want to steal an E-boat and do what?"

"It has torpedoes on it doesn't it? And maybe a deck cannon or two?"

"Well, yeah. But none of us knows how to pilot a craft like that."

"Oh, come on, Dave. It's like riding a bike isn't it?"

Cross gave Dunn an aghast expression. "Do you have any idea what it takes to run one of those?"

Dunn gave Cross innocent. "How hard can it be?"

Cross turned apoplectic. Before he could speak Dunn pointed at the sub.

"Maybe instead of arguing, we should get aboard the E-boat and figure things out as we go before the target disappears."

Cross swiveled his head to look at the advancing sub. He shook his head.

"It's our only chance, Dave. That thing is not going out for sea trials. I'd bet a nickel on it."

Cross realized Dunn was right and they had no choice. But it had been several years since he'd piloted a boat of any kind, let alone trying to figure out a German attack boat. Not to mention the language problem of the buttons and dials. Although he would have Goerdt's and Schneider's German language skills, so maybe that would work out okay.

The German E-boat, the *schnellboot*, fast boat, was similar to American PT boats as Cross had mentioned. It was 107 feet long with a beam of 17 feet, and a displacement of about 80 tons. It had a shallow draft of a little less than five feet. Powered by three huge Daimler Benz MB 501 marine diesel engines, it carried a crew of about 25 men, four twenty-one inch diameter torpedoes, two in the launch tube and one on a loading rack behind each tube, a double-barreled 20mm cannon on the foredeck and 37mm antiaircraft cannon on the aft deck. It could reach a speed of almost 44 knots and was extremely maneuverable.

"Man, Tom. Okay."

Dunn grinned and patted Cross's back. "Good man."

Cross grunted.

Dunn waved the men closer and they formed a semicircle around him. He explained what they were going to do. Some of the men exchanged glances with each other, but they said nothing. They were used to Dunn changing directions on a mission. And they knew he was always right.

Dunn took point and they started west again. They only had to travel another hundred yards to reach a point directly across from the E-boat that was first in line. Dunn stopped the squad and watched the boat and the pier. He was about to give the men the order to move when motion to his left caught his eye.

Two sentries were slowly striding toward the E-boats' position along the pier. Their rifles were slung over their shoulders. They seemed unalarmed.

Dunn looked to the east and saw the sub also closing in on the E-boats' position. Perhaps another minute or so and it would be past them. He couldn't just wait for the sentries to leave the area on their rounds.

The woods curved closer to the wharf, but there was still a distance of over two hundred yards to the E-boats, and it was all wide-open space. Nothing to use as cover. The distance exceeded the accurate range for the Stens by fifty yards.

"Jonesy," Dunn called out softly.

The sniper edged up next to the squad leader.

Dunn pointed. "Both have to go down."

"Okay, Sarge"

Jonesy got into a prone position and readied his weapon. He lined up the sight's reticle on the nearest target.

"Ready, Sarge."

"Fire."

Jonesy squeezed the trigger and the rifle bucked against his shoulder and the suppressor made a spitting sound. The nearest German fell straight back and crashed to the ground. The other soldier slipped his rifle off his shoulder and looked around, clearly unable to determine where the shot had come from. Like Dunn had noticed, there was no place for the man to hide. He dropped to the ground and aimed generally toward the woods as it seemed the likeliest place. His aim was off by fifty feet to the east.

Jonesy worked the bolt and sighted on the man's left shoulder, the one without the weapon tucked against it. He didn't want to try a shot through the helmet, even though he was pretty sure the high-powered round would penetrate from this distance. He calculated that a shot through the left shoulder of a prone man from this angle and distance would burrow through the body's interior and strike the heart, in essence from what would be above if the man had been standing.

He squeezed the trigger. The man's head simply flopped down as if he'd suddenly fallen asleep. His rifle rolled off his hands.

"Targets down, Sarge," Jonesy said, as he racked the bolt once more. He stood.

"Good shooting."

"Thanks."

"All right, men. Column formation on the double heading toward the first of the three long boats right in front of us." He pointed. "Follow Cross. Keep your eyes peeled for any movement. Let's go."

Cross bolted from the trees and the men formed up on him with a gap of about two yards between them. As Cross ran, he looked at the other two E-boats tied up behind his selected E-boat. There was no movement there.

He reached the edge of the pier. A gangplank had been left in position for the E-boat crew. He darted up the gangplank and boarded the sleek craft. He located the structure that housed the passageway to the lower deck, where the crew, if sleeping aboard, would be. He pointed at Higgins and Martelli, who were nearest to him, and they joined him. He told them to check things below and to be careful. They opened the door and started down the steps.

Cross grabbed Schneider and Goerdt and they went into the compact bridge. When he entered the bridge he was amazed by what he saw. It was beautifully designed. There were windows all around providing excellent visibility. He looked at the instrument panel and gave them a verbal list of words he was looking for and they split up to examine the panel on either side of the ship's wheel. It was a finely worked wooden wheel with silver spokes. There wasn't enough moonlight coming in through the windows, so each Ranger had to flick on his flashlight, which like Jonesy's had tape across the lens to allow only a sliver of light.

Dunn hadn't reached the gangplank yet. He stopped on the pier and stared at the sub as it glided abreast of the E-boat. The bow wave had grown even larger. It was still picking up speed. He thought he saw motion on the front of the conning tower, but wasn't sure.

He stopped long enough to direct the rest of the men: Jonesy and Lindstrom on top of the bridge, ready to take out anyone advancing on the boat from land; Wickham and Kelly to the bow to set up crossfire with Jonesy. He also told those two to see if they could figure out the cannon there.

Running up into the bridge, he joined Cross and the others who were intently examining the instrument panel.

"How's it look? The sub's passing by us right now."

Cross glanced out the starboard windows. "Terrific," he muttered.

Higgins and Martelli poked their heads inside.

"All clear below, Sergeant Cross."

"That's great."

"You guys go to the rear deck and figure out how to use the cannon there," Dunn said.

"Got it, Sarge," Martelli said.

"On it, Sarge," Higgins replied.

The two men disappeared.

A few thumps came through the ceiling. Cross looked up, then at Dunn. "Jonesy?"

"Yep."

Cross went back to what he was doing. He looked down at the cabinet below the panel, and opened one of the small wooden doors. Hanging on the back of the door was a clipboard with about twenty pages clipped to it. He aimed his flashlight at the top paper.

"Eureka, Tom!" He held it up, grinning. "I can't read it, but this is a checklist." He flipped a few pages. "Ha!" He held it so Goerdt could see it. "Is this a how-to on firing the torpedoes?" It had a diagram of a torpedo and its launching tube with notations and arrows.

Goerdt leaned over. "Yeah, Sarge. Hold on. It says where the firing switches are."

He looked at the instrument panel, toward the right side. "There they are." He pointed to a pair of silver toggle switches. Below each switch was a black button. Both switches were in the down position. He looked back at the paper, reading it farther down. "Down is unarmed."

He turned the page. "It gives the instructions for setting the fuse on the torpedoes. It's either contact or magnetic proximity."

Dunn looked over at Cross.

"Better set for magnetic," the pilot said. "More margin of error. Goerdt take the pages for the torpedoes and set the two you'll find in the launch tubes to magnetic."

"You got it, Sarge." Goerdt grabbed the paper and took off.

Cross found the page with an instrument panel diagram on it and asked Schneider to translate it. That took a few minutes. Cross identified all the gauges, switches and buttons he needed on the instrument panel. He looked at the gear shift for each engine's drive to make sure it was in neutral. The fuel gauge showed full and the batteries were fully charged.

"Cross your fingers," he said, looking over his shoulder at his friend. He flipped the switch for one engine, and pressed the button.

Somewhere in the rear bowels of the boat an engine rumbled to life. The boat vibrated even at the low idle of a single engine. Cross grinned. "Better tell the guys on deck to release the lines so we can get underway. Man, I love the sound of that engine!"

Dunn ran out onto the deck, first to the front where Wickham and Kelly were examining a double-barreled weapon that Dunn took to be a 20mm cannon.

"Hey, guys, come get these lines off the boat. We're about to get underway. After you release the lines, push the front of the boat away from the pier to help Cross get us underway. Wave at the bridge when we're free." Dunn pointed at a couple of inch-diameter ropes securing the boat to the pier.

Under his feet, he could feel the deck vibrate as another massive engine fired up.

They nodded and ran over to work loose the lines.

Dunn took off for the rear and stopped suddenly at the midpoint. He grabbed the end of the gangplank and pushed it off the boat. There was a safety chain dangling from a metal post. He unhooked one end and latched the other to the next post, blocking the space where the gangplank had been. Moving onward, he found Martelli and Higgins at a 37mm cannon. The barrel rested at a forty-five degree angle. Dunn figured it was an anti-aircraft gun and hoped its barrel could be lowered to horizontal. He gave the pair the same instructions, including pushing the boat's rear end away from the pier. They ran to the pier side of the boat and started work.

Dunn ran back to the bridge.

Cross started the third engine. He grinned at Dunn again.

Dunn moved to stand next to him and looked out the window at Wickham and Kelly. Kelly threw the end of a line onto the deck. He and Wickham both pushed off the boat and Kelly turned to wave at the bridge. Dunn looked the other way to find Martelli and Higgins. They also threw the lines off and pushed away, turned and Martelli waved.

"We're free," Dunn said.

"Excellent."

With his right hand, Cross turned the wheel to the right about a quarter turn. With his other hand he engaged the drives to the propellers. He pushed the currently connected three-part throttle forward. The below-deck rumble increased and the boat began to move. Cross's gaze shifted from the panel to the bow to the pier in a repeating cycle.

The boat glided away from the pier. Cross turned the wheel more to the right and gave the engines more fuel. The boat surged forward, aiming for the clear river. He shoved the throttle much farther forward. The bow lifted and the aft dipped. The boat leapt forward, happy to go fast again, its natural state.

Dunn looked out the back window.

"Uh oh," he said.

Without looking at Dunn, Cross asked, "What's the matter?"

"Those police trucks are coming back on the road. They're slowing down. Well, now they've pulled up to where we just left. No, wait, one is speeding ahead."

"Why are they after us? They can't know we're aboard, can they?" Cross asked.

"Someone must have seen us. Or they simply deduced we're the ones who shot those policemen."

31

Saunders had somehow caught up on rest during the submarine trip home. Most of his waking hours had been sitting with Tim Chadwick. The wounded Commando finally woke up around midnight the night before and wanted something to eat. The doctor had checked him over and said he could have broth, but nothing else. Chadwick had grumbled for an hour about that. Saunders just commiserated with him. Even though he was starving himself, he refused to eat real food that was banned to Chadwick in front of the wounded man.

The trip had been uneventful, something Saunders and Barltrop were quite thankful for. Their last excursion across the North Sea had not been uneventful. On the trip home following a mission to attack the Wilhelmshaven submarine pens, the submarine had been depth charged. Saunders had taken quite a fall and got himself a knock on the head. Barltrop was just glad anytime a boat trip was over, not being fond in any way of bodies of water. He'd once asked a sub captain if the boat always came back up. He'd been less than happy with the navy man's grin and reply of "usually."

Saunders told Barltrop he could have a few days off to go to London to be with his girlfriend, almost fiancé, Kathy.

Saunders, Colonel Jenkins, and the aide, Lieutenant Mallory were the only ones present.

"How's Chadwick?" Jenkins asked, concern on his face.

Saunders nodded. "Very well, sir." He shook his head. "If you hadn't insisted on attaching a doctor to our submarine missions, he never would have made it home. So thank you, sir."

Jenkins blew air from his nose, completely relieved. "Glad it turned out to be valuable. Had to call in some heavy-duty favors for that to happen."

"Of course, sir. Tim will have a long road to recovery because it was a lung shot. They'll be watching him extremely carefully for infection, which, as you know, can be the real killer."

"Yes. What about the prisoner?"

"He's recovering and under guard at the hospital. He's very young. I don't know how valuable he'll be during interrogation, but you never know."

"Right you are. So everything was destroyed? Every pound?"

"Yes, sir. Except for the sample packages of each denomination we brought back." He lifted a small satchel into his lap, opened it, and handed a fiver package to the colonel.

Jenkins pulled one five pound note from the package. He examined the German craftsmanship closely, turning the note this way and that. He placed the note on the desk. Leaning over, he pulled his wallet from his back pocket. He removed a fiver from it and pocketed the wallet. He laid the real money on his desk next to the forged one. He compared them to each other.

He shook his head. "Hopeless. I can't see the difference."

He picked up a pen and made a tiny mark on the back of the forged note. Flipping the notes around he shoved them across his desk to Mallory, who leaned forward. His eyes darted back and forth, one note to the other.

"No difference I can see."

He pushed them back toward Jenkins, who left them on the desk.

"Good job on the mission. I would like to see your report tomorrow."

"Certainly, sir." Saunders had written so many of these post-mission action analysis reports that the Americans loved to call post mortems. Lovely dark humor.

Someone knocked on the closed office door.

Jenkins smiled and immediately said, "Come in."

The door opened and a young man in his thirties stepped through. He glanced at each of the men, and stepped out of the way. A man in his sixties stepped into the office. Jenkins and Mallory jumped to their feet. Saunders joined them and turned to see who it was.

"Welcome, Sir John," Jenkins said, walking around the desk to shake Sir John Anderson's hand.

Saunders recognized the name of the Chancellor of the Exchequer.

"Thank you, Colonel Jenkins."

"Allow me to introduce my aide, Lieutenant Mallory."

Sir John shook Mallory's hand.

"And this is Sergeant Major Saunders."

Sir John shook Saunders' hand, staring into his eyes and holding the grip longer than usual.

"You're the Commando who solved our problem."

"Yes, Sir John, along with my squad."

"Of course. I'm quite pleased to meet you."

"You, too, Sir John."

Sir John let go of Saunders' hand. "Please sit, gentlemen." He sat down in the chair to Saunders' right, and the others seated themselves. The young man stood guard at the door, which he had closed quietly.

Sir John had brown hair with a severe widow's peak and gray at the temples. He had a thin face and a long pointed nose.

"Thank you for coming all the way from London, Sir John, at such a late hour. We know how busy you must be."

"My pleasure. It's nice to escape London on occasion." He glanced at the notes on the desk. "Is one of those a fake?"

"Indeed, Sir John." Jenkins slid the two notes closer.

Sir John leaned over and examined both. He shook his head. "Identical to my eyes."

"The fake has a pen mark on the back, sir," Jenkins said.

Sir John flipped them over and saw the mark. He flipped them over again and reexamined them.

"Even knowing which one it is, I cannot tell."

"No, sir."

Sir John looked at Saunders. "All destroyed?"

"Yes, Sir John."

"Heavens, this would have been a disaster. Thank you. I hope the mission went well otherwise?"

Saunders glanced at Jenkins before replying. The colonel nodded. Saunders realized he would have already told Sir John about Chadwick.

"Yes, Sir John, except we did have a man wounded in a firefight. He's expected to recover."

"His name so I can send him a get well card?"

"Sergeant Timothy Chadwick."

The man by the door wrote that down in a little notebook that appeared out of nowhere.

The Chancellor turned back to Saunders. He sized up the Commando, taking in the red hair and red mustache, as well as the impossible to miss bulk.

"You and your men have done our country a great service. I'm going to put in for some medals for all of you. Don't know which one, but I'll work that out with Colonel Jenkins."

He glanced at the colonel, who smiled and nodded.

"Also, by any chance do you think you and your men, and their wives or girlfriends would enjoy a night out in London?"

Saunders grinned, the tips of his handlebar mustache twitching. "Oh, I'm certain the lads would be, er, quite appreciative of that, Sir John."

"Jeeves here will set it up and let the colonel know the details as well as coordinate the date, which should be sooner rather than later, don't you think?"

"Yes, Sir John. Thank you very much."

Sir John picked up the forged note from Germany, turning it over to make sure it had the pen mark. He also picked up the package of fivers on the desk.

Saunders lifted the satchel. "Here's the rest, Sir John. We got packages of tens and twenties also."

"That's wonderful, thank you."

"You're quite welcome."

Jeeves stepped closer to take the satchel from him.

"Well done, Sergeant Saunders."

"Thank you, Sir John."

Sir John rose and the soldiers jumped to their feet. He shook hands with everyone, and said his goodbyes. Jeeves closed the door behind them as they left.

Everyone sat back down.

Saunders looked at Jenkins closely, noting something different.

"Sir, if you don't mind my saying so, you seem rather . . . happy. Has something happened?"

"What are you, a detective?" Jenkins snapped.

"Not at all, sir. I'm sorry if I've overstepped."

Jenkins harrumphed, but said, "You're not wrong. I'm seeing an old flame again. Things seem as if twenty years hadn't passed us by at all."

Saunders kept his face still. Jenkins never talked about his personal life and this was more of a shocking revelation than just a surprising one.

"I'm glad to hear that, sir. Might I ask her name?"

Jenkins grinned like a young man. "Alice. Well, Lady Alice, now."

"Wonderful, sir. I'm happy for you. Okay to tell my Sadie?"

Jenkins thought about that briefly. "Yes, but no one else, please."

Saunders nodded. "Certainly, sir."

"Well, that'll be all."

Saunders left the office and as he was going down the outside stairs, he couldn't help but grin at learning the colonel had fallen in love. Who knew? War was so weird.

He jumped into the staff car and roared away, anxious to tell the men they were going to get medals and a night out in London courtesy of the Chancellor of the Exchequer himself.

He was pretty sure which prize the men would value the most.

RONN MUNSTERMAN

32

Aboard the captured German E-boat
Elbe River
Hamburg, Germany
1 December, 2147 Hours, Berlin time

As Jonesy watched, the lone police panel truck flew by, obviously trying to find a place to get ahead of the moving E-boat. He changed positions so he could aim farther ahead. The boat was evidently racing across calm water because it was pretty smooth. He wondered if that would hold up. The boat was a hundred yards from the wharf and angling away, and about two hundred from the road. The panel truck braked hard and turned onto a street running perpendicular to the river. Jonesy gauged that it would reach its stopping point well ahead of the E-boat.

He turned to Lindstrom and raised his voice so his spotter could hear over the roar of the engines and the slap of the hull slicing through the water.

"We're going to have to be quick on this one, Eugene."

"I'm ready, Jonesy."

Jonesy nodded and aimed at the rear of the truck, where he expected the bulk of the men to get out. His sight picture bounced a little from the boat's movement. It looked like the crosshair was moving at least two feet at the target distance with each bounce. He'd just have to anticipate and compensate.

The panel truck stopped hard. The driver and passenger hopped out, and a stream of eight men bolted from the rear. They were carrying rifles.

One of the men who got out of the front seat ran to the dead sentries. He turned to the riflemen. He pointed a finger at the slowly moving E-boat.

"Tell Sarge we might be taking fire from the police. Eight rifles spotted."

"Okay." Lindstrom lifted his walkie-talkie and passed the word.

Dunn listened to Lindstrom's message and acknowledged it. He told Cross what the message was and that he'd be right back. He ran out of the bridge headed for the front of the boat where he found Wickham and Kelly working on the 20mm cannon.

"Targets kneeling. Rifles coming up," Lindstrom said sharply.

Jonesy lifted his head to get a wider field of view of the targets for a second. He lowered his head. He picked his first target and laid the crosshair on the man's upper chest. The boat bounced. The sight picture was completely lost. The boat settled back down. The crosshairs were off by a foot. Jonesy adjusted to the center of the man's chest and fired as the boat jumped again.

The bullet was wide and slammed into the man's left shoulder, spinning him around and to the ground. The rifle bounced silently on the ground. Jonesy worked the bolt and acquired his next target; the man to Jonesy's right of the first one.

He sighted and fired. The man took the round in the throat and he dropped the weapon, grabbing his neck. He fell onto his back, his legs thrashing.

The six remaining riflemen all fired at the same time. Long bright orange and yellow muzzle blasts flared in the dark.

Rounds plinked into the boat's upper structure, just below Jonesy.

Working the bolt, Jonesy fired again. The boat lurched sideways. He saw a spark on the truck's passenger door. He'd missed by five feet.

From his left, Jonesy suddenly heard the roaring and ripping sound of the 20mm cannon firing. He watched its tracers light up the night. Whoever was firing the weapon was doing pretty well for a first time. The shells walked right up the pavement into the line of Germans, who fell in all directions. A few survivors ran off. Shells struck the panel truck, destroying the hood, and likely the engine underneath, and shattering the windshield.

The cannon grew silent.

The E-boat left a path of destruction behind as it continued to gain speed.

Lindstrom's walkie-talkie popped to life. "Dunn to Lindstrom."

He keyed the mike. "Lindstrom here."

"You guys come on down into the bridge."

"Roger. Out."

"Out."

Lindstrom told Jonesy and the two scrambled on their hands and knees to the ladder at the rear and were soon in the relative warmth of the bridge.

Dunn joined them.

"Who fired the cannon, Sarge?" Jonesy asked.

"Wickham."

"Pretty good shooting for a first timer."

"Sure was."

Jonesy and Lindstrom moved away to stand by the left windows and out of the way.

Dunn walked up next to Cross and peered out at the river.

"I see it."

"Ayup."

The German submarine was about five hundred yards ahead. The E-boat was gaining fast. Dunn glanced down at what looked like a speedometer. It read forty knots; just over forty-five miles an hour.

"How fast do you think the sub is going?"

"Probably about eight to ten knots at the most," Cross replied without taking his eyes off the sub and the platforms trailing behind.

"What's our plan?"

"Remember the river has an island ahead that splits the Elbe into two deep channels?"

"Yep."

"The north one is about three-quarters of a mile wide. The other channel where we came in and where our sub is waiting is much narrower. I'm sure he'll take the north channel. I plan to get on whichever side of him has the most room to maneuver. We'll come up from behind slowing for the turn. Make the turn and speed up and launch the torpedoes while I'm aiming ahead of the bow."

Dunn nodded as he pictured the attack.

"What about the platforms?"

Cross told him what he had in mind.

Dunn nodded again. "Excellent." He made a quick walkie-talkie call explaining the plan to the men outside.

Goerdt, who had just returned to the bridge, stepped closer.

"I set the torpedoes for magnetic trigger. I also set the extra two that are on the deck behind the launch tube. I set the depth for two meters. Is that okay?"

"Dave?" Dunn deferred to Cross.

"Yeah, that sounds perfect."

"Okay, good. I figured out how we load the tubes in case we need the other two."

"Great job, Rob. How many people does it take to load the tube?" Dunn said.

"The second set of torpedoes are locked on a huge rack with rollers behind the tube. All we have to do is push it into the launch tube. Maybe three of us, just in case."

"Okay. Go grab Higgins and Martelli. Fill them in."

"Will do."

"Rob, did the manual tell you what the torpedo's maximum speed would be?" Cross asked.

"Oh, yeah, I found that. It said forty knots."

"Okay, great. Tom, how long for it to cover a hundred yards?"

Dunn looked at the bridge's ceiling as he calculated. It didn't take long. "About two seconds, maybe a little more since it won't be going that fast right away. Could be as long as four seconds."

He frowned. "Crap. Wait. I didn't use nautical mile." He recalculated. "Four and a half seconds at full speed, so maybe five or six from launch."

Cross seemed to be doing some calculations of his own. "Okay, we'll need to lead the sub by about fifty feet to strike it just back of the bow."

"Okay, whatever you think best."

Dunn turned to Goerdt. "Thanks, Rob. Off you go."

Goerdt left.

Cross throttled back so as not to overrun the sub. He could see the smaller wake of the platforms as they slid through the water. He'd have to keep them in mind as he approached so he wouldn't get caught in their tow cables.

"There he goes. Taking the east side."

Dunn looked. A dark shape close to the water was on the left; the long thin island.

Cross throttled back some more and turned the boat to the right toward the north shore. The sub was heading down the middle of the channel, its deepest point.

Cross turned left paralleling the sub. They passed the platforms one by one missing them by a quarter mile. Pulling past the rear of the sub, Cross kept the boat as far to the north as possible without having to worry about running aground. They passed the conning tower.

Two German sailors were there, both staring at the sudden arrival an E-boat. One of them lifted a pair of binoculars.

"Why are they on the conning tower?"

"Can't navigate a sub in a river without someone on deck to guide the helmsman," Cross replied.

Dunn raised his walkie-talkie and broadcast to everyone. "Everyone on deck, wave at the submarine and smile!"

The men on deck turned and waved at the sub. The sailors didn't lift a hand. One of them turned away, possibly talking on some communications device to the sub's interior.

"Uh oh. I don't think they believe we're Germans," Dunn said.

"Doesn't matter now, we're about to attack."

Cross wheeled hard left. He gauged the sub's speed and his distance from it. He steered toward a point about a hundred yards ahead of the sub's bow. He would make any final corrections just before they reached the launch point.

Four sailors suddenly popped out of a hatch on the rear deck and ran toward a deck cannon there. Two ripped off a cover. The others began loading a round.

"Uh, Dave?"

"Still doesn't matter. We're okay. Do you want to do the honors of firing the torpedoes?"

"Sure."

He stepped close to the toggle switches and buttons that would fire the torpedoes.

Schneider leaned toward Dunn. "The left switch and button are for the torpedo on the left side of the boat, Sarge."

"Got it."

He looked out the window in front of him. The sub was easy to see, the moonlight glinting off its long wet shape. Cross was taking them on an angled heading to lead the sub.

Dunn raised his walkie-talkie and called for Kelly, who was with Wickham at the 20mm cannon.

When Kelly responded, Dunn said, "Kelly, tell Wickham to light up the men at the rear deck gun."

"Roger. Out," Kelly replied.

"Out."

A flame shot out of the sub's cannon.

Wickham fired his 20mm cannon, its own flames brightening the night.

The sub's cannon shell blew up in the E-boat's wake, just twenty yards away. Its geyser shot upward about fifty feet.

Wickham's rounds sparked off the sub's deck. One sailor went down. The other three stood in place, loading another round.

Goerdt radioed Dunn to tell him he and the others were ready to load the next torpedoes.

The sub grew larger.

"Tell everyone we're going to make a hard, fast left turn after the torpedoes are launched," Cross said.

Dunn passed on the message and rested his hand near the switches.

Jonesy and Lindstrom grabbed onto silver handles set in the bridge's wall.

"Flip on the toggles."

Dunn did that.

Cross measured the rapidly closing distance. "Get ready to fire both."

The boat bounced a little.

"Fire!"

Dunn used both forefingers and stabbed at the black buttons. He looked out the window to the right.

A long silver shape flew out of the tube with a *fwooping* sound. It splashed into the water and raced away. He followed its wake. The other torpedo was running parallel to it.

The men on the bridge watched the torpedoes.

Cross cranked the wheel to the left and the boat heeled over hard, heading back east.

A second cannon shell from the sub missed, this time hitting the spot where the E-boat had been just prior to Cross's sudden turn.

"Criminy!" Schneider shouted.

Dunn turned to keep an eye on the torpedoes. It was like watching slow motion tracers. At first they were aimed at a spot ahead of the sub's bow. Next, they were aimed at a point about twenty feet back from the bow.

The two Germans on the conning tower stared at the torpedoes.

The explosions erupted at a point one third the way back from the bow. Water jetted fifty feet into the sky and an orange and black fireball followed it, roiling in the air.

The men on the bridge cheered.

The sub came to a stop almost immediately, dead in the water.

The men at the deck cannon disappeared over the side, blown off the boat by the explosion. The two on the conning tower simply disappeared from sight.

The bow broke off and sank below the surface. The new front of the sub angled downward as water rushed into the metal tube turned coffin.

The conning tower disappeared, the rear end of the sub rising out of the water.

Cross turned the boat to starboard and slowed down. "Tell Wickham to have at it. He better target the first one first."

Cross had placed the boat a couple of hundred yards from the middle platform pointed at the platforms so Wickham would have clear sightlines.

The sub's rear was nearing the water's surface and would soon be under. It would drag the first platform with it if Wickham didn't blow it up first.

Dunn radioed Kelly and gave him the green light.

The cannon fired a long burst as Wickham was finding the range to the target.

Dunn watched the fast motion tracers walk up to the lead platform. Wickham found the range and the huge, high velocity rounds tore into the platform's skin and through into the V2 rocket.

The liquid oxygen ignited first. Dunn had counted on the rockets being fueled for the trip to the coast of the United States. Immediately, the 2,200 pound amatol warhead exploded, too. The fireball looked just like the ones at the liquid oxygen storage tank facility, just on a much smaller scale. The water's surface rippled as the pressure wave flew across it.

"I hope we're far enough away," Cross said.

Wickham aimed at the second platform. It went up in an equally impressive explosion.

The first one's pressure wave petered out prior to reaching the Rangers' boat.

"One more, Stan!" Dunn shouted as if cheering on his fullback on the football field.

The last explosion matched the other two.

Cross wheeled left and hit the throttle. The boat leapt ahead.

"Nice job, Dave!" Dunn shouted.

Cross nodded as he gauged the water for the turn he wanted to make. They would have to go west past the island and cross over to the other channel, which was where their own sub would be waiting.

Motion far ahead, east in the same channel, caught his eye.

"Ah shit!"

"What?" Dunn asked, alarmed.

Cross pointed.

Five hundred yards ahead one of the other E-boats was churning through the Elbe's calm water.

Aimed right at them.

Loaded with torpedoes.

RONN MUNSTERMAN

33

Aboard the captured German E-boat
Elbe River, North Channel
Hamburg, Germany
1 December, 2204 Hours

Cross kept the boat on its east bearing in the north channel toward the other E-boat.

Dunn keyed his walkie-talkie. "Kelly, tell Wickham to fire at the oncoming boat. Over."

"Already prepared. Out."

Dunn could see Wickham and Kelly through the front windows. Kelly knelt to open another ammo box. He looked farther ahead. The enemy E-boat seemed to be slowing.

"Tom, the magnetic setting won't work on that boat. It has a wood hull like our PT boats. Also, the draft is really small. He should set the depth to zero."

"Understood." Dunn called Goerdt and gave instructions to reset the remaining torpedoes.

Goerdt acknowledged.

Flames over three feet long erupted from Wickham's 20mm cannon and the roar was deafening.

Dunn couldn't tell whether Wickham had hit the other boat, but it heeled over to his left, toward the northern shore, and turned back toward him.

Dunn keyed his walkie-talkie again. "Goerdt! Load the other torpedoes! Over."

"Way ahead of you, Sarge. Just finished. Over."

Flames appeared on the twin muzzles of the other E-boat's cannon.

Cross spun the wheel right to put more distance between the boats, then turned left again.

"Send Martelli and Higgins to the back to get on that other cannon back there! Over!" Dunn couldn't make himself stop shouting over the din.

"Roger. Out."

"Out."

"I hope you have a plan, Dave."

Cross shrugged. "Working on it. Never had the fish shoot back before, I have to say."

The boats were passing each other in opposite directions, both of their cannons brightening the night.

Loud *thunking*, slapping sounds came from the left side, somewhere in the hull, Dunn thought.

And the boats were past each other.

Cross looked over his shoulder out the rear of the bridge. The other boat was still on the same heading.

"Which way? Which way?" he asked.

"What'd you say?" Dunn shouted.

"Which way is he gonna turn?"

"Left! It'll be left!"

Cross turned sharply to his right.

"Get ready to fire the port, uh, left torpedo."

"Okay."

Dunn grabbed onto the panel and moved closer to the firing switches. Something occurred to him and he looked down in alarm. He expected the toggle switches to still be in the firing position, but they had flipped back down to disarmed. He guessed it was automatic when the firing buttons were pushed. Clever.

He looked ahead. The German boat turned left as he predicted. When it finished its turn, they would be on a collision course. Cross's plan.

"How'd you know they'd turn that way?" Cross asked.

"Fifty-fifty chance. I guessed."

Cross nodded, but said nothing as he concentrated on piloting the huge craft. Both boats were picking up speed and closing on each other at close to a hundred miles an hour.

Cross rolled the wheel to the right just enough for the boat to change directions slightly.

"Get ready, Tom."

Dunn flipped the left arming switch.

The enemy boat changed course following Cross. "Fire!" he shouted.

He whipped the wheel back left.

Dunn punched the Fire button. The torpedo launched making its odd *fwoop* sound. It splashed into the water.

The German boat changed directions again, the pilot following Cross's every move. It was crossing in front of the torpedo's path.

Wickham fired the 20mm again.

Dunn could see the huge rounds striking the other boat's bow.

The other pilot must have seen the torpedo because the boat practically stood on its right side as it curved away to safety. The torpedo's wake missed by a good twenty feet.

"Bob!" Dunn called out.

Schneider, who had been holding onto a rail for dear life due to Cross's maneuvers, replied, "Yeah, Sarge?"

"See if you can raise the *Sea Tiger*."

Schneider shrugged off his radio and knelt. Turning it on, he lifted the microphone to his lips and began calling the sub's name.

Cross checked the position of the German boat. It had turned to go east. He thought it was going to try to come up from behind. He was worried he might not be up to the task of fighting off the far more experienced pilot.

As if reading his friend's mind, Dunn said, "You can do this, Dave."

Cross glanced at Dunn and nodded.

He turned to follow the other boat. He changed course more to the right, angling ahead of the German boat, guessing where it would be. He was about two hundred yards away when the gun on the German's rear deck flared.

"Oh shit," Cross muttered.

He slapped the throttles to the highest point and cranked the wheel to the left.

The round exploded in the water to the right of the boat, rocking it.

Wickham fired at the rear of the German boat. His rounds raked the hull just under the deck, and Cross changed directions again and he lost his firing angle.

The German boat seemed to almost spin on its axis in a tight turn to the right. It was coming toward Dunn's boat again.

Cross adjusted to the left.

The German boat fired its left torpedo. The pilot changed course and fired its second torpedo.

Dunn's boat was bracketed between the two torpedoes.

Cross slammed back the throttles to full stop.

"Dave?"

"Hang tight."

Cross maintained heading as the boat's speed bled off.

The first torpedo zinged by on the right, missing by about ten feet.

The bow cannon on the German vessel fired. Rounds shredded the ceiling of the bridge. Everyone ducked, but Cross stayed put at the wheel.

Cross pushed the throttles to the top. The engines roared and the boat sped toward the other torpedo and the German boat.

Cross made a hard right turn.

Wickham fired his cannon.

Pieces of the German boat's bow deck disintegrated. It reversed course and sped away to the west.

The second torpedo ran past Dunn's boat, missing by fifty yards.

"Sarge, I got the *Sea Tiger* on the radio."

"Ask them which way they're pointing."

Schneider did. "West."

Dunn looked at Cross, who nodded, reading Dunn's mind this time.

Cross spun the wheel and completed a half circle to go back west. The German boat was a good five or six hundred yards ahead and still going away from Dunn's boat. Maybe Wickham's shooting had given them pause.

"Tell them we're bringing company from the west. Tell them we need help," Dunn told Schneider.

Schneider explained the situation. A minute passed before he got a reply.

"They'll be ready. Bring the German boat straight down the middle of the channel. The sub is located half way along the length of the island."

"Tell them thank you."

Cross aimed the boat left, heading for the western point of the island in the middle of the river. They were only a few hundred yards away.

The boat skimmed across the water going as fast as possible, which was about fifty miles an hour. *Under peaceful conditions, this would be a wonderful ride,* Cross thought.

The German boat began a large turn to the left to come about.

Cross slowed his boat and rounded the western tip of the island. Heading east, he moved the boat into the center of the narrower south channel.

The German boat was about six hundred yards back coming straight at them.

Dunn realized the trailing Germans couldn't fire their second set of torpedoes because his E-boat could actually outrun them. He looked forward trying to pick out where the sub was lying in wait.

A flash of movement much farther ahead caught his attention. He squinted his eyes to see better.

"Ah, crap."

Cross looked at Dunn. "What?"

Dunn pointed.

Far ahead another German E-boat was aimed their way.

34

Aboard the captured German E-boat
Elbe River, South Channel
Hamburg, Germany
1 December, 2215 Hours

Cross held his course, but slowed the boat.

"We're outmatched. Any ideas?"

Dunn immediately said, "Bob, call the sub back and tell them another German boat is coming from behind them."

Schneider made the call. He listened to their reply and signed off.

"The captain said he'd make ready the aft torpedo room. He wants you to slow down. Also to maintain course even if you see his torpedoes coming our way. He expects us to be too close and they won't have come up to attack depth until they pass us. Plus they'll be set for contact explosion because of the enemy's hull being wood. He said it would be best if we avoid running into his periscope as he kind of needs it."

Dunn looked at Cross.

"Oh, man, Tom."

"Think it'll work?"

Cross shrugged. "I sure as hell hope so. Not much other choice." He slowed the boat to twenty knots and kept the bow lined up in the center of the channel.

The boat following grew larger as did the one coming from the east.

Cross checked their position relative to the island on the left.

"We're coming up to the half way point," he announced.

"Sarge!"

Schneider was pointing through the front windows.

Twin torpedo tracks were visible, like white chalk lines in the moonlight. They seemed to be headed straight toward them.

"I hope the captain is right," Cross managed to croak.

The tracks grew closer and closer.

Just as they seemed about to hit, Cross made a guttural sound something like, "Gah . . ."

They looked forward and saw a single torpedo track heading east toward the other boat.

The tracks reached Dunn's boat, but nothing happened.

The Rangers, except for Cross, turned and looked to the rear. The pursuing E-boat was only two hundred yards away. The front cannon began firing. Dunn saw Martelli and Higgins hit the deck behind the 37mm cannon.

The torpedo tracks disappeared.

The German E-boat blew up.

Debris and flames shot out in all directions.

Cross, keeping his gaze on the water ahead spotted a glint of moonlight on a thin metal object right in front of the boat. The sub's periscope.

He wheeled right and put the boat through three quarters of a circle and stopped. This placed him in the dead center of the channel about fifty yards west of the periscope and perpendicular to the oncoming E-boat. He spun the wheel right and pushed the throttle for the port engine only forward. This rotated the boat toward the enemy E-boat.

Wickham fired the 20mm cannon.

Cross lost sight of the sub's eastbound torpedo.

Bright flashes erupted on the German E-boat as it fired its own bow double-barreled cannon.

"Down!" Cross shouted as he ducked behind the instrument panel.

Everyone dropped flat on the floor.

The front windows exploded as high velocity 20mm rounds tore through the glass and wood frames.

A giant explosion sounded and the cannon shells stopped.

The Rangers rose unsteadily to their feet and looked at another burning hulk of a German E-boat two hundred yards east.

"Oh my God," Dunn said.

Cross wiped his face with a shaking hand.

Schneider stared at the burning debris, first in front and then behind the boat. He held onto the instrument panel for support. "Wow . . ." he muttered.

Jonesy and Lindstrom scrambled to their feet and looked out.

"I've been in a lot of firefights, but this one definitely takes the cake," Dunn said.

"Yeah, it does," Cross said.

He looked out the destroyed windows and noted the boat's position. He had slammed back the port engine's throttle, so the boat was drifting backwards and westward with the channel's current.

Turning the wheel to the right, he gave the engines a little goose. The boat glided out of the center of the channel. He turned her around and reversed the engines long enough to come to a complete stop.

Water on the surface ahead began to churn. A moment later, the submarine popped up and lay there, a long black line. The conning tower looked like a waterfall as liquid drained from it.

"Bob, radio the sub again and tell them we're ready to get the hell out of here."

"Yes, Sarge," Schneider said.

"I can pull us alongside," Cross said.

"Okay, go ahead. I'm sure they'll figure out what we're doing. I'm going to get the guys together. Which side should we be on?"

"Port. Left."

"Got it." Dunn told Jonesy and Lindstrom to make their way to the left side of the boat for the transfer.

"Sub says they'll have men on deck in a few seconds," Schneider said.

"Thanks, Bob."

Schneider shut down the radio and hefted it onto his back.

Dunn went down a set of stairs to the front deck. His greatest fear came to full realization.

Wickham and Kelly were down, Goerdt was working on Wickham. Martelli and Higgins were kneeling by Kelly, but they were sitting perfectly still.

He turned around and yelled at Schneider on the bridge through the destroyed window openings, "Bob! Two men down!"

Schneider took off.

"No!" Dunn shouted as he ran to Kelly.

He dropped to his knees. Kelly's chest was a bloody mess. He'd been struck several times by the German E-boat's 20mm cannon shells. His sightless eyes were open.

Martelli looked at Dunn, his face a mask of pain and failure.

"There was nothing we could do, Sarge."

Dunn touched Martelli's shoulder gently. "I know, Al. I know. Why don't you and Chuck go over there with the other fellas? We're going to get out of here."

"Okay, Sarge. I'm sorry."

"Not your fault, Al."

Dunn looked at Higgins, who had tears running down his cheeks.

"Same goes for you, Chuck."

He stood up, grabbing Higgins under the left armpit and lifting. The young man rose shakily.

Martelli closed Kelly's eyes and got up. The two men helped each other away.

Dunn spun around and ran to Wickham.

Goerdt had pulled off Wickham's jacket and cut away the top of his shirt to expose his right shoulder. Blood poured from Wickham's big right trapezius muscle. His face was scrunched up in pain.

"How bad, Rob?" Dunn asked.

"Looks worse than it is."

"Easy for you to say," Wickham muttered. "Hurts like the dickens. It's on fire." Fire came out fi-yar.

Dunn noted that Wickham's Brit-Tex accent had disappeared, as it always did when he was under stress. He sounded pure Texan.

Schneider arrived and dropped to his knees still carrying the radio on his back. He left it there as he put his first aid kit on the deck beside him and opened it. "Want me to help?" he asked Goerdt.

"Yes, take over, Doc." Goerdt decided to call the big man by the name he'd earned.

Schneider glanced at Goerdt and smiled. He bent to look at the wound. "The round gouged a trough through the muscle, maybe a quarter inch deep."

"Feels like a damn mile, Bob!"

"I know it does, buddy. Hold on." He grabbed a morphine ampoule, broke it open, and said, "Ready for a pinch?"

"Yeah."

Schneider jabbed the needle into Wickham's upper arm, squeezed, and withdrew it. He tossed it onto the deck.

Wickham closed his eyes.

Schneider set about dressing the wound as Wickham's breathing began to slow and his face relaxed.

"Thanks for taking care of him, Bob."

"You bet, Sarge."

"We're pulling alongside the sub now. We'll get some help to get him aboard. You know about Kelly?"

"Yeah, poor kid."

"Yeah." Dunn looked over at the body. "Damn it." He shook his head and turned away.

"See you in a bit."

"Okay," Schneider replied.

The boat was already alongside the sub and about a dozen sailors were on deck. They'd thrown a couple of lines over and Jonesy and Lindstrom had grabbed them and tied them to the railing, snugging the E-boat's gunwale against the sub. The sailors hooked up a short gangplank and rested it on the E-boat's port opening.

Cross suddenly appeared next to Dunn.

"Hey, I went below and opened the seacocks to sink the boat. We need to get out of here."

"Good idea. That'll make three German E-boats destroyed."

Dunn set about getting the men off the E-boat and safely aboard the HMS *Sea Tiger*. When all were on the deck and making their way to the hatch, two sailors carried Wickham on a stretcher and two carried Kelly's body. Two more sailors unhooked the gangplank, and then cut the lines to the E-boat, which was already settling lower in the water.

Soon thereafter, the men were below, the hatch closed, and the sub began to move slowly westward. She avoided the debris field of the west E-boat and began to submerge. The black water closed over where she'd been and grew calm.

Except for the debris of two E-boats, and a slowly sinking third one, it could look like any other calm night on the river.

After thanking the sub's captain, Dunn called for his men to meet in the galley. Wickham was safely asleep in the infirmary, and Kelly's body had been gently and reverently wrapped and placed in the aft torpedo room. A torpedoman volunteered to stand vigil. He shaved, changed into his dress uniform and took up station outside the torpedo room. Dunn had shaken his hand and thanked him.

Dunn eyed the seven men looking at him. Their faces were a mess. Their black grease paint was smudged like a woman's makeup in a heavy rain.

"Tough night, men. Let's take a moment for Hugh."

He bowed his head as did the men.

Dunn shook his head. Another man lost. Another wounded, but thankfully alive. Even though it was the nature of war to lose men, it always hurt. He wondered, not for the first time, how much more he could stand. He'd lost eight men since May. Well, seven if you didn't count the traitorous Griesbach, who Dunn himself had killed in hand-to-hand combat aboard a train in Germany. Seven, then. Seven souls. Seven families suffering unimaginable pain.

But he knew he would withstand it. That was the job and he'd volunteered for it. He would see it through, regardless of his personal cost.

He opened his eyes.

"A job well done, men. Thank you. No speeches, but a special thanks to Sergeant Cross for his skill tonight."

"Hear, hear," the men said in unison.

Cross blushed.

"Let's all go get some shuteye. Sleep as long as you possibly can. Good night."

The men nodded and filed out, leaving Dunn and Cross alone.

Dunn walked over to his best friend and extended his hand, which Cross took.

They pulled each other into an embrace and patted each other's back.

Separating, they looked at each other.

"You did a hell of a job driving the boat tonight."

Cross smiled at the compliment, and decided to let his friend get away with calling "piloting" "driving."

"Thanks. Good night, Tom."

"Good night, Dave. Get some good rest, you sure as hell earned it."

RONN MUNSTERMAN

35

Colonel Mark Kenton's office
Camp Barton Stacey
3 December, 1045 Hours, 2 days later

December brought a surprisingly warm day to England. The sun shone with a wintery intensity on the camp. Dunn and Cross had decided to walk to the colonel's office because they felt like they needed to do something physical to help relieve the stress of the last two missions. They'd arrived in London the evening before. Dunn had contacted the American graves unit in London from the sub, and they'd picked up Hugh Kelly's body. As the men from graves carefully carried Kelly from the sub, Dunn and his men watched while standing at attention on the deck. The captain, his XO, and several of the officers in the crew joined them. When the body passed the men, they saluted, and held it until he was completely off the boat.

After lowering his hand, Dunn sighed and struggled with moisture in his eyes. He glanced at Cross, who stared back. His eyes were wet, too.

"This is terrible," Cross said.

"Yes."

Dunn profusely thanked the captain for about the fourth time.

The captain kindly acknowledged it and the two men saluted each other.

On the ride to Barton Stacey, everyone slept, including Dunn. It was a merciful mental timeout.

Sitting in their usual places in front of Colonel Kenton's desk, Dunn and Cross glanced at the young red-headed second lieutenant sitting in what used to be Captain Samuel Adams' seat. He caught them looking and blushed.

Dunn suppressed a smile. The epitome of the pink-faced newbie. Probably a ninety-day wonder.

Kenton entered the room, running a little late. The men stood and saluted. Kenton returned it as he whipped by to get to his seat.

"Morning, gentlemen," he said, plopping down.

They all replied, "Good morning, sir."

Colonel Mark Kenton was a forty-one year old West Point graduate. He had dark hair with streaks of gray along the temples. He called them his sergeant stripes since his sergeants caused them. He only stood five-nine, but you didn't become a Ranger colonel if you couldn't stand up to people. Originally from Kansas City, Missouri, he'd met his wife, Mary, when he attended West Point and she Columbia in New York City. They'd married the month after he graduated from the academy.

Dunn and Kenton met in Italy during the Anzio misery, when Kenton commanded a Ranger battalion. Afterwards, they'd both been transferred to their current roles of executing top secret missions whenever and wherever intelligence gave them a target. So far, Dunn and his men had gone on over twenty missions since the previous May.

"Let me introduce you to Captain Adams' replacement. This is Lieutenant Fred Tanner. He comes highly recommended."

Dunn and Cross stood, and offered their hands. Tanner shook with them.

"Tom Dunn. Good to meet you, sir."

"I'm Dave Cross, sir. Nice to meet you."

"You, too," Tanner said.

Tanner was Dunn's height of six-two, but Dunn must have outweighed him by thirty pounds. Dunn couldn't help but think that Texan Stan Wickham would call him "a long drink of water."

The men seated themselves and looked at Kenton.

"I'm sorry about Kelly," Kenton said.

Dunn nodded. "Yeah, me, too. It was pretty bad: twenty millimeter rounds."

Kenton sucked in air through his teeth and grimaced. He shook his head. "He's been taken care of?"

"Yes, sir, in London. I wrote the letter to his parents last night. I mailed it on the way here."

Kenton nodded. "Okay, thank you. Fill me in on the second mission."

"Sure thing."

Dunn had sent a long coded message from the sub the night before telling Kenton that the mission had taken a turn that required intervention, and was successful, but the message had lacked detail. He also told Kenton about being successful in placing the number seventeen on top of the V2 rocket platform construction facility.

Dunn verbally gave the colonel a detailed accounting of destroying the sub along with its three V2 rocket platforms.

As Lieutenant Tanner listened, his mouth dropped open.

Kenton noticed. "This is what we do here."

"Uh, yes, sir."

Dunn laid a large envelope on the colonel's desk and pushed it closer.

Kenton opened it.

"Those are pictures we took of the submarine with its three rocket platforms, and also the platforms' assembly line, which is in the building with the number seventeen on top."

Kenton pulled out the pictures and took his time looking at them. When he was done he passed them to Tanner.

"Those are great photos. I sent on the info about that building to the Eighth Air Force. I heard back last night that they were sending a mission to hit it today. Might already be over."

"I sure hope they get it, sir."

"Me, too. Nazi subs and rockets off the coast of the U.S. makes my skin crawl."

Dunn and Cross nodded their agreement with this assessment. "I imagine there will be a lot of upset Nazis about this one."

"Yes, sir. We saw Admiral Dönitz there on the wharf. A whole bunch of naval officers and suits. They were really pleased with themselves when the sub left for a sea trial the day before." He didn't bother explaining that he'd ordered Jonesy to stand down on the shot he had lined up on the admiral.

"I just bet they were."

Kenton looked at Cross. "So you turned out to be a navy man instead?"

Dunn laughed.

Cross shook his head. "No sir. Never be a *navy* man. A boat man, maybe, never *navy*."

Kenton chuckled. "I sit corrected. Nevertheless, you did a whale of a job getting that sub and keeping the men as safe as was possible."

Cross smiled at the word choice. "Thank you, sir."

"Tom, please tell the men 'great job' for me."

"Will do, sir."

"I hope they understand what they've done."

"They do, Colonel. They really do."

"We might be thinking about some promotions."

Dunn nodded. "My thoughts exactly, sir. I'll start working on it right away."

"What are the men doing right now?"

"Weapons clean up. I was planning on giving them the night off. Let them go into town around eighteen hundred."

"Sure. Good idea. What about you and Cross?"

"Letter to my dad about missing fishing with him. And then hours and hours of sleep," Cross said.

Kenton smiled and nodded.

"Sunday lunch with Pamela and her parents at the farm."

"How is Pamela?"

Kenton always asked how Dunn's wife was doing.

"Good. Feeling pretty good right now."

"Glad to hear that." He turned to Tanner. "Sergeant Dunn's wife is expecting in May."

Tanner stuck out his hand. "Congratulations, Sergeant. That's terrific news."

Dunn grinned. "Thank you, Lieutenant. We're really happy."

"I can tell." Tanner smiled, his freckled cheeks puffing out.

"Anything else, sir?" Dunn asked.

"Nah. Get out of here. Say 'hello' to Pamela for me."

Dunn stood up, and Cross followed.

"Will do, sir. Oh, how's Bobby doing at West Point?"

Kenton's son was in his first year at the academy.

"Good. Settled in and feeling good. It's hard, but he enjoys the challenges. Well, at least for the most part. They can be pretty tough."

"I'm sure."

Dunn and Cross saluted and headed out. They stayed silent for about half the trip back to the barracks. A few jeeps and trucks rumbled by.

Cross glanced over at Dunn, who was wearing a deep frown.

"Out with it, Tom."

"What?"

"Better spit it out so you can move on."

"How'd you know?"

Cross stopped walking forcing Dunn to stop. "Really? How'd I know?"

Dunn tipped his head. "Okay, okay. Don't get your shorts in a knot."

"I'm not."

"I was thinking about what I could have done different. To keep Hugh alive."

"You go through this every time."

Dunn sighed and started walking. Cross kept pace.

"I know I do. But what else can I do? I need to do it, so maybe I can learn something."

"I understand that. I realize that's the analytical part of you, but it's also prompted by guilt."

"Well, I damn well *know* that!"

"Take it easy, buddy. Trying to help you here."

"Well, it's not helping."

An angry Dunn sped up. Cross had to run a couple of steps to catch up.

"Come on, Tom. Don't be angry."

"Well, I am," Dunn snapped.

They walked the remaining quarter mile in complete silence. Cross glanced over at his friend a few times, but Dunn kept his face forward.

When they got to the barracks, Dunn yanked the door open and walked straight back to his private quarters and slammed the door behind him.

Cross stood in the center of the barracks with his hands hanging limply by his side. The men had stopped what they were doing and stared at Cross. He shook his head and went to his bunk and sat down. He got his boots off and lay back on the bunk, his hands clasped under his head. He tried to figure out exactly why his best friend had grown so angry. It was the first time he'd been that upset with him. Sure they'd had their disagreements along the way, what best friends didn't? This was also the first time he'd received the silent treatment from Dunn, who typically preferred to get things out in the open, discussed, or argued, and be done with it. He shook his head, just not understanding. He closed his eyes and took some deep breaths. Ten seconds later he was out.

Dunn tore off his garrison hat and threw it across the room. He sat down at his desk mad at himself for a lot of things. Not protecting Kelly. Almost losing the entire squad because he wanted to be the hero and sink the sub and the platforms. Well, okay, maybe not because of the hero thing. That had never been his motivation. But losing it with Cross. That was so wrong.

"Idiot," he mumbled to himself. He got up and went to the barracks. He walked toward Cross's bunk. His men watched him, carefully staying quiet. When he got close he could tell Cross was sound asleep, his chest rising and sinking slowly.

He turned around and went back to his desk and sat down. He grabbed a piece of paper, ready to write an apology to Cross. He would put it on Cross's trunk by the bunk. He wrote Cross's first name and stopped. He dropped the pencil. It wasn't right. You don't apologize to your best friend on paper. He crumpled up the paper and threw it in the trash can nearby. Getting up, he retrieved his cap, put it on, and left his quarters.

He stopped midway to the front door.

"Gentlemen, Colonel Kenton wanted me to tell you 'great job.' "

The men nodded, noticing Dunn's calmer demeanor.

"You all have the night off, starting at eighteen hundred."

The men cheered the news.

"I'm heading home. See you tomorrow."

He received a few "see you later, Sarge" replies.

He glanced at Cross once more. Still knocked out.

Going outside, he jumped into the canvas-covered jeep.

Leaving the camp, he drove through Andover's downtown, passing the Star & Garter Hotel, and on out of town, never checking his rear view mirror.

He really should have.

Ronn Munsterman

36

The Hardwicke Farm
5 miles south of Andover
3 December, 1145 Hours

Dunn turned off the highway and headed up the long driveway.

A black car with two occupants slowed when the jeep in front of them did. After it turned off the road, SS Major Dedrick Förstner sped up and drove past the farm entrance. He stopped at the same point he had the other day when he and Evelyn had done a recon of the farm. Getting out, the two met at the rear of the car. He opened the trunk lid, but looked over the top of the car to the east. No cars. Checking behind he saw nothing there either. Reaching inside, he lifted his MP40 and checked the magazine for the tenth time. Full. Reinserting it, he charged the weapon.

Evelyn wore a dark, but expensive coat, a black skirt and a white ruffled blouse. Her blond hair was brushed up and back and she wore a red cloche hat. Around her neck was a gold chain holding a diamond. Overall, she looked like a movie star. She pulled a Luger from a shoulder holster under her right armpit inside her coat and checked her own magazine.

They both grabbed extra magazines for their weapons and pocketed them.

Förstner closed the trunk. He wore the same dark work-style clothes as the other day, boots, and the newsboy black cap.

He removed his own Luger from a similar holster to Evelyn's and checked the magazine. He holstered the pistol and patted his left pocket. Two magazines for the Luger.

"Ready to meet the happy little family?"

"Ja," she replied, her eyes holding a dangerous gleam.

"Remember, no one survives."

"Understood."

"Stick to the plan exactly." He handed her the car keys.

She nodded.

He started across the road. Evelyn got in the car, started it, turned in a big circle, shoulder to shoulder, and drove back to the Hardwicke's driveway. She turned in and went up the hill slowly. Stopping after about ten yards, she checked her wristwatch so she'd know when to continue.

Dunn held the main house's door open for Pamela. She stepped through. Her two dogs darted inside before Dunn could even move. He grinned at them. They were, frankly, a hoot to be around. He'd always loved animals, growing up as he did in a city surrounded by farms. His best friend, Paul, lived on a farm, and Dunn spent days at a time out there in the summer helping with the daily chores. Paul had dogs and barn cats, which were a whole different kind of cat from city cats, and some enormous rabbits. Dunn loved dogs, favoring them over cats. He'd tried repeatedly to get a dog for the Dunn household, but there were already three cats in the house, thanks to older sister Hazel who beat him to the "I need a pet" punch by luck of birth. Also, Mrs. Dunn was afraid they would terrorize any dog. Dunn secretly believed she really thought the dog would spend every day chasing the cats.

The dogs circled the food-filled table, their tails wagging hopefully, their noses in the air the whole time. Baked chicken smells did that. Dunn took a deep breath, inhaling the wondrous odors of Mrs. Hardwicke's famous cooking. She was standing by the stove, stirring the mashed potatoes. Mr. Hardwicke was already seated at the head of the table, but he stood and hugged Pamela, who pecked him on the cheek, and sat down

Hardwicke held out his hand for Dunn, who shook it.

"Good to see you, Tom."

"You, too, Mr. Hardwicke."

"Earl," the father said automatically.

"Yes, sir," Dunn said, grinning.

Hardwicke shook his head. "Maybe one of these days."

"Yes, sir."

Hardwicke smiled and sat back down.

"Hi, Mrs. Hardwicke," Dunn said, going over and giving her a gentle hug from the side.

"Mom, Tom," she said sternly.

"Yes, ma'am."

She looked at him. "You're hopeless, aren't you?"

"Yes, ma'am."

"Just for that you can scoop these into the bowl." She pointed to a large bowl next to the stove.

"Glad to help." He took the huge wooden spoon from her and began plopping the thick, creamy potatoes into the bowl. It was hard work. When he was done, he put the spoon in the sink and picked up the bowl. He thought it weighed at least five pounds. He put it on the table between the platter of chicken and the gravy bowl. Also on the table was a bowl of baked carrots.

He sat down across from Hardwicke. The mother and daughter faced each other on the sides of the table.

Mrs. Hardwicke held out her hands. Everyone grasped the two on either side of them. Hardwicke said grace and everyone said, "Amen."

The food was passed around the table and, at the same time, they all started in, although Hardwicke pulled the skin off his chicken leg and thigh and held it down for the dogs, each getting some and licking his fingers to boot.

"Earl!"

Hardwicke looked at his wife innocently. "What, dear?"

"Oh, my gracious, you're . . . so in trouble."

"Ah, a new experience."

Everyone laughed, including Mrs. Hardwicke.

"Did you go read to the men today at the hospital, honey?" Dunn asked Pamela.

"Yep, at eight o'clock for about an hour."

He nodded and chewed some chicken. He swallowed. "I know the guys appreciate it."

Pamela smiled. "Yes, I think they do."

Dunn waved his drumstick in the air. "Forgot to tell you that Colonel Kenton says 'hello.' "

She smiled. "Tell him 'hello' right back. He's always so nice to us."

"He sure is."

"How's Dave?"

Dunn's cheeks flared red and he looked at his plate.

"Something happen?"

Dunn shrugged. "Yeah. I . . . got upset at him for no reason."

"I see. Are you two okay?"

"I was going to apologize, but he had fallen asleep. We're all pretty tired from the trip."

The Hardwickes watched the young married couple, but neither wanted to say anything.

Dunn looked at each of them and said, "Sorry to air this out in front of you."

Mrs. Hardwicke patted Dunn's hand. "You're family, Tom. It's quite all right."

Hardwicke nodded.

"Okay, thank you. Dave's my best friend."

"We know, dear. We remember him from the wedding. He was your best man."

"Yeah, he sure was."

Deciding it was time to change the subject for Dunn's sake, Mrs. Hardwicke asked, "Have you thought about what you'll do after you and Pamela go home?"

The Hardwickes had been incredibly supportive of the idea that Pamela was going to live thousands of miles and weeks of travel away from them.

Dunn glanced at Pamela. She tipped her head slightly.

Dunn took the cue. "I'll go back to school first and get my degree in history. Too late to change that since I'm only one semester away. But after that, I'm going to apply to the Cedar Rapids Police Department."

Hardwicke grinned. "I say. A constable in the family again! My youngest cousin was a copper in London."

Dunn smiled. "Wow, I had no idea. Of course, Cedar Rapids is so small compared to London, but it seems like a good place to start."

"Like they say, you have to start somewhere," Hardwicke said.

Förstner crept up to a tree located twenty yards east of the Hardwicke main house. He leaned against the cold wood and eyed the rear of the house. Smoke curled skyward from the chimney, which was in the center of the roof. A back door stood dead center in the back wall, with two windows on either side. The door and all of the windows were closed, but the curtains on the windows were pulled or tied back, presumably to let in daylight.

He checked each window and was satisfied no one was actually standing at one of them. Checking his watch, he nodded to himself. Anytime.

Evelyn was right on schedule. He could hear her tires crunching on the driveway as she drove toward the barnyard.

Both of Pamela's dogs got up and looked toward the front door, their ears perked. The collie suddenly woofed and ran to the door, his tail trailing stiff behind him. The Labrador followed. Everyone at the table looked at the front door.

"Must be someone coming up the driveway," Pamela said.

Mrs. Hardwicke got up. "I'll go see who it is."

She went to the door and opened it.

A black car pulled into the barnyard.

"I don't recognize the car."

The car stopped and a drop-dead gorgeous blond woman climbed out carefully, making sure her skirt didn't flare in the breeze. She pulled her coat tighter.

"It's a young woman," Mrs. Hardwicke said over her shoulder. "I expect she's lost. I'll be right back." She lifted a coat from a hook by the door and slipped it on. She opened the door and the dogs burst out, barking. She went out the door, closing it as she left.

The people at the table went back to their meals.

Mrs. Hardwicke walked along the well-worn path to the barnyard.

The blond woman gave her a radiant smile and a little wave. The dogs were barking at her from a distance.

"Hello," she called out. "I'm lost."

Mrs. Hardwicke grinned. "Thought you might be, dear. Where are you trying to go? Andover?"

The dogs approached the woman, tails wagging because now they recognized her smell from a few days ago. She took off her left glove and lowered her bare hand so the dogs could sniff it to their hearts' content. When they finished, she petted each one. Both sat down.

The blond woman didn't reply. She looked over the older woman's shoulder at the front door, noting it was closed. She walked past the dogs, closing the distance to the other woman. The dogs followed her, and circled around Mrs. Hardwicke. When they were about two steps apart the two women stopped and eyed each other in a friendly fashion. Country strangers meeting for the first time. The dogs sat down by Mrs. Hardwicke looking at the guest.

Florence held out her hand, smiling. "I'm Florence Hardwicke."

Evelyn smiled in return.

Instead of taking Florence's hand, Evelyn reached inside her coat with her left hand and drew her Luger. She aimed at Florence's heart and shook her head.

"Not a word, Florence."

Evelyn's mistake was underestimating a British farm woman and two dogs.

Florence screamed at the top of her lungs, "Earl! She's got a gun!"

The dogs, frightened by the sudden change in the emotional air, growled and barked. The collie attacked first, going for the blond woman's left hand, which was holding the gun.

The gun went off and the collie dropped to the ground, bleeding from the gunshot.

37

The Hardwicke Farm, main house
3 December, 1214 Hours

Everyone in the house heard Florence scream and the gunshot. They jumped to their feet. Pamela and Earl started toward the front door, but Dunn stopped them.

"Earl, what weapons do you have?"

"Weapons? I have a couple of shotguns in the living room. The shells are in the desk."

"Pamela, go down to the cellar and hide yourself."

Pamela stared at Dunn as if she didn't comprehend what he'd said.

He started to repeat himself, but she held up a hand. "No, I'm ringing for help." She ran to the phone.

"Okay, but when you're done, get downstairs. Lock yourself in."

"I will," she replied as she picked up the party line phone.

Dunn and Earl dashed into the living room, which was north of the kitchen.

At the sounds of the barking dogs, the screaming woman, and the subsequent gunshot, Förstner cursed Evelyn and ran to the back door. He tried the doorknob, but it was locked. He took a step back, and leapt forward kicking the door beside the knob. The wood cracked, but held. He repeated his attack on the door and this time it burst open, slamming hard against an interior wall.

Pamela reached the farmer closest—two miles away—and he promised to come with weapons, and to ring for more help. She hung up and rang Barton Stacey. When the operator answered she screamed, "Colonel Kenton! It's a life or death emergency!"

When his deep bass voice came over the line, she told him what was happening. He said he'd send someone.

She ran to the living room.

Earl handed Dunn one of the double-barreled shotguns and got the other down for himself. Dunn was already getting a couple of boxes of shells. Each held twenty-five shells. The two men loaded two rounds each and pocketed the rest of a box each. Dunn was regretting not having his Colt .45 with him. But why would he have it with him?

The blond woman backhanded Florence with the butt of her gun and the farm woman went down. The Labrador attacked, biting the woman's left leg.

She screamed, lost her footing because he was yanking on her leg with incredible strength, and fell down beside Florence, her red hat rolling across the ground. The gun bounced out of her hand.

Florence was holding her bleeding forehead with one hand and crying from the pain and anger. The Lab let go to get a better grip and the woman tried to scramble free but he snapped hard on her lovely ankle. Blood spurted onto the ground and she screamed.

Florence had trouble seeing because of the blood in one eye, but she saw enough to spot the gun on the ground. She got to her knees and dove for it ungracefully.

The blond woman managed to roll over and kick the Lab on the nose. He let go and snarled, a frightening, guttural sound that made the woman's hair on the back of the neck stand up. He raced up her body snapping at her neck, but she found the strength to roll over and get into a tucked natal position. She wrapped her arms around her head and buried her throat. He bit her hands and wrists, but she stayed tucked in, screaming all the while.

Florence saw what was happening and yelled, "No, Sammy, No!"

He was too deep into his protective instincts to stop biting.

Florence got to her knees and crawled over to him. She grabbed him by the collar. He turned toward her, his bloody mouth open for another attack.

"It's all right, Sammy. It's all right. Good boy. Good boy," she said in a soothing voice as she pulled his head closer to her. She wrapped her other hand around his body and hugged him. He sat down and whimpered.

The woman raised her arms to look at Florence with terrified eyes.

Florence raised the Luger with a steady hand.

"I know how this thing works."

Instead of rushing inside, Förstner stood flat against the outside wall next to the broken door. He stuck the barrel of his weapon into the opening and fired a short burst.

Dunn recognized the sound of the MP40. He grabbed Pamela by the hand and pulled her into the corner of the living room behind the huge, heavy wood desk.

"Get down, honey! Cover yourself with these." He snatched a couple of seat cushions off the sofa. She did as he asked. They wouldn't stop a bullet, but they'd help with wood splinters and shattered glass. At least until he could clear the house and get her to the cellar from the kitchen.

He looked at Earl and held up a hand as a stop sign. Earl nodded.

"That's a German soldier."

Earl's eyebrows went up. "A German? Here?"

Dunn nodded.

Earl started to ask why, but the expression on his son-in-law's face explained it. Someone had come here hunting him. And found him.

Dunn advanced to the door to the kitchen. Kneeling, he peeked down the hallway that led to the back door. A shadow moved and he raised the shotgun. A man's figure appeared briefly, in and out. Dunn almost fired, but didn't. Instead he rose and ran across the kitchen to a point on the right side of the hallway. He peeked again, weapon aimed down the hall. Once more the shadow appeared. Then a head and shoulder.

Dunn fired both barrels.

The boom of the shotgun inside the house was enormous.

Pieces of wood shattered under the buckshot, but the form had retreated just in time.

Dunn ducked as more 9mm rounds tore down the hallway and into the front wall of the kitchen. He reloaded.

The German weapon ceased firing, Dunn thought perhaps so the man could also reload. He peeked around the door jam. The hallway was clear. He ran back to the living room and drew Earl close.

"I'm gonna lie down and aim down the hallway. Can you lean over me and fire both barrels. I want to see if he exposes himself," Dunn whispered. "You back up as soon as you fire."

"Bloody hell I can," Earl replied, a determined look on his face.

Dunn got down and pointed the shotgun down the hall.

Earl stepped into position and raised his weapon. "Ready," he whispered.

"Fire," Dunn whispered back.

Earl fired and stepped back into the living room, barrels up. He broke the shotgun open, ejected the two empties, reloaded, and snapped the barrels back into position.

Dunn sighted over his two barrels.

A head appeared, but at floor level. The other guy had been in firefights before.

Dunn blasted one barrel, lowered his aim and fired the second one.

The man yanked his head back before the second shot.

More wood splinters flew in all directions.

The MP40's ugly snout appeared around the corner of the door frame.

Dunn scooted back into the living room as another half magazine of 9mm rounds zinged by, inches from where his head had been. He stood, listening, and broke the shotgun and reloaded. He was going to have to do something else. Trading hot punches down the hallway wasn't going to work. He looked around the room briefly and made his decision.

"Earl, I have to get outside. Can you keep an eye out on the hallway?"

"Yes."

"When you hear his weapon firing from someplace outside, get Pamela and yourself into the cellar."

Earl shook his head. "I'll get Pamela down there, but I've got to get to Florence."

Dunn was torn. He didn't want to leave Pamela alone in the cellar, but he understood Earl's need to go help his own wife.

"How about this? If the gunman leaves to follow me, which I think he will, you check on Florence from the doorway. Get her inside and into the cellar. All three of you."

Earl thought it over, recognized the prudence of such a move, and said, "Sure. Yes, that makes more sense than me barging outside. I'm not quite used to getting shot at. Training was a long time ago."

Dunn nodded. "Understood. Are you ready?"

"Yes."

Dunn eyed his father-law briefly checking the man's state of mind. His eyes reflected not panic and fear, but resolve. That's what he needed to see.

"Let's go," he said.

Earl got down on the floor where Dunn had been, shotgun near the floor, aimed down the hallway.

Dunn knelt beside Pamela and told her what was going to happen. She nodded, reaching up to touch Dunn's cheek. "Come back to me, Tom Dunn."

"Yes, ma'am."

He gave her a quick kiss and went to the north window. He looked out from each side to get the best view of the opposite direction. Nothing moving. He unlocked the casement window, the kind that opened on hinges on the sides, and pulled both sides open.

He leaned out just enough to make sure the man wasn't right there along the north wall waiting to take his head off. It was clear. Now or never.

Lifting his left leg through the window, he let his boot touch the ground, and ducked his way through, pulling his other leg behind him. He immediately dropped to a knee with the shotgun up, aimed toward the back of the house. He scanned the trees that were farther away, perhaps twenty yards. No movement.

He began combat walking along the wall toward the rear of the house, the shotgun stock nestled against his cheek.

Sudden movement near one of the trees caught his eye.

The shotgun barrel traversed left and he fired one barrel.

Chunks of bark flew off the tree.

The enemy ran northwest aiming for another tree, firing blindly as he ran.

Dunn dove to the ground. Rounds splatted and sparked against the house's rock foundation just above his head.

38

Dunn's barracks
Camp Barton Stacey
7 miles from the Hardwicke Farm
3 December, 1219 Hours

Eugene Lindstrom had lost his patience with the phone in Dunn's quarters that just wouldn't stop ringing. He'd run in and picked it up. He'd listened to Colonel Kenton's instructions and said "yes, sir," and slammed the phone down and dashed back into the barracks.

Lindstrom had shouted, "Dunn's family is under attack!"

Minutes later the men were up and dressed in combat gear, including their Thompson .45 caliber submachine guns. They ran outside just in time to see their truck—ordered by Kenton—arrive.

Cross, his face craggy and puffy from sleep and exhaustion, climbed up in the cab. He gave the driver terse directions and the encouragement of, "Drive like hell, buddy!"

The Hardwicke Farm

Florence turned at the sounds of the shots coming from the woods north of the house. As her body turned, the Luger's barrel swung away from Evelyn. In spite of her pain, Evelyn scrambled to her feet and lunged forward. Florence inadvertently blocked out Sammy the Lab.

Evelyn tried to grab the gun away from Florence, but the older woman spun away with an unlikely athleticism. She backed up a few feet and aimed the gun at Evelyn's right eye.

Sammy stood up, growled again and tensed his muscles to attack, but Florence said, "Steady, Sammy. Stay."

Sammy sat back down, but he continued to voice his displeasure.

Florence wiped some more blood from her left eye with her coat sleeve.

She bent over the collie, whose eyes were closed, but he was breathing. The bullet had gouged a crease along the top of his head.

She gave the blond woman a hate-filled look. "Pick up my dog and carry him into the house, woman," she commanded.

Dunn fired his second barrel at the fleeting views of the fast moving target, but missed by yards. He reloaded and jumped to his feet. It was obvious where the gunman was headed, so Dunn ran toward the barn. He sprinted in front of his own small house and headed toward the barn's door facing the barnyard. Half way across bullets hit the ground at his feet. He looked up to see a man in the loft. He was swapping out a magazine while watching the Ranger with what Dunn thought was a supercilious smirk. He stopped and raised the shotgun. The man stepped back out of view. Dunn held his fire. He only had nineteen rounds left. What he'd give for his Thompson safely locked up back at the barracks. He ran to the east wall of the barn and stood at the corner thinking about what to do.

He looked up at the opening for the loft, but the attacker was not in sight. Glancing left, he couldn't believe his eyes. A bleeding Florence was holding a gun on a blond woman, who was carrying Winston toward the house. Earl burst through the door carrying his shotgun, hopefully after stashing Pamela safely in the cellar. He ran to his wife, staring at the blood on her face. He grabbed the blond woman by the arm and forced her forward faster. Dunn couldn't see his expression but had no trouble picturing it. He imagined it matched his own.

They reached the door. Florence stepped around the woman and opened the door. She gestured with the pistol. Dunn saw that it was a Luger. Sammy darted indoors. The trio entered and the door swung shut. Dunn shook his head at the sight.

Satisfied the Hardwicke family was safe, he turned back to his problem: how to get at the lone gunman. To charge inside was out of the question, a sure way of getting shot if the attacker had run downstairs from the loft. He could use a few more men. Like his squad. Or if he had a smoke grenade maybe he could confuse and blind the man long enough. That triggered another thought.

He jammed a hand into his pocket and pulled out his Zippo lighter. Its speckled black surface reflected the noon sun. That would be one way to get the man out. Except for the not so small detail that it would destroy Earl's barn. He slipped the lighter back in his pocket. He raised a hand to his brow in frustration.

Suddenly, there came the sound of vehicles crunching along on the drive. Dunn looked south. A pair of older pickup trucks crept into the barnyard. Dunn thought there were two men in each. They would be sitting ducks. They were well inside the effective range of the German weapon, which was about 150 to 200 yards. Dunn stepped to the side and waved his arms, one hand holding and waving the shotgun back and forth. He held up his left hand as a stop sign. The trucks stopped. Dunn pointed up at the loft, and pointed his shotgun at the trucks. The lead driver waved a hand in acknowledgement, and motioned for the trailing truck to back up.

Within seconds the trucks began backing down the drive.

From above, the MP40 fired a short burst and a few rounds peppered the lead truck's metal bumper.

The trucks disappeared back the way they'd come.

Dunn sighed in relief. Pamela must have gotten through to someone for help.

He knew the attacker had to have entered the barn from the north door. To get to the loft, he would have run south through the big open space that took up about three-fourths of the barn on the right. The stables were built against the west wall. He would have climbed the ladder, the only way up. Next, he would look for the best hiding place with a clear field of fire on the ladder's opening.

Dunn had been in the barn a number of times to help Earl with various chores. He pictured the interior and the exterior and a detail came to mind. Would it be in the right position?

Silently, he moved north along the east wall. When he got to the northeast corner of the barn he stopped, knelt, and peeked around the corner. Clear. Good. He looked up at something dangling from a support beam sticking out at a point midway along the back of the barn and to his side of the opening to the loft. Dunn smiled grimly. Luck was with him.

Earl called out Pamela's name softly after knocking on the locked cellar door. He heard rustling and footsteps. A key turned in the lock from the other side and she entered the kitchen. She immediately spotted her bleeding mother, noticing the gun in her hand, unwaveringly aimed at a blond woman seated at the table. The woman was bleeding around her neck, and hands, which were on the table and tied together with thin rope.

"Mum, are you all right?"

She ran around the table to her mother.

"I'm fine. Just a cut."

Looking quickly around the kitchen, her expression grew worried. "Where's Tom?"

Earl answered. "He's after the gunman. I'm going to go help."

In her fearful state, Pamela could only nod. She turned away and opened a drawer by the sink and pulled out first aid supplies, and two clean kitchen towels. She wet one of the towels in the sink.

Earl went to the door, looked once more over his shoulder at the people he loved most, and left to go help the one other person he also loved.

Pamela told her mother to sit down and quickly set about cleaning and patching her wound.

Florence, sitting across the wide table from the blond woman, rested the pistol butt on the table and kept it aimed at her.

"Pamela, this *woman* shot Winston. I don't know how he's doing." Florence pointed to a crumpled Winston lying on his favorite blanket by the door. Blood was seeping from the wound across the top of his head.

Pamela sucked in a breath, but said nothing as she finished bandaging her mother.

She went to the side of the blond woman.

She stiffened. "I recognize you! You were here saying you were lost."

The woman shrugged.

"What's your name?"

"Evelyn."

"Let me see your neck."

Evelyn looked up at Pamela in surprise.

"I'm a nurse."

"Thank you."

Pamela started working on cleaning the bites and claw marks that Sammy had inflicted on the woman.

"Why did you come here?" she asked as she dabbed the area on the neck with a cotton ball soaked with alcohol.

The woman flinched at the sting. "Ow, watch it there. Don't you have some oath to do no harm?"

"That's doctors. My job is to keep you healthy even if it hurts you temporarily."

Evelyn frowned but said nothing.

"Why are you here?" Pamela persisted.

The blond woman smiled evilly. "I would have thought it obvious: to kill all of you, especially your precious husband."

39

The Hardwicke Farm
3 December, 1227 Hours

Earl ran to Pamela's house and peeked around the corner. He could see no movement around the barn, which was where he thought Dunn and the German must be. Just as he was about to dash off, as much as a fifty-year-old farmer could dash, he heard a rustling sound behind him, south of the main house. Raising his weapon, he peered into the trees there, about ten yards away he was able to see Mr. Jackson, his closest neighbor, and three other farmers who lived within five miles. They all carried double-barreled shotguns. He lowered his shotgun.

Earl waved at the men to join him. Mr. Jackson looked at the opening of the loft, and started walking fast; running was out of the question for the seventy-one-year-old. The other three followed. When the four men reached Earl, he said, "Thank you for coming."

Jackson nodded. "Whatever you need, Earl."

"There's a German in the barn somewhere. I heard automatic gunfire. I think he came here to kill my son-in-law."

"A German here? To kill Sgt. Dunn?" Mr. Jackson asked, incredulous.

"Yes. And my family, I think."

"Bastard."

"Yes. I want one man to go in the house. Florence is holding a gun on a woman who attacked her. She's part of the team that came here."

"I'll go," volunteered a man who was a little older than Jackson.

"Thank you, Mr. Miller."

The man took off toward the house in a shuffling fast walk, but his head was held high and the shotgun at the ready.

The three others turned to Earl expectantly.

"I'm not sure where Tom is or the German. I thought we'd approach the barn from the east and make our way to the door."

The men nodded.

Earl started to move, but drew his leg back, thinking. He didn't see his son-in-law anywhere. Was he already in the barn? Or attempting to access it quietly?

"I have an idea that might help."

He explained.

The two farmers nodded.

Dunn examined the rope hanging from a large wooden pulley near the peak of the roof. The rope had a huge knot tied at both ends to prevent it from whipping on through the pulley. He pulled down on the rope and made sure the upper end was snug in the pulley and secure enough to hold his weight. The excess rope coiled at his feet. The pulley was attached to a beam that swiveled. It was currently on his side of the loft's opening. Luck was indeed with him. He did, however, have a problem. How to climb the rope and carry the shotgun. It didn't have a sling. Undoubtedly, he could find a thin rope inside the barn, but where would it be? There wasn't any outside.

Desperation breeds inspiration. Dunn leaned the shotgun against the barn, and ripped off his uniform jacket, and his long sleeved shirt. Slipping back into the coat, he buttoned it. He tied one of the sleeves to the butt, right behind the trigger guard and the breech. Next, he tied the other sleeve onto the barrel. There was no natural point that would hold the sleeve in place, so he tied a double knot as tight as possible. He realized he would have to carry it barrel down. He hoped that wouldn't turn out to be a problem.

Finished with the jerry-rigged sling, he draped the end near the butt over his right shoulder. He practiced lifting the barrel and getting into a firing position a couple of times. Finally ready, he jumped and grabbed the rope.

From somewhere on the south side of the barn, gunfire erupted. Several shotguns were firing single barrels at a time until six shots had been completed. He clearly heard the buckshot hitting the barn. It sounded like they had aimed at the area just under the peak of the roof, above the opening to the loft.

Seemed like a good distraction to him.

He put his boots together and began to climb as fast as possible. It was like boot camp, but now it really was life or death.

Förstner resisted the urge to scoot close to the opening to see who was shooting at him. Judging by the number and ferocity of the shots, it was more than just his target, Sgt. Dunn and the old man firing. Somehow they'd gotten reinforcements, the men in the trucks he shot at. Because the weapons were all shotguns, he thought they were locals, probably neighboring farmers. He patted his pocket. He had three magazines left. In theory, it should be enough.

No more shots came, so he decided it might be worth a look. Maybe he could take out one or more of them with a short, but accurate burst. He got down on his stomach, his weapon in front of him and he combat crawled toward the loft opening. He stopped at the left edge for a moment to gather himself. Inching forward, he craned his neck and peeked into the barnyard. His eyes swept across its entirety, then focused on the two houses. He saw no one at first, but then a shadow appeared on the ground by the smaller house to his left. He aimed the MP40.

A man's head and torso appeared.

He fired a three round burst.

The man dropped back and screamed.

He smiled. One down.

He inched back and rose to a kneeling position, thinking. What would he do if he had reinforcements to act as a diversion? He immediately turned his head toward the north end of the barn where the blue sky greeted him.

Of course.

He rose, weapon at the ready. Dodging various farm items strewn about on the floor, he headed toward the opening.

"Jesus, Earl," Jackson said as he knelt beside his friend. "Let me see."

Earl was on his back and had his hand to his left side. His coat was blood soaked already.

Dunn heard the MP40 go off and a scream. *Dear God*, he thought. He sped up. Reaching the point where he could step into the barn, he wrapped the rope around his left forearm and used his right hand to bring up the shotgun's barrel. He would have to fire one handed, so it would have to be one barrel at a time to have any hope of retaining a grip after the massive kick of the shot.

Pamela heard the shotguns go off, and the automatic weapon. She heard a scream. She looked at Evelyn with steady, furious eyes.

"If anything happens to my husband or father, I will kill you."

Evelyn, noting some panic in the nurse's eyes, laughed and shook her head. "You don't have the guts. Never happen, darling."

Rather than argue with a prisoner, Pamela ran to the kitchen drawer and pulled out a big roll of her dad's black friction tape. She stuck the end of the roll against Evelyn's cheek and wrapped several layers of tape over her mouth and around her head.

"I've had enough of you," she said through clenched teeth. When she was done, she asked, "Mum, are you okay with guarding her?"

Florence gave her daughter a glance and went back to staring at Evelyn. "More than."

The older farmer, standing nearby, looked at Pamela in alarm.

"Ma'am, your dad wanted me to keep you safe in the house."

She shook her head. "Mr. Miller, someone's hurt out there." She grabbed the medical supplies and dropped them in an empty bread basket from the table. "I'm going."

"Be careful, ma'am."

Pamela nodded as she put on her coat. She knelt beside Winston. She'd cleaned and dressed the wound, and wrapped his head with a bandage, but he was still unconscious. She patted him on the shoulder.

Sammy got up to follow, but she pointed at him and then at his own blanket next to Winston. He lay back down looking up at her with sorrowful eyes. He snuggled close to Winston and sniffed his friend's bandage. He whimpered.

She rose, went to the door and looked out. Two men were kneeling next to someone on the ground. She couldn't tell who it was because they blocked her view. Then she realized that neither of the men wore a coat like her dad.

"Oh, no."

With no regard for her own safety, she bolted through the door.

Dunn put his right boot on the barn's second level floor and leaned in. A shape materialized to his left.

He yanked the shotgun barrel left and fired.

He heard a scream and a thump of a body hitting the floor and the clatter of the MP40 bouncing away.

His grip on the shotgun failed and it dangled from his shoulder in danger of sliding off. Fumbling for it, his right foot slipped off the floor and he began to spin left.

The make-shift sling slipped off his shoulder and he gripped the rope with his right hand. The sling caught in the bend of his elbow. Catching the loft's floor with his right foot again, he stopped spinning. The weight of the weapon, being in an unusual place, the elbow, began to drag his fatigued arm down the rope. Thinking fast, he let go of the rope and drew his arm back like a sidearm pitcher and flung it forward.

The shotgun, propelled by the motion and its own weight flew toward the loft. Dunn prayed it wouldn't go off and kill him. It didn't, instead simply landing on its side, so to speak, and sliding a few feet, the barrel pointing away.

Dunn grabbed the left side of the barn opening and pulled himself inside. He looked left and saw blood droplets on the floor nearby, and the MP40, but the German was gone. Dunn ran to the shotgun and picked it up.

He knelt looking around the large space, his eyes growing accustomed to the gloom. To his left was a stack of hay which covered an area about ten feet in diameter. To the right of that stood a cabinet of some sort. Dunn turned right.

And met a huge fist.

40

The Hardwicke Farm
3 December, 1234 Hours

"Turn here! Hurry up!" Cross yelled at the young driver.

The truck bounced up the long driveway.

Suddenly, the driver slammed on the brakes.

Cross looked ahead. Two pickup trucks were blocking the way.

"Is there room to get around?" he asked.

The driver eyed the space between the trees lining the road and the trucks. "I'm sorry, Sarge, but no way."

"Stay here," Cross told the driver. Then he yelled through the small window to the cargo area, "Everyone out!"

He jumped down and met the men in front of the vehicle. He checked them over quickly. Satisfied, he said, "Let's go."

Eight deadly U.S. Army Rangers threaded their way toward their friend and his family.

Pamela had torn open her dad's coat and shirt. The bullet had entered in the lower left abdomen. Earl's eyes were closed and his breathing shallow.

"Help me roll him over, Mr. Jackson."

Jackson gripped Earl by the shoulder and lifted and pushed.

Earl groaned.

Pamela lifted the back of his shirt. A bloody exit hole greeted her. She dressed it expertly and they rolled him back over and she began working on the entry wound.

Without looking up, she said, "We have to get to the hospital as soon as possible. You two go in the house right here and take a bedroom door off the hinges. You'll find tools in a drawer by the kitchen sink. We'll use that as a stretcher."

"Yes, ma'am," replied Jackson.

Florence stood, wobbling slightly from the hit in the head.

She handed the Luger to the farmer, Mr. Miller. He handled it like someone who knew exactly what to do with it. He flipped the safety on and stuck the pistol behind his back. He swung the shotgun's double-barrels toward the bound and gagged traitor.

To her they looked like cannons.

"If she moves, shoot her. Understood?"

"Completely, Mrs. Hardwicke."

Florence put her coat back on and ran out the door. She saw Pamela working on someone lying in the grass.

She was ten feet away when she realized who it was.

"Earl!" she screamed.

Dunn took the hit almost on the point of his chin. He rocked back and fell down on his ass. The German dove and landed on Dunn, his big hands closing like clamps around the Ranger's throat.

The killer's right bicep was bleeding heavily from several buckshot holes.

Dunn grabbed the man's wrists with both hands and tried to break free.

Didn't work.

He rocked and kicked, but had no leverage.

The German stared into Dunn's eyes and grinned. "Just so you'll know, I have a message for you from Minister Speer: time to die, Sgt. Dunn."

Dunn knew he only had a few more seconds before he would pass out.

He let go of the attacker's right wrist and punched the man in the wounded bicep with his left fist.

The German grunted in pain, but held tight.

Dunn let go with the other hand and clapped his hands together like he was praying. His hands were under the German's arms, close to the German's chest. He forced the hand wedge up between the man's elbows and spread his own elbows, like opening a vice.

The German's elbows gave way and bent slightly. Not enough to break their grip on the throat, but it brought the German's face closer.

Dunn's hands flew upward and grabbed the attacker's head from both sides, thumbs inward.

He gouged at the man's eyes.

The man grunted and tried to shake his head loose from Dunn's grip.

Instead of instinctively pushing the man's face upward, Dunn suddenly grabbed both ears and snapped the face downward.

He head butted the German square on the nose. Blood gushed all over him. Next he pushed up on the head and slammed it back down into his own forehead again.

The attacker roared in pain and let go.

Dunn gasped in some air and rabbit punched the man's ribs twice lightning fast. He heard at least one rib crack from the twin shots.

Pushing the gasping man to the side, Dunn scrambled behind him.

He threw his right elbow around the man's throat.

His left hand snaked around under the enemy's left arm and behind the back of the enemy's head, clamping onto Dunn's right arm.

The German tried to turn his head into Dunn's elbow to reduce the pressure on his throat.

Dunn squeezed harder and flopped onto his back wrenching the man's head and body with him.

He wrapped his legs around the man's thighs and tightened his muscles, immobilizing the man's legs like a python.

The German's hands flailed, trying to scratch at Dunn's face.

Dunn leaned his head back as if he were looking up.

He squeezed harder.

Thirty seconds passed.

The man's efforts grew feeble.

His hands thudded to the loft's floor.

Dunn squeezed more.

Five minutes later, Cross clambered up the ladder. He looked around wildly and finally spotted two men lying on the floor on the opposite side. He darted over and leaned down.

Dunn's arms were still locked around the enemy's throat.

The German's face was purple. Eyes bulged. His dark, swollen tongue hung limply from the mouth.

"Tom."

No answer.

"Tom. It's over, buddy. Come on."

Cross snapped his fingers a couple of times.

"Tom!"

Dunn looked up, suddenly aware. He let go of the German, pushing the body away. He scooted backwards as if to get away from something terrifying.

Jumping to his feet, he shouted, "Where's Pamela?"

Cross grabbed him by the arm.

"She's fine. She's okay, Tom. Come on, let's get you outside. I'll send a couple of guys up for this one. Here, hold still, you can't let Pamela see your face like this." He pulled a handkerchief from his pocket and wiped some of the German's blood from his friend's face. It was better, but blood still streaked across his skin.

"Thanks."

"Ayup."

Dunn ran over to Pamela, who was standing by their front door, and pulled her into a bear hug. She fell into his embrace and started crying.

"You're okay?" she asked into his chest. "Is that your blood on your face?"

"Not mine. I'm not hurt."

She nodded and began crying harder.

"What is it?"

Between sobs, she was able to say, "Daddy got shot."

Dunn looked around. "Where is he? Is he . . .?" he stopped, unable to ask the question.

"He's alive, and a couple of neighbors carted him to their truck. They're on the way to the camp hospital. I told them to tell everyone there he was my dad."

Dunn nodded. "Good idea." He pushed her gently away, holding her upper arms so she wouldn't collapse. "Let's get you and your mom to the hospital."

She looked up at him, her arctic-ice blue eyes filled with tears. "Mum went with him. I do want to go, but . . . there's the woman inside. She was in on it. She shot Winston. She was the woman who took our picture the other day."

"What?"

Dunn realized he'd been snookered by a German agent.

"Son of a bitch. I ought to kill her, too."

Pamela touched his cheek gently. "No. No, Tom. It's all right."

Calmed by her touch and soothing words, Dunn nodded. "Okay. I'm okay."

By this time, Cross had given instructions to Lindstrom and Higgins to bring the attacker's body down. He wandered over nearby, not wanting to intrude.

Dunn looked over his wife's shoulder at him. "Dave."

Dunn let go of his wife and waved his friend closer. He grabbed Cross and pulled him into a hug.

"I'm sorry for the way . . ." Dunn trailed off, embarrassed by losing his temper with Cross just hours ago.

Cross patted him on the back. "It's okay, Tom. Don't worry about it."

They separated and Dunn nodded to his best friend. "Thanks for coming here. How . . .?"

"Pamela called the colonel, who called us."

Dunn looked at Pamela. "Good job, honey."

She smiled.

"What can I do to help?" Cross asked.

"Take a couple of men inside. Grab the woman in there. She was in on it, whatever it was. Take her to the MP Headquarters. Call the colonel and fill him in with what you know. I'm taking Pamela to see how her dad's doing."

Pamela raised a hand. "Oh, there's a neighbor in there guarding her. His name is Mr. Miller. Could you make sure he's okay? By the way, he's armed with a pistol and a shotgun."

"Ah, thanks for mentioning that. Will do, Pamela," Cross said. Like the rest of the men in the squad, he'd do anything for Pamela.

"Oh, Dave, could you get my collie? I want to take him to the vet."

"Of course."

He whistled at the rest of the men standing in front of the barn.

They looked his way and he held up two fingers.

Martelli and Goerdt immediately took off toward him.

When the two men joined him, they left the young couple and entered the house, Cross first. He stopped by the door and said, "Hello, Mr. Miller. I'm Sergeant Dave Cross. I'm one of Tom Dunn's men. Okay to come in?"

Miller stepped into view, keeping the double-barreled shotgun aimed at Cross as he moved. His eyes were narrowed and wary. When he saw for sure it was an American, he relaxed, lowering the barrels.

Cross stepped farther inside and stopped when he saw the blond woman tied up and gagged at the table. "Huh, how about that?" He grinned and laughed.

"Looks like you're having a day, ma'am."

She mumbled something whose syllables could have belonged to "up yours."

Cross continued grinning and walked over in front of the woman, who looked into his blue eyes with fury. He bent over to get right in her face. He thought that if her mouth wasn't sealed shut by black tape, she would have spit in his face.

"Ayup, I'd say definitely you're having a day. And guess what? It's gonna go from bad to worse to nightmare before the day is over. Enjoy it."

He straightened up and waved at the other Rangers. They each got a hand under an armpit and lifted. She refused to walk.

Cross sighed and nodded at Martelli and Goerdt. They lowered her back into the chair and her eyes flared victory. Cross laughed.

Martelli stood behind her and pulled her chair back from the table, spinning it to his left.

Goerdt picked up her feet, which she started kicking. He spun quickly to face away from her, and got her ankles under his arm, pinning them tight with both hands. Martelli lifted her upper body and they carried her out, her head shaking and her legs trying to kick loose to no avail.

Cross turned to look at Miller, who had watched the whole thing with an amused expression.

"Well done, you. Not too bad. For a Yank."

"Thank you, sir. I'm heading outside. Care to come along?"

"Would do."

Cross bent over and picked up the collie. The dog snorted, and took a deep breath. Cross held the dog's face on his left. He looked down at the beautiful creature.

"Hey-ya, puppy. Gonna wake up for me?" He stroked the brown and white fur on Winston's side.

The dog opened his brown eyes and looked at Cross.

"You're okay, puppy." He kissed the dog on the nose, thinking of his own dog at home, a brown and white spaniel named Buddy.

He was rewarded with a tiny tail wag.

When Cross got outside, Pamela spotted him and noticed the tail, which was still wagging.

She ran over and rubbed the dog's body gently. She bent over and kissed him on the nose.

"Thank you, Dave."

"You're welcome. I'll go ahead and carry him to the jeep if that's okay?"

"Yes, please."

Dunn, sporting the beginnings of a bruise on the side of his chin, another one on his forehead, and purple finger marks around his neck, put an arm around Pamela's shoulder.

"Let's get going, honey."

She patted him on the chest. "Right."

As they walked toward the jeep, the Ranger squad gathered together near it forming something like a reception line. Dunn walked the line, gratefully shaking hands with each of his men.

Pamela followed and kissed each one on the cheek. When Dunn reached the end he turned and faced the squad.

He fought back tears of pride and gratitude.

"Men, thank you for coming out here. We appreciate it. Very much. You're the best."

Cross leaned close to Dunn. "We're the best because of you."

Dunn smiled and patted Cross's arm.

He and Pamela got in the jeep and drove away, heading for the veterinarian's office in Andover, and after that to the hospital.

Cross and the men finished gathering the German's weapon from the barn and cleaned the blood as best they could. When they were done, they marched back to their truck, which had driven up into the barnyard after Dunn's jeep drove off, and Miller left in his pickup truck. The prisoner sat on one of the benches in the back, close to the cab, where Martelli and Goerdt had put her. They sat one next to her and one across to make sure she stayed put.

The dead German lay at her feet, black tongue still lolling.

She averted her eyes the whole trip.

41

The Farm, Area B-2
In Maryland, 70 miles northwest of Washington, D.C.
3 December, 0800 Hours, U.S. Eastern Standard Time

Gertrude was having some trouble adjusting to the new hours. At Bermuda Station, she'd worked the second shift from 3 p.m. to 11 p.m. There, she'd stayed up until midnight or 1 a.m. chatting with her friends or reading. Here, wake up was 5:30 a.m., breakfast at six, and to the first classroom or training area by six forty-five. Rubbing some sleep from her eyes she thought back to her first Trainazium exercise a couple of days ago, right after the five mile run. Not one of the women had been able to walk from one eighteen inch diameter disc of wood to another all the way through the course. Once fallen, you had to start all over again. She came to realize that she was not as fit as she thought she was. She understood that Rick the instructor had purposely had them do the Trainazium right after the run to teach them that exact lesson. Later in the day, they were lined up in two rows and began a series of calisthenics obviously designed to strengthen their bodies, both upper and lower muscles.

Following the physical exercises, they'd been herded back into the recreation center / classrooms building. There they'd been given a lesson in writing coded messages while under time pressure. They discovered that their fine motor skills had become severely hampered. Writing block letters neatly was too much for all of them.

Today, the plan appeared to be different. They were all standing on the firing line of the new pistol range. It had human shaped targets set at ten and twenty five yards. The ones farther out were turned sideways and would be rotated to face the shooters when needed. Lying on a wooden table directly in front of each shooter was a shiny, black .38 Police Special with a five-inch barrel. Next to the weapon was a box of ammunition.

They were lined up alphabetically left to right using their new names, so Gertrude/Peggy was on the right side of the group. They'd spent the hour previous in the classroom going over weapon safety, learning about sight picture, handling a weapon, and muzzle awareness. Next had been taking the sideways, one-handed firing stance favored by the military, aiming at paper human targets taped to the walls, and dry firing the weapon to get used to the trigger pull. Finally they'd been taught how to open the cylinder and load and unload the weapon properly.

Rick stood behind them. He had a silver whistle hanging on a lanyard around his neck. He blew the whistle once.

"Pick up your weapons. Be extremely aware of exactly where your muzzle is pointed, which should be down range at all times."

Gertrude picked up her weapon in her right hand, holding it with the barrel pointed at the targets. She wasn't nervous. She had been a hunter at home, although that had always been done with a rifle. Her dad had taught her how to handle a revolver, and she'd fired a few rounds so she would have that experience under her belt. Her sister Hazel had refused to hunt, or shoot the handgun. Guns scared her.

"Open the cylinder," Rick said.

She pushed on the release button with her thumb and the cylinder swung out to the side.

"Load six rounds. Keep your muzzle pointed down range."

She loaded six lead and brass rounds into the empty slots.

"With your free hand, close the cylinder."

Gertrude did that.

"Grip the weapon in your shooting hand and take the firing stance. Remain vigilant with your muzzle awareness."

Gertrude gripped the weapon in her right hand and raised it, sighting through the rear sight and lining up the front sight.

"On my command, fire one round only."

"Ready . . . Aim . . . Fire!"

Gertrude remembered to squeeze the trigger, not jerk it, and to use the pad of her forefinger, not the knuckle. The weapon fired, bucking slightly in her hand.

"On my command, fire your remaining rounds."

"Ready . . . Aim . . . Fire!"

The staccato sounds of ten unsynchronized pistols firing echoed around the range.

Gertrude took her time, letting the weapon return to its position after the kick from the fired round. Regaining her sight picture, she fired again. She repeated the process until all five had been fired.

Lowering the weapon, she opened the cylinder. She dumped the expended shells into a bucket hanging from the right side of the table. She laid the pistol down and stepped back.

Rick watched as one by one, the trainees finished firing their five rounds and clearing their weapons. When all had stepped back from their table he said, "Retrieve your target."

Each woman walked down to her target and pulled it free from the wooden frame. They picked up a clean target from a stack nearby and tacked it in place.

Gertrude examined hers right there. The first and second shots were about two inches to the right of the target's heart. The other four had drifted down and to the right in a line about six inches long. She frowned, turned, and walked back to her table.

Rick started with the first woman and critiqued her target. He moved down the line and he took Gertrude's from her. He noted the two close shots and the others that straggled away.

"What's happening here is when the weapon rests after a shot, it's coming down lower than it was. When you're reacquiring your sight picture, the weapon has also rotated horizontally due to your wrist being slightly more bent to the inside than you realize. Does that make any sense to you?"

"Yes, sir."

"Good. Make the adjustment the next time."

He moved on.

Soon the women were ready for their second session at the ten yard range.

This time, Rick had them fire all six rounds consecutively.

When Gertrude picked up her target, she was excited to see a true cluster just to the right of the heart. All six shots fit inside a circle the size of a baseball. She practically ran back to the table, and could hardly wait for her turn with Rick.

He finally made it and grunted when he saw her tight grouping

"Pick up your weapon, take the firing stance, and get your sight picture."

She obliged him.

He walked around her examining her position. He stood behind her and looked down her arm.

"Your whole body's position is off to the right. That's why you're missing."

"Thank you, sir."

A few minutes later, Rick gave them the commands and they readied for another ten yard firing session.

Gertrude made a tiny adjustment to her stance.

She fired her six rounds and when she checked her target, she couldn't believe her eyes. The cluster had moved to the left and had nearly obliterated the heart target.

When Rick returned to her station he muttered, "Hm." He handed her target back. He leaned close so the others couldn't hear. "I don't usually like to compliment new trainees, but you seem to be very coachable. That's an excellent result you have there. Just remember how you did it. And do not let it go to your head, young lady."

"Thank you, sir. I won't."

"Good."

The range work was done for the day. The trainees emptied their weapons and slid them into the holster on their hips.

On the way back to the classroom, Gertrude caught up with Ruby, the woman who'd won the five-mile race.

"How'd it go?"

Ruby, a willowy blond about Gertrude's height replied, "I think I need a lot of practice. Kept missing all over the place. How about you?"

Gertrude had grown to like Ruby and didn't want to show her up unnecessarily. "Not too bad. Could use some work myself."

"Maybe we can get some extra time on the range. Help each other."

"Works for me. Where's Edna?"

They looked around and found the third place finisher back a few people. They stopped and waited for her.

When she caught up, they headed for the classroom building together.

"How'd you two do?" Edna asked.

"Need some more work on the range," Gertrude said.

"Ha, me too. Holy cow, some of my rounds completely missed the target. Rick was not too happy about that."

Gertrude and Ruby chuckled.

"I bet he wasn't," Ruby said.

The three had hit it off after the running event, and in spite of Gertrude shouldering Edna out of the way and Edna trying to trip Gertrude, they got along pretty well. Since no one was allowed to say where they were from, Gertrude guessed from Edna's speech that she must be a New Yorker and Ruby might be from the south, what with her drawl.

"Where do you suppose they'll send us?" Edna asked.

Gertrude shook her head. "No idea really."

"Do you want Europe or the Pacific?" Ruby asked them.

"Either," Edna replied immediately.

"Not sure," Gertrude said.

The other two nodded.

They walked the rest of the way in silence as they thought about what their future might actually have in store for them.

42

After dropping Winston off at the vet, and Pamela at the hospital, Dunn rushed to the MP headquarters. Once there he made sure the woman attacker was in the hands of the MPs, and he gave his statement.

He drove like mad to get back to the hospital. He was desperate to learn how Earl was doing, or heaven forbid, if he hadn't survived. He had no idea what he could possibly say to Pamela or her mother if Earl died. He'd somehow brought a killer right to their home. His grip on the steering wheel was so tight his hands were white. His pulse raced, his breathing fast, yet somehow ragged, as if his lungs just couldn't keep up. He passed slower vehicles with a long honk of warning, whipping the wheel over to speed past them, and back to get in the proper lane.

He slowed to make the turn into the drive for the hospital, but was still going too fast. The rear end began to slide left. He corrected into it, and the tail end whipped back to the right just enough to stay on the road. With the vehicle straight on the driveway, he stomped on the brakes and clutched for a downshift. By the time he reached the parking area, he'd gotten his speed down to about fifteen miles an hour. He nosed into a space between a couple of British cars and shut down the engine.

He ran into the hospital right to the "Inquiries here" desk, where a young woman wearing a dark blue dress sat.

She raised an eyebrow when she saw his red and purple face and neck bruises.

"I'm looking for Earl Hardwicke."

"One moment," she said, looking down at a clipboard on her desk. Running a finger down the list, she found Earl's name. She looked up.

Dunn tried to read her expression, but it was noncommittal.

"He's out of surgery and in the recovery ward. It's—"

Dunn ran off down the hallway, calling over his shoulder, "Thanks, I know where it is."

He slowed enough to open the recovery room's door quietly and slip inside. He spotted Pamela and Florence. They were sitting one on each side of Earl's bed.

Walking over to join them, he passed several men who were in various stages of wakefulness.

One of the men, wearing a bandage over his chest and one on his right cheek waved a hand.

"Hey Sarge," he said.

Dunn paused long enough to look more closely at the soldier. He finally recognized him as another Ranger. "Oh, hey, Ralph. You doin' okay?"

"Yeah. Took one in Belgium while we were sneaking around."

"Sorry to hear that. Get well, buddy."

"Thanks." Ralph waved.

Dunn made his way over to Earl's bed and looked down at the man. His eyes were closed. Dunn put a hand on Pamela's shoulder. "Hi, honey."

She started, but stood and hugged him.

"How is he?"

"Doctor said he'll make a full recovery, but it was a close one."

"Oh, man."

He let go of her and looked at Florence. She had a bandage on her left forehead where the blond woman had pistol whipped her.

He swallowed. It felt like his heart was trying to climb out through his throat.

"Florence, I'm . . . I'm so sorry."

He went around the bed and pulled her into a hug. She patted him on the back.

"It's all right, Tom. It's not your fault the Germans did this."

"I feel like it is."

She shushed him and held him tight.

Pamela grabbed another chair from an empty bed nearby, putting it next to Florence's.

"Tom, have a seat here."

He let go of Florence and sat down hard. He leaned close to the bed, a hand on the railing. He watched Earl's chest rise and fall smoothly.

"Jesus, Earl, I'm so sorry." He dipped his head and closed his eyes. He said a silent prayer of thanks, and opened his eyes.

Earl's eyelids fluttered a couple of times and then opened. He found Florence first and smiled.

"Welcome back," she said.

He tried to speak, but couldn't. He made a drinking motion.

Pamela poured him a half-full glass of water. Thankfully, the bullet had missed his stomach and intestines, so water as okay. He'd be able to eat later in the day.

He drank the glass quickly and handed it back.

"Better. Hi everyone."

Florence leaned over to give him a careful squeeze and a kiss. Pamela went next from the other side.

"How do you feel, Dad?"

He gave her a weak smile. "Not as bad as I expected."

"Good."

Earl looked at Dunn, whose expression was crestfallen and guilt ridden.

"I'm glad you're okay, Earl."

"Me, too. So you're calling me 'Earl' now?"

"Oh, yep. Being in combat with a man forges an unbreakable bond with him. First name seems right now."

Earl nodded. "It does."

"I'm so, so sorry. This is all my fault."

Earl lifted his hand for Dunn to take. Dunn gripped it gently.

"It's okay. It's not your fault. The war came home, that's all. Everything worked out, didn't it?"

"I suppose."

"Did you catch him?"

"Yes. He's dead."

Earl nodded. "You?"

"Yes, sir."

"Good. The woman?"

"In MP jail."

"Good."

"Earl, you showed some real courage going out there against him."

Earl shrugged. "Had no choice, right?"

Dunn stared at the older man and saw what kind of soldier he would have been if he'd made it to the front line in the Great War.

"Thank you for helping. I am really sorry this happened."

"No apology is needed."

"But—"

"You don't seem to quite understand, so let me help you."

Dunn frowned, totally confused.

"We love you. You're part of our family and will be forever."

Dunn's throat closed over, so he nodded.

"You've given us something we've deeply needed."

Dunn swallowed again. "I don't understand."

Earl smiled.

Florence put her hand around Dunn's shoulders and squeezed.

"You've become a son to us, Tom. We have a son again."

Dunn leaned into Florence's hug and cried.

43

Military Police Headquarters
Camp Barton Stacey
4 December, 1608 Hours, the next afternoon

Colonel Kenton entered the Military Police Headquarters building. His new aide, Lieutenant Tanner, accompanied him as well as a man wearing a black suit and somber face from the British Home Office. Dunn trailed the group.

Kenton stopped at the desk and said to the corporal sitting there, "Colonel Kenton for Colonel Walton."

The corporal nodded. "One moment, please, sir."

He rose, walked to a closed office door nearby, and knocked. He evidently heard a reply no one else could and opened the door, disappearing inside the office. He returned, followed by the MP commander.

"Hello, Colonel Kenton. Ready to interrogate her?"

"We sure are."

"We have an interview room ready."

"That's great, thanks."

The MP commander turned to the corporal. "Take someone with you and bring her to interview room one."

"Yes, sir."

The corporal disappeared again, this time through a door across from the entry.

Kenton turned to his Ranger. "Sergeant Dunn, why don't you grab yourself a cup of coffee and wait here."

Dunn frowned, but said, "Yes, sir." He'd wanted to be in on the interview.

"This way, Colonel."

The MP commander led the way down a hall on the right, past his office. He opened the first door on the left. He held his hand out indicating for the visitors to enter first.

Dunn got himself a cup of hot coffee and stood looking out the front window at the landscape. Trees were naked. Heavy clouds covered the sky. The grass was brown. *Just like Iowa this time of year,* he thought.

Taking a seat behind one of the empty MP desks, he took another sip of coffee. Dear God, it had been so close. Pamela and the baby could have been . . . he couldn't even think the word. Tears began to run down his cheeks as he thought of all that would have been lost. Moving to the states. Watching Tom, Junior grow up, hopefully with brothers and sisters. Growing old with Pamela. In his mind's eye, he saw all of these things. They could still come to pass. All he had to do was survive the war.

He wiped his face with his sleeve.

If it hadn't been for Cross's boating skills, and some quick action on the sub captain's part, they might not have made it home at all. He shook his head to get that thought out of his mind.

Some time passed and he nodded off, mentally and emotionally exhausted.

The room was plenty large enough for a table and chairs. One window was built high in the wall behind the table. A single overhead light hung from the ceiling.

Three chairs were set on the side of the table facing the window, and a lonely chair sat opposite. Two extra chairs were placed by the wall on the left.

"I was thinking I would start the questioning, Colonel Walton," Kenton said.

The MP cleared his throat. "I'm okay with that."

"Thank you."

Kenton took the middle chair, and motioned for the other officer to take the one to his right.

The British Home Office representative seated himself to Kenton's left. Lieutenant Tanner sat in one of the extras. He opened a notebook and pulled a pencil from his shirt pocket, ready to take notes.

The corporal from the front desk and two other MPs entered with the prisoner. The men in the room did not stand.

The MPs led the limping woman around the table and pushed her down into the chair. She wore the same clothes she been captured in, and a pair of handcuffs. One of the MPs reached over and yanked her hands toward a small steel ring set in the table. He attached another pair of handcuffs, one cuff to the ring and the other around the chain between her cuffs. He rattled them to make sure they were secure. The MPs lined up one directly behind her and the other two on either side of her. Marks from the black tape Pamela had used to shut her up marred her face. Shortly after her arrival, a Barton Stacey doctor had been summoned. He'd changed the dressings Pamela had put on her wounds, including Sammy's bites on her ankle. Due to the infection danger from dog bites, he'd given her a shot of penicillin.

Kenton started by introducing himself and the two others at the table.

"Your name?" he asked.

She looked as though she had no interest in speaking, and looked at the ceiling.

"I highly suggest you cooperate, miss. You are in a world of trouble," Kenton said.

She lowered her gaze, a smug smile on her lips. "I . . . am . . . not . . . talking." She chopped off each word.

The Home Office man, Stanley Oliver, looked at Kenton. "Perhaps I might clarify the legal situation for the young lady?"

"Certainly, sir."

Oliver leaned forward, his hands planted flat on the table. In a dangerously soft voice, he said, "Let me make this simple for you, miss. You are charged with the four counts of attempted murder, namely of a U.S. soldier and three British civilians. You are also charged with espionage as an agent of a foreign power, namely Nazi Germany, with whom England is in a state of war. The first charges carry a lengthy prison term. The second, however, will result in you hanging by the neck until you are dead. I have the authority to determine which charge becomes final. Perhaps you should consider this before refusing to speak."

She swallowed. "Evelyn Harris."

Oliver stared at her, annoyed she'd lied to his face. "Your real name!"

Her smug smile disappeared. Cowed, she answered, "Elsa Hoffman."

"How did you come to be at the Hardwicke Farm?" Kenton asked.

"I was ordered to locate a Ranger who was exceptional in skill. I didn't have a name."

"How did you decide on Sergeant Dunn?"

She looked away, obviously trying to find a way to use her information to her best advantage. She looked directly at Oliver, since he would be the one deciding the charges. "If I tell you what I know, will you take espionage off the table so I don't hang?"

Oliver thought for a long time before finally answering. "It depends on whether I believe you."

She drummed the fingers of her left hand on the table. She nodded slowly.

"I received orders from my handler in London."

"How do we find this person?"

"I never met him. We have a cutout system. He marks a particular phone box by King's Cross Station. I mark the next one east of it. He leaves coded instructions taped under a bench across from my phone box."

"How do *you* initiate contact?"

"I mark my box with a different shape, an oval with a line through it."

"You've never seem him?"

"No."

"Or her?"

"No."

"Why were you hunting Sergeant Dunn?"

"I told you: I didn't have a name."

Oliver frowned and sighed. "Why were you after a Ranger?"

"I don't have the details of why."

"Speculate."

She shrugged. "A Ranger made someone really high up angry."

"High up where?"

"Where do you think?" she snapped.

Oliver glanced at Kenton, and back at her. "Berlin?"

"Of course, Berlin!"

Oliver rose and nodded for Kenton to follow him out of the room. He closed the door behind them.

"I know you can't divulge operational information, but can you tell me if your Sergeant Dunn could have been involved in any . . . missions whose results might have attracted the attention of the higher up levels in Germany?"

Kenton didn't bother to hesitate. "Almost all of them, sir. A lot of serious, serious damage to the German war machine."

Oliver blinked at the news. "One Ranger?"

"Well, not by himself, of course."

"I understand. Right, thank you, Colonel."

They went back in and sat down.

Evelyn looked at Oliver hopefully.

"Are you certain you were not given Sergeant Dunn's name?"

She laughed. "Oh, bloody hell. Yes, I'm certain. I figured it out on my own. I had a slim description, is all."

Exasperated at dragging information from the woman piece by painful piece, Oliver slammed his hand down. She flinched.

"Tell me all of it now, or we'll quit right here and you'll dangle from that rope."

"All right, hold your horses." She looked at her hands, preparing her words. She looked up at Oliver.

"I got lucky. I found a newspaper article about him getting the Medal of Honor from that . . . President Roosevelt." She practically spat out the name. "It showed a picture of him and his pretty little wife. It even said where they lived. How about that for easy? I went out to the farm and actually met them, and took some photos of them and the farm for the man who was with me. They thought I was a freelance photographer."

"You met them?" Kenton asked, his face red. "You talked to them?"

"Well, of course."

"And then you decided to try and kill them all?"

She shook her head. "No. I was *ordered* to help kill them all."

Kenton could think of nothing to say to that at first, but then something occurred to him.

"His wife is pregnant."

She looked at him with disdain and shrugged. "So?"

Kenton turned red again and seemed about to leap across the table.

Oliver quickly asked another question. "What do you know about the dead man?"

"Nothing. We're all compartmentalized. He behaved the way someone would who'd had training. Lots of it. And experience."

"No name?"

"Fake."

Oliver sat back, thinking. Then he turned to Kenton. "Any more questions?"

Kenton shook his head, still red-faced.

"Do you, Colonel Walton?"

"No, sir."

Oliver stood. "We'll charge her with the attempted murders and espionage."

She started to complain, but he leaned on the table with both hands. "If your phone box story leads us somewhere productive, I'll consider dropping the latter. That's the best you'll get from me."

She put her face in her hands.

The three interrogators and Lieutenant Tanner departed, leaving the woman in the hands of the MPs.

Kenton, who had calmed himself before going out to face Dunn, told him most of her story, leaving out how she found him and her despicable reaction to Pamela's pregnancy.

Dunn knitted his brow, his face turned red and his eyes flashed black. He made a move toward the interview room.

Kenton understood the warning sign in the eyes and grasped the infuriated Ranger's upper left arm. "Sit . . . down."

Dunn stared at Kenton.

In a barely controlled voice, he said, "She's responsible for Pamela's dad almost dying and hurting her mom. They were going to murder my family!"

"Yes. And she will pay with life in prison at the minimum."

"I want to talk to her."

"Not a good idea, Tom."

"Tell me you wouldn't want to do the same thing if you were in my shoes." Dunn looked around the room at the MPs, the Home Office man, and Lieutenant Tanner. They seemed sympathetic, but said nothing.

The MP commander walked over by Kenton and Dunn.

"Perhaps Sergeant Dunn should go be with his family."

Kenton looked at Dunn thinking of his wife and son, Mary and Bobby. He nodded. "I do understand. But I want you to go, Tom. Be with Pamela and the family."

"Life?"

"Without a doubt. At the minimum," Oliver said.

"How'd she find me?"

Kenton cleared his throat. "Another time, Tom. Okay?"

Dunn nodded reluctantly. He shook hands with Kenton, Walton, and Oliver. "Thank you."

He turned and left ready to get back to the hospital to see how Earl and Florence were doing, and to hold Pamela.

The two colonels looked at each other.

"I don't see any problems with the prosecution of the woman," Oliver said.

"Good," Walton replied. He looked at an MP nearby. "Go tell the men to take the woman to her cell. I want a twenty-four hour watch on her. I will not allow her to kill herself in my jail."

"Yes, sir."

He turned to Kenton and Oliver. "I didn't want to mention this in front of Sergeant Dunn, but the man he killed was SS. The examining doctor found the SS tattoo on his arm."

Kenton stared at Walton, thinking. Dunn had told him what the man had said while trying to squeeze the life out of him. A message from Speer, who had obviously called in a favor, probably from Himmler himself.

"I see. Thank you for telling me."

Walton nodded.

Kenton shook hands with Oliver and the colonel.

"Gentlemen, thank you. I'm going to take off unless you need anything from me."

"We're all set, Colonel," Walton said.

"Very good."

Kenton and his aide left. Tanner drove them back to Kenton's office.

All the way Kenton could think only of one thing: what if it *had* been his family?

44

**Dunn's barracks
Camp Barton Stacey
5 December, 1500 Hours, the next afternoon**

Dave Cross sat upright on his bunk and stared at the envelope in his hand. Mail call had arrived a few minutes before. It had come from his home town of Winter Harbor, Maine, and it wasn't from his parents. She'd written back! Betty Warner had written to him. The girl from high school he'd admired from afar. He started to open it, but became so nervous his hands began to shake.

He finally regained control of his limbs and ripped the envelope open. A one-page letter fell out into his lap. He snatched it up and unfolded it. He began to read:

Dear Dave, (do you still go by Dave? You did in high school, I remember that)

I had heard you were in Europe. I hope this letter finds you well and safe. I've been meaning to ask your mother how you were doing, but you know . . .

He looked up. Yes, he did know. She'd been afraid to ask in case he was dead. He continued:

I was really pleased to get a letter from you. I figured you'd have forgotten all about me. I don't know if I should tell you this in a letter, Dave, but I liked you, a lot. I have always wished we could have . . . grown closer. If you feel something similar, is that why you wrote me? perhaps we could continue writing to each other until you come home. Then we could see where this might take us. Oh, dear, is that too forward? I'm sorry. Well, no I'm not really.

Please write me back,

Betty

Cross smiled to himself. His heart pounded. He grabbed some paper and a pencil, and a book for something solid to write on. He started his reply:

Dear Betty,

I'm so glad you wrote back! I had no idea you liked me. I sure did like you, too. Yes, that's why I wrote to you. Yes, I'd love to write you and see where this might take us!

Star & Garter Hotel Restaurant
Andover
5 December, 1600 Hours

Dunn and Pamela sat side by side at their favorite table by the window looking out on High Street. It was growing dark outside thanks to winter coming. Sitting across from them were Malcolm and Sadie Saunders. The men were dressed in their uniforms and each woman wore a colorful dress; Sadie a pale pink one with puffy sleeves at the shoulder, and Pamela a light blue one that accented her blue eyes.

Everyone looked at the menu, paying attention to the piece of paper clipped to it showing the evening special. The waiter came and took their orders, which were identical: the special of fried chicken, and fried potatoes with onions and peppers. He gathered up the menus and left.

"How's your dad?" Sadie asked.

"Recovering well. Doctor says he'll be fine. No lifting for a while due to the surgery across the stomach muscles. I already talked with our neighbor, Mr. Jackson. He'll pop round whenever dad needs help. Mum's head is better. Fortunate that she didn't get a concussion. She hasn't left his side except to go home, change clothes and go back."

"What about your dog? That crazy woman shot him?"

Pamela shook her head at the thought. "Yes. It knocked him out for a long time, but the vet says no lasting damage. He's back home on his favorite blanket."

Dunn, who had been unusually quiet, continued to stare off at the distance behind Saunders.

Saunders had noticed. "I'm so sorry about Kelly."

Dunn's eyes zeroed in on Saunders'. "Yeah. Thanks. He was a good kid."

Pamela leaned into Dunn and laid her hand on his. He wrapped an arm around her shoulders.

"This damn war," he said.

"Aye," Saunders replied.

"Chadwick doing all right?" Dunn asked.

"Aye. Barely, though. If we hadn't had a doctor aboard the sub with us, he wouldn't have made it. We owe Colonel Jenkins big for always insisting on sending one along." He sighed deeply. "Tim's lucky to be alive plain and simple. He's going to be out a very long time. Months."

Dunn shook his head. He liked Chadwick. "I'm so sorry. I'll make sure I get over to the hospital to visit him."

Saunders nodded. "He'd like that." He leaned forward and lowered his naturally loud voice. "She found you from a newspaper article?"

Kenton had told Dunn about that earlier in the day. He shook his head ruefully. "Yeah. I can't believe it."

"Any ideas on who the bloke was?"

"Colonel Kenton told me all we know is he was SS. The MPs gave his picture to intelligence, but we'll probably never hear back from them."

"The SS? But why'd they target you?"

"I've thought about it. Without going into details, I came face to face with Albert Speer recently. I was wearing some . . . extra gear so I don't think he saw my face clearly, but my gear did have a Ranger patch on it. He was furious that we were, uh, stopping something. The man who came here gave me a message direct from Speer."

"Albert Speer, the Minister of Armaments, tried to have us all killed?" Pamela asked quietly.

"I believe so. Maybe it started out as being just me, but someone along the line of the mission changed it. Maybe the killer did it on his own. Never will know the truth. The woman knows nothing else."

"What'll happen to her?" Sadie asked.

"She may avoid the noose depending on what the Home Office discovers about her handler. It amounts to life in prison, is what I heard for four attempted murders. Something like fifteen to twenty years for each count."

"Good. Too bad they couldn't hang her anyway for being part of such a horrific plan," Saunders said.

Everyone nodded their agreement to that.

Dinner arrived and the starving foursome dug in with relish. Dunn poured a liberal amount of catsup on his plate for the chicken and potatoes. No one reacted to his condiment predilection anymore.

After dinner everyone had coffee.

"Your neighbors were a big help out at the farm," Dunn said to Pamela.

"They sure were. Bless their hearts. They showed a lot of courage."

"Yep. So did you and your parents."

She nodded. Tears suddenly welled up. She dabbed at them with a napkin. "Do you think it's over?"

"Yes. The Germans, Speer in particular, will never know what happened. They'll just assume it was a failure, and decide against going through the trouble again."

"I wish we could punish him, too."

"After we win the war, this time, I think the Germans in power will be tried for war crimes. He'll get some kind of punishment, mark my words."

"Good, I hope so."

Dunn decided to change the subject. "Sadie, are you feeling okay these days?"

"Yes, although I am having some morning sickness."

"Oh, sorry to hear that. Do you have crackers?" he asked. "Or biscuits, rather."

She smiled. "Yes, they help."

"Good"

"You know, the anniversary of Pearl Harbor is coming up in a couple of days. The day after is my third anniversary of joining up."

"Three years," Saunders said. "A long time."

"It seems like a lifetime, doesn't it, Mac?"

"Aye. A lifetime."

The two tough men looked at each other, Ranger to Commando. From antagonists to close friends, they'd covered a lot of ground, some of it together. Saunders held out his hand across the table and Dunn shook it. They nodded once to each other and that ended the moment.

Sadie and Pamela watched their husbands share that moment and glanced at each other. They were part of the war in ways some people could never, ever fully understand. The fear and uncertainty that had become central to their lives could have become unbearable if not for each other and their families. The two young, pregnant wives tipped their heads to each other, their own singular bond forever sealed.

The upright piano over near the bar suddenly started up and the four friends looked over.

A young man, another patron of the restaurant or bar, had seated himself at the piano. He was playing a pretty, slow song that Dunn didn't recognize. He was smart enough to stand up and hold out his hand to Pamela.

"Care to dance?"

"Would I!"

She got up and they headed for the more open space by the piano.

Saunders took the hint and he and Sadie joined them.

A few other customers watched with smiling faces. Another, older, couple joined them.

The pianist glanced at the couples and grinned.

He finished the song and immediately went into another slow one.

"It feels great to dance with you, Tom. We don't get the chance often."

He pulled her tight. "I love it, too."

The song ended and the pianist turned to the dancers. "Anyone up for swing?"

The dancers all shouted "Yes!"

They danced for an hour, working up a good sweat on the swing, and resting on the slow songs.

At the end, the pianist stood up and closed the lid over the keys.

Everyone in the audience applauded and he grinned and bowed. He made a sweeping motion with his right hand to acknowledge the dancers and the applause started up again. The three male dancers dug into their pockets and laid some pound notes on the piano's top for him.

"Thank you," Dunn said, shaking the young man's hand.

"My pleasure, sir."

The couples returned to their tables.

The foursome had another cup of coffee and chatted about the coming life with kids.

A young American soldier, who couldn't have been over eighteen, walked up to their table. He looked right at Dunn.

"Sergeant Dunn, I have a package for you." He held out a flat package.

Dunn raised his eyebrows, but took it. He started to dig in his pocket for something to give the soldier, but the young man warded him off with a wave of the hand.

"No, Sergeant. All taken care of. Good night." He started to turn away, but noticed one of Dunn's ribbons and stopped.

"Could I shake your hand, Sergeant Dunn? I've never met someone who won the Medal of Honor."

Dunn smiled and rose, extending his hand. The kid shook it.

"Thanks!"

"You're welcome."

The soldier practically ran out of the restaurant.

"Probably going to tell all of his buddies, don't you think, Tom?" Saunders asked.

Dunn nodded as he sat down.

Dunn tore off the brown paper and exposed an eight-by-ten picture frame. It was the black and white photo Cross had taken of him in Hamburg. Dunn set it on the table. Pamela picked it up to examine it. She grinned.

There was neat writing in pen across the bottom. She read it aloud.

"To the best friend a man could ever have, Dave."

"Wow, Tom," Saunders said.

Dunn's eyes filled with tears.

Pamela patted his arm. "I love this picture. It's wonderful."

"Thanks," Dunn replied.

The conversation resumed, but after fifteen minutes, it was clear that Pamela and Sadie were flagging.

"The dancing take it all out of you, ladies?" Saunders asked, patting Sadie's arm gently

Sadie and Pamela nodded.

Pamela turned to Dunn. "Take me home, Tom," she paused, "however, don't get your hopes up, I am really knackered!"

Dunn grinned.

"No problem, dear. I'm 'knackered' myself."

Dunn and Saunders left money for the check and a sizable tip on the table.

Everyone got up and they made their way outside into the cold evening air. It was cloudy and windy.

"Drop you two off?" Dunn asked.

Sadie looked up at her husband. "I'd rather walk."

"As you wish, darling."

Everyone exchanged hugs. The women pecked each other and the opposite husband on the cheek.

The Saunderses walked away holding hands, heading up High Street toward their flat.

Dunn helped Pamela into the canvas covered jeep and got in himself. He leaned over and kissed her.

"I love you, Pamela Dunn."

"And I love *you*, Tom Dunn."

He started the jeep and drove off.

He glanced over at Pamela when they reached the city limits.

His gorgeous, wonderful wife was sound asleep.

A peace settled on him.

He smiled to himself in the darkness.

Author's Notes

The two main story lines for this book, the V2 rocket platforms and the counterfeit British money came from the list of WWII operations that I've used for several books. This book starts out vastly differently from previous ones, with a game of flag football. Dunn's and Wickham's last play is called the option play, which came into the NFL in 1941, and is still around today. I just made up the penalty on Saunders. He deserved it, right?

Just a tidbit of information about brown eyes: they make up 55% of world population. No wonder it didn't help character Evelyn Harris. Operation Bernhard was a plan by Nazi Germany to forge British bank notes with the intention of wreaking the British economy. Jewish prisoners at the Sachsenhausen concentration camp were forced to do the work.

Dunn's second mission, at the Hamburg shipyards, is based on the Prüfstand XII (Test Stand XII) project. As depicted, the Germans would tow three V2 rockets to about 300 miles off the U.S. coast and fire the rockets at New York City. The German U-boat 2508 was real and of the type XXI. The Blohm & Voss Shipbuilding Company was real and still exists today. It built the type XXI U-boats and the infamous battleship Bismarck.

The two British submarines, the HMS Sea Spray and the HMS Sea Tiger both in the S-class, have fictional names.

I hope you enjoyed Gertrude's new adventure in the world of the OSS agent. Women were indeed recruited and sent to The Farm. You can expect more of this story line. The location is accurate.

Duck tape, nowadays called duct tape, was invented in 1942 by Johnson & Johnson. It gained the name "duck" because it was waterproof and made from a cotton material called duck. Military personnel quickly discovered what we all know today: this stuff can fix anything! Using this miracle substance to seal Chadwick's wound seemed a logical choice for Saunders.

The German E-boat was a beautiful craft. Our pilot hero, Dave Cross, did a fantastic job with this 100 plus foot long boat. The battle on the Elbe River Waterway was complex enough I had to draw it out on graph paper to make sure every boat was where I described it. Blowing up the U-2508 was a lot of fun to write as was the Sea Tiger sinking both E-boats.

Here are my research failures that were, fortunately, found. Steve Barltrop caught a silly mistake: like American PT Boats, the E-boats had wood hulls, so a magnetic setting on torpedoes wouldn't have worked. I completely missed that. Nathan Munsterman wanted to know how the doctor on the submarine knew Chadwick's blood type. I thought, mistakenly, that it would be on his ID tag, like it was on American dog tags. Bzzzt. Not there. Nathan also wondered whether Dunn's use of "You don't pass go and you don't get two hundred dollars," was accurate. Did the game Monopoly exist then? I researched it and it did, although the amount for passing Go might have been different back then. The modern version or something similar came out in 1933 when Dunn was thirteen. Bob Schneider found several. Here are a couple of them: the coffee pot in The Farm's house is shown as a silver pot. I originally had it as the glass pots you see today in restaurants that sit on a heated platform. Another bigger one was a scene at the Hardwicke farm. Dunn is exiting the house through the window. I had him cutting a screen first. Bob pointed out that in England screen windows were pretty much nonexistent due to climate. These are just some of the things ALL of my FIRST READERS help me with.

Albert Speer certainly picked on the wrong man. Sending an SS assassin to hunt Sgt. Dunn was fatal mistake for the SS major. Obersturmbannführer (Lieutenant Colonel) Otto Skorzeny really did rescue Mussolini and fly him out in an overloaded airplane. He also paraded him in Munich as mentioned.

RM
Iowa
January 2019

Please consider following me on my blog and or Twitter to get up-to-date info on what's happening with upcoming books.

www.ronnmunsterman.com
http://ronnonwriting.blogspot.com/

https://twitter.com/RonnMunsterman
@ronnmunsterman

The Sgt. Dunn Photo Gallery for each book:
http://www.pinterest.com/ronn_munsterman/

RONN MUNSTERMAN

About the Author

Ronn Munsterman is the author of the Sgt. Dunn novels. His lifelong fascination with World War II history led to the writing of the books.

He loves baseball, and as a native of Kansas City, Missouri, has rooted for the Royals since their beginning in 1969. He and his family jumped for joy when the 2015 Royals won the World Series. Other interests include reading, some more or less selective television watching, movies, listening to music, and playing and coaching chess.

Munsterman is a volunteer chess coach each school year for elementary- through high school-aged students, and also provides private lessons. He authored a book on teaching chess: *Chess Handbook for Parents and Coaches*.

He lives in Iowa with his wife, and enjoys spending time with the family.

Munsterman is currently busy at work on the next Sgt. Dunn novel.

RONN MUNSTERMAN

RONN MUNSTERMAN

Made in the USA
Columbia, SC
15 August 2019